Dear readers,

I'm so excited to be releasing this sequel to *The Kissing Booth* after all this time. I know it's been long-awaited for so many of you, and it's been several years of hard work on my part to get here now. Some of you may have known Elle, Lee and Noah since their first appearance on Wattpad in 2011, and some of you may have been introduced to them through the Netflix movie adaptation in 2018.

Speaking of the movie – it's absolutely incredible that we'll soon be seeing a second movie of *The Kissing Booth* on Netflix. And while that *is* based on my manuscript and what you'll read in this book, you'll also see some differences when the film does come out. Which isn't surprising: the second movie has to follow on from the first movie, and there were a few differences in that from the first book, too.

I adored the script to the second movie, and honestly liked the changes made from my book – I thought they made a lot of sense, and after all, it's called an 'adaptation' for a reason. But I also believe that the second movie stays true to the characters, their challenges, their successes, their conflicts, and their relationships – as you will also see in this book. I can't wait to see the finished version of the movie, and I hope you all love it, and this book, as much as I do.

Beth x

Beth Reekles penned her novel *The Kissing Booth* when she was fifteen and began uploading it to story-sharing platform Wattpad, where it accumulated over 19 million reads. She was signed by Random House UK at the age of seventeen, and was offered a three-book deal whilst studying for her A Levels. Beth now works in IT, having graduated from Exeter University with a physics degree, and has had four books published with Penguin Random House Children's: *The Kissing Booth*, *Rolling Dice*, *Out of Tune* and *The Beach House*.

Alongside writing exciting new fiction novels, Beth blogs regularly about writing and being a twenty-something. She has been shortlisted for the Women of the Future Young Star Award 2013, the Romantic Novel of the Year Awards 2014 and the Queen of Teen Awards 2014. She was named one of *Time* magazine's 16 Most Influential Teenagers 2013, and in August 2014 she was listed in *The Times* at No. 6 on their 'Top 20 under 25' list.

THE KISSING BOOTH 2

GOING THE DISTANCE

BETH REEKLES

PENGUIN BOOKS

PENGUIN BOOKS

UK | USA | Canada | Ireland | Australia
India | New Zealand | South Africa

Penguin Books is part of the Penguin Random House group of companies
whose addresses can be found at global.penguinrandomhouse.com.

www.penguin.co.uk
www.puffin.co.uk
www.ladybird.co.uk

First published 2020

001

Text copyright © Beth Reeks, 2020

The moral right of the author has been asserted

Set in 11/17 pt Palatino LT Std
Typeset by Jouve (UK), Milton Keynes
Printed and bound in Great Britain by Clays Ltd, Elcograf S.p.A.

A CIP catalogue record for this book is available from the British Library

ISBN: 978–0–241–41322–7

All correspondence to:
Penguin Books
Penguin Random House Children's
80 Strand, London WC2R 0RL

For Gransha, who has been my biggest fan
from the very start

Chapter 1

'Senior year, baby!'

Once the car door slammed shut behind me, I tilted back my head and let my eyes slide closed, drawing in a deep breath. The sun tickled my cheeks, and a smile played on my lips. The school smelled of freshly cut grass, and the air was filled with the bubbly chatter of teenagers running around the parking lot, meeting up with their classmates again after summer. Everybody always complained about how much they hated the first day of school – I was sure that everyone secretly loved it, though.

There was just something about the new school year that meant new beginnings. Which was kind of ridiculous, because it was *high school*, but it didn't stop it feeling true.

I turned to Lee, eyes open again now, and he shot me a grin.

It may have been a Monday morning, but I felt

weightless. My smile mirrored his. 'Senior year, here we come,' I replied softly.

If there was anything worth being excited about, I was sure that the start of senior year was it.

I'd heard people say that your college years were supposed to be the best years of your life – but college sounded like it was going to be so much more hard work than high school, even if it did mean more freedom. Lee and I were convinced that senior year was the last year to *really* enjoy ourselves, before adulthood hit.

I moved round the car to lean against the hood, next to Lee. He'd always made a fuss about his precious car, the '65 Mustang he cherished so dearly; hell, it practically sparkled.

'I can't believe it's finally here. I mean, think about it: this is our *last* first day of high school. This time next year, we'll be at college . . .'

Lee groaned. 'Don't remind me. I already had that speech off my mom this morning – complete with tearful eyes. I don't even want to *think* about college.'

'Tough luck, buddy. It's inevitable. We're moving up in the world.'

Even though the thought of college applications made my stomach twist, too; I'd tried to work on my application essay over the summer, but still hadn't made any progress on it.

I didn't even want to *think* about the possibility that Lee and I would end up at different colleges. That he'd get accepted somewhere I didn't. That we might end up apart next year. We'd spent our entire lives practically joined at the hip. What the hell would I do without him around?

'Unfortunately,' Lee was saying, drawing me out of my thoughts. 'Look, you're not going to start waxing lyrical about the future or something, are you? Please say if you are. I'll leave you to your thoughts and go find the guys.'

Playfully, I shoved my shoulder into his. 'I'll stop talking about college now. Promise.'

'Thank God for that.'

'Although, speaking of the guys – has Cam told you anything about this new neighbor?'

'I'd almost forgotten about that.'

Cam, one of our closest friends since elementary school, had sprung the news on us last week that some guy had moved into the house opposite his and, since he was our age, Cam's parents had suggested he take the new guy under his wing and introduce him to us – and the way Cam had said *suggested* made it sound like they'd given him an ultimatum about it.

Lee carried on. 'I know he's from Detroit. And his name's Levi. Like the jeans. I don't know much else about him, though. I don't think Cam knows anything else about him, either, really.' Then he stood up off the Mustang. 'I'm just hoping he's not a total asshat, since we promised Cam we'd try and help him fit in. Help Levi fit in, I mean.'

'I know what you mean,' I mumbled, but I was distracted by my cell phone, which had started to ring in my hands.

Lee's gaze went to the caller ID, and he sighed. I looked up to give him an apologetic smile just in time to see him roll his eyes at me and start to stroll away, backpack slung over one shoulder.

'No phone sex, Shelly. This is a school. Keep it PG,' he said.

'Oh, like you and Rachel never made out in the janitor's closet!' I shot back. He just gave me a thumbs-up over his shoulder.

I answered the phone. 'Hey, Noah.'

Lee's older brother, Noah, was half the reason I'd not made progress on my college application essay: after sneaking around with him behind Lee's back for a couple of months last spring (which ended in total disaster when Lee caught us kissing), and then officially dating him since the summer, we'd spent as much of our vacation together as possible. He was in college at the other end of the country, now, at Harvard.

4

He'd been gone barely a couple of weeks, and I couldn't get over how much I missed him. How was I going to cope with not seeing him until Thanksgiving?

'Hey, how are you?'

'I'm good. Start of senior year excitement. How's college?'

'Eh. Not much different from when I called you last night. I had class this morning. Math. It was pretty interesting. Second-order differentials.'

'I have no idea what you're talking about, and I don't think I want to know.'

Noah laughed, a soft, breathy sort of chuckle that made my heart melt. Almost everything about him made my heart melt or my knees go weak or my stomach fill with butterflies. I was a goofball, a cliché straight out of a movie. And it felt great.

I missed that laugh as much as I missed feeling his arms wrapped round me, or his lips on mine. We spoke all the time – video chat, Snapchat, messages, good old-fashioned phone calls . . . but it wasn't the same. And I was a little cautious to let on just how badly I missed him, in case it made me sound too clingy. I still wasn't really sure how to go about all this relationship stuff.

'You're *such* a nerd,' I told him.

I'd never thought of Noah as a nerd. I mean, I knew he was smart. He'd had a 4.7 GPA (his mom had told

5

me that recently – that was when I'd realized just how smart he was). He'd narrowly missed out on being top of his class, yet he had a reputation all through high school as the resident bad boy. Up until we got together, I'd never really thought that underneath his image he might actually *like* learning stuff like second-order differentials. Whatever they were.

'Shh, someone might hear you.' I could hear the smirk in his voice. 'Anyway, enough about me. I talked to you for, like, an hour straight last night about college. I just wanted to wish you luck for your first day of senior year.'

I smiled, even though he couldn't see. 'Well, thanks. I appreciate it.'

'So, what's it feel like? Being the big kids in school?'

'Kind of scary, kind of nauseating and a lot exciting. I'm trying not to get too stressed out about college and stuff.'

'Scary, right?'

'Thinking about college makes me feel grown up when I feel like anything but a grown-up. I mean, my kid brother had to come kill a spider in my room last night.'

'Tell me about it. I had to ask someone how to use the dryer in the laundry rooms the other day. I felt so stupid.'

'You've never done laundry?'

'My mom is *very* particular about how the laundry should be done, Shelly, you know that.' I did – she'd asked Lee to spread sheets to dry once, when she went out, only to redo them as soon as she got back. She didn't ask him to do it again. 'Besides, those four teddy bears on your bed probably don't help with the not feeling like an adult.'

'I bet there are a bunch of girls at college – some guys, too, probably – who have a teddy bear or two on their beds.'

'But not four.'

'Hey, now, don't you say a word against Mr Wiggles.' I couldn't help but let a pout slip on to my face. 'Anyway, you're the one with Superman boxer shorts.'

Before Noah got a chance to defend himself, there was the sound of someone pounding on a door in the background on his end of the line. He sighed. 'Looks like I've got to go. Steve was in the bedroom, so I came in the bathroom to talk to you, for some privacy –'

'Flynn, come on, man, I need to take a piss!' his room-mate, Steve, yelled. His voice was muffled, probably by the bathroom door.

'I should go, too. The guys will be here by now, and we're supposed to meet Cam's neighbor and help him feel welcome.'

'Is that the guy from Detroit? 7 For All Mankind?'

'Levi.'

'That's what I said. Well, good luck with that. And hey, tell Lee good luck at tryouts from me. I text him, but he never replied.'

A rattling noise sounded at his end, and more knocking. 'Flynn! *C'mon!*'

'Have a good last first day of school,' Noah said.

'Thanks. I love you.'

I heard the smile in his voice, and could practically see the dimple in his cheek that accompanied that smile, when he said, 'I love you, too.'

We both lingered on the line a moment longer, neither of us saying anything, just listening to the sound of each other's breathing. Then I took the cell phone away from my ear and hung up, making sure the ringer was off before shoving it into my satchel, where it promptly buried itself among my brand-new notebooks and other first-day necessities (namely a hairbrush, a candy bar, a tampon and a pair of very tangled earphones).

'Elle! Hey! Over here!'

I craned my neck at the sound of my name, standing on tiptoe to look. Dixon was a few yards away, with Lee and our other friend Warren waving me over. I waved back, just so Dixon knew I'd seen him, before heading over.

I weaved between a couple of cars to get to the guys

8

and, just as I began to scoot past an unfamiliar green Toyota, the driver's side door opened into my hip and knocked me back against the Ford behind me.

I sucked in a sharp breath, waiting for the Ford's alarm to wail – and I let the air out in a rush when it didn't.

Guess I won't be the school klutz this year. New beginning, here I am.

'Oh, shit. Oh, man, I'm so sorry, I didn't see you there . . .'

'It's totally my fault, don't worry about it,' I said, brushing the hair out of my face before taking a look at the driver. I didn't recognize him at all: he was all long limbs, but not actually much taller than me, and his eyes were hidden behind sunglasses so dark I could see myself in them. He pushed the sunglasses up into his curly brown hair in a fluid motion, then his arm hung limp at his side, one hand clenched round a backpack handle.

He had nice eyes. Friendly sort of eyes. They were green and they crinkled in the corners. I had to squint a little, because the sun was just behind him. He shifted his weight to his other foot, and blocked out the sun.

He was cute.

'Are you okay? Did I hurt you? I'm so sorry –'

'Seriously, don't worry about it. I'm fine. Really.' I smiled for emphasis, even if my hip did hurt a little.

The sound of the passenger door opening caught my attention, and I immediately recognized Cam, with his floppy blond hair and battered blue backpack that he'd had since, like, the eighth grade. He grinned over at me.

'Why am I not surprised? Dude, we've told you, you need to watch where you're walking.'

I pulled a face at him before turning back to the long-limbed guy with the sunglasses, about to say something like, 'You must be Levi,' but Cam beat me to the punch.

'I guess I should introduce you two. Elle, this is Levi. Levi, my friend Elle.'

'Nice to meet you.' He held a hand up in a wave, and flashed a smile that showed teeth so white I thought they had to be bleached.

'Nice to meet you, too. Sorry for walking into your car door. When Cam told us we should meet his new neighbor, *klutz* wasn't exactly the first impression I was going for.'

His smile went wider. 'So are you always this clumsy, or is this just an off day for you?'

'She's a klutz,' Cam pitched in, and I thought he sounded kind of snappy. Did he not like his new neighbor, or was he just stressed? Sensing something off, I changed the topic.

'Dixon's just over there, with the others.'

'Awesome.' Cam started off in the direction I'd gestured, spotting the guys quickly, but Levi made no move to follow him.

'Come on,' I said to the new guy, 'you should come meet everyone else.'

When introductions had been made, and Levi started asking about the sports here (he was on the lacrosse team back in Detroit), I nudged Cam in the side gently.

'What's the deal between you two?' I kept my voice low. 'Tell me to shut up if I'm crossing a line or something, but . . . I don't know, it just seems like you don't really like the new guy much.'

Cam's grumpy expression became something more abashed. 'It's not that I don't like him – I don't really know him that well yet,' he mumbled. 'I just hate being responsible for the new kid, you know? I feel like I have to reign in the sarcasm and be super nice.'

'It'll be fine. He seems nice. At least try not to look like Brad when my dad tells him to eat his broccoli.'

'Easy for you to say,' he muttered. 'The guy drives like a maniac – and my car's still in the garage.'

'I'd like to remind you of the time that you backed into a post.'

'Ugh, don't.' But he smiled, and I grinned back. Lee's shoulder bumped into mine as he gestured in conversation to Warren and Levi about football, and I caught his eye briefly.

Senior year, here we are.

Chapter 2

I quickly remembered why the first day of school was so bad: hordes of students around us were clamoring to get to their homeroom to grab a seat for their friends before all the good ones were gone, and the freshmen stood in tiny groups, blocking the corridors, looking lost and overwhelmed – even a little sick, in some cases.

It was weird not to spot Noah's head somewhere, cutting a path through them all.

Lee's shoulder bumped against mine, and I locked my fingers round his wrist so we didn't get separated.

I looked over my shoulder. 'I've lost the others.'

'They know their way.' Lee paused for a moment, and someone barreled into me from behind before cursing at us and moving round. Lee tugged me down the nearest corridor, taking a detour to our homeroom class. Any other day, this way would have taken twice as long, but today at least we avoided being trampled.

Mr Shane, our senior-year homeroom tutor, was an English Lit teacher, so his classroom was covered in posters of the books his classes would be studying, and A4 pictures of authors like John Steinbeck, Shakespeare, Mary Shelley and F. Scott Fitzgerald.

Mr Shane himself looked like the stereotypical fresh-out-of-grad-school teacher: he wore thin-framed glasses, his tie was slightly askew, and his shirt was only tucked in at the front. And he didn't have that hard look on his face that some of the older teachers did, when they were sick of having taught the same syllabus for twenty years straight. He smiled at us individually as we came into the room.

Rachel and Lisa had clearly arrived only moments before, since they were just putting their bags down on desks near the window. Lee made a beeline for the desk next to his girlfriend, Rachel, and kissed her on the cheek. I looked at the desk on his other side, but it was already taken.

'Elle! Sit by me!' Lisa chirped when I hesitated, gesturing at the desk next to her, in front of Lee. She'd started dating our friend Cam a few months ago and had become part of our group ever since. 'Did you guys meet Levi yet? I was over at Cam's for dinner just after he'd moved in, so we went to say hi together. He was kind of shy, I think, but he seems cool. And I'd *kill* for eyelashes like his! And his hair – it's just *so* curly. I'm in love with it.'

I smiled in reply and she turned to resume her conversation with Rachel. Lee had pulled his chair closer to Rachel's, looking at her with a gooey expression, and I tried not to feel *too* stung that he'd picked a desk beside her over one next to me. I was still getting used to the new dynamic that Lee going out with Rachel had created. I hadn't really noticed it until our time at the beach house this summer, and now Noah wasn't around to help soften the blow of Lee choosing his girlfriend over me.

Once almost all the desks were filled, Mr Shane started with the typical first-day-back speech – how he hoped we all had a good summer, but now we had a 'really big year ahead' and how important this year was for each of us, and that some of us would need to 'knuckle down and work hard'.

He was about halfway through this spiel when there was a knock at the door, and the school secretary stepped inside with a polite smile.

'Sorry to interrupt . . . You have a new student in your homeroom, and I thought I'd bring him up here. My fault he's late – there was some paperwork that needed to be checked.'

I turned to look at Lee, who raised an eyebrow at

me. Our heads swiveled to look at the new student, though I had a feeling I already knew who it was.

And I was right. Levi stepped in from behind the secretary timidly, and his mouth twitched, like he wasn't sure if he should smile or try to look cool. He was still wearing his sunglasses on top of his head, and where they pushed all the hair back from his face I realized how long his face was. And how his chin was sort of pointy; his jaw was defined but not as square as Noah's. Actually, seeing him from a distance, he looked taller than he was. A few of the girls across the room started to whisper to each other.

His shirt was free of creases, but only tucked in on one side, and his sweater was slung over his shoulder, underneath the strap of his backpack. It was like he was trying to make his uniform untidy to look cool, but he still looked pretty clean-cut.

Mr Shane smiled warmly at him. 'Well, welcome. Come on in, find a seat. What's your name?'

'Levi Monroe.'

When Levi spotted Lee and me, his face brightened up. Before he could zigzag between the desks to the empty one in front of me, he tripped, arms pinwheeling, alarm taking over his face. He grabbed at a nearby desk for balance, only to bring that crashing down with him.

Someone coughed, trying to cover a laugh, and

then Lee and I burst into giggles. One guy got up to give Levi a hand, another one righting the desk he'd knocked over. Even Mr Shane was laughing, though he was trying not to.

'Looks like you've got competition for class klutz,' Lee whispered to me.

Levi, without so much as a blush, tossed his head back and dropped his shoulder, turning gravely to the class. 'Let it never be said that I don't know how to make an entrance.' He bowed, and Lee whooped behind me, more people laughing as Levi made it to the seat in front of me – this time, without falling over his own feet.

He swung the chair sideways, so he could see us and the teacher.

'Hey again,' he said tentatively. I could understand why Cam hadn't wanted to be stuck with the new kid, but I felt sorry for the poor sap. It couldn't be easy, moving for senior year. I smiled to put him at ease.

'It's . . . Ella, right?'

'Elle,' I corrected him. I jerked a thumb over my shoulder. 'And that's –'

'Lee, I remember. Yeah.' He looked at Lisa. 'We met the other day, didn't we?'

'Yeah. Lisa.'

He nodded. 'Lisa. Got it.'

'And this is Rachel,' Lisa said, gesturing behind her. 'Lee's girlfriend.'

'I'm going to have to start making a list. I'm never gonna remember who's dating who. I'm bad enough at remembering names.'

'If you yell "dude", I can almost guarantee one of us will look up,' Lee suggested.

Mr Shane started talking again, and we fell silent; he might've been pretty cool as far as teachers went, but we knew he wouldn't exactly appreciate us talking through his little speech.

When our class schedules were handed out, everyone started buzzing with conversation, comparing theirs with their friends'. I snatched up Lee's immediately, poring over it.

'Well? What's the damage?'

'Different classes for English Lit,' I said. 'And you're in AP Calculus. I'm in Algebra II. Everything else looks good.'

'Phys Ed?'

'Phys Ed at the same time.'

'*Yes.* You know how much I love watching you take people out in dodgeball.'

'You know how much I love taking you out in dodgeball.'

I passed back his schedule so he could compare it

with Rachel's, but she was still busy comparing with Lisa. I looked up and saw Levi chewing his thumbnail, looking at all of us out of the corner of his eye – like he was too shy to join in, but he wanted to.

I leaned forward, and said, 'Come on, hand it over.'

His relief at being included was palpable.

We had a couple of classes together, but as we talked about our classes and teachers Levi began to look more nervous.

'Everything okay?' I asked.

He stuck his chin out, looking defiant. 'You know, I don't want you to feel like you have to hang out with me just because I'm the new kid. I told Cam he didn't have to carpool to school with me, but he said he didn't mind, at least not for the first couple of days, especially while his car's still in the shop getting repairs. But just – you know, don't feel obligated to be nice to me, or anything.'

'You haven't given me a reason to *not* be nice to you. Not yet at least. Besides, if we're in the same first class together, you may as well walk with me. Right?'

His smile was apprehensive. 'You don't have to.'

'Why? Are you an ax murderer? On the run from the cops in Detroit?' I fake gasped. 'Oh my God. I've got it. I bet you're the kind of person who agrees to terms and conditions without reading them.'

He laughed, the tension and anxiety falling away from his face. 'You caught me.'

The bell sounded, and I picked up my bag. 'Come on, newbie. The hell on earth that is algebra awaits us.'

Morning classes flew past, and my head felt like a car that kept stalling. It was like I'd forgotten how to take notes properly over the summer, and forgotten how to just sit down and learn stuff. Plus, I got distracted every time my phone buzzed, wondering if it was a text from Noah. (It never was.)

But now it was lunch, and I could breathe a sigh of relief that the day was half over.

I joined the end of the lunch queue and leaned my head back so it rested on Lee's shoulder. His chin sat on top of my head.

'Mm, smell those tacos.'

'Don't drool on my hair,' I told him sternly. 'I washed it this morning.'

Lee made a gargling noise in response and I ducked away before he did *actually* drool on me.

We were the first of our friends to the cafeteria, and once we got our food we made our way to an empty table near the middle of the room. It was one that some of the seniors used to sit at and, now that they'd moved on to college, I guessed that made it ours. As Lee and

I took seats opposite each other, he gave me his usual impish grin, and I knew he was thinking the same thing as me: being seniors was *definitely* cool.

It didn't take the others long to join us – Cam, Dixon, Warren, Oliver, and now Levi, too. Lisa and Rachel weren't far behind, taking the empty spots next to their boyfriends. A couple of girls they hung out with sat at the end of the table by Lisa.

As people started swapping stories from their mornings, I noticed Levi looking awkward again, trying to keep up with it all.

Lee was too busy giving Rachel gooey-eyes to notice anything else, so I turned to Levi. 'How're you liking California so far?' I asked him brightly. 'Hot enough for you?'

'The girls are,' he joked, with a wink that made me blush. Warren snorted, only to choke on his soda so hard that Oliver had to thump him on the back several times. Lee waggled his eyebrows at me, trying not to laugh.

'I'm kidding,' Levi said. 'Well, not – I mean, obviously you're pretty, but – no, no offense – I just . . . God, this sounded a lot smoother in my head. I was gonna sound all suave and cool and funny.' Everyone laughed then, Levi included. 'That was supposed to be a joke. And now I sound like a loser.'

'Why'd you move here, anyway?' Warren asked. We

were all wondering it, but every one of us gave Warren a wide-eyed, pursed-lips, *what are you thinking* look. Catching on, he added hastily, 'Sorry, dude, I didn't mean to pry.'

Levi didn't seem to mind too much, though. 'Nah, it's cool. My dad's a dentist and my mom was the accountant at the place where he worked, but then the company went bust and my parents lost their jobs, so we decided to move. We have some family not too far away, and my mom managed to get another job, so . . .' He trailed off, then cleared his throat. 'So, yeah. Here we are.'

'Is it just you and your parents, then?' Rachel asked, prying much less bluntly than Warren had.

'My sister, too.'

'Sister?' Oliver's eyebrows quirked and he leaned forward. 'Single?'

'Uh, well, considering she's eight years old and still thinks boys have cooties . . .'

The guys jeered at Oliver, and he blushed. Levi grinned, running a hand through his curls, relaxing. 'I take it back,' Olly mumbled, head in hands. 'Next time, specify *little* sister, maybe.'

'I'll bear that in mind.'

'Anyway,' Dixon said, 'speaking of siblings . . . Lee, how's your brother doing at college?'

'He loves it there. I'll be surprised if he even wants to come home for Thanksgiving.'

Wait, what?

I shot Lee a look, but he seemed oblivious. Had Noah said something about not coming home for the holidays? When was I going to see him next? But, no – surely he would've told me.

I took a breath. He definitely would've told me. I was definitely overreacting.

'Have his classes started yet?' Cam asked me.

'Uh . . . Yeah. He had Math this morning.'

'Ugh.'

'He loved it.'

Warren snorted again. 'Who'd have thought Flynn was such a geek, huh? He hid it pretty well. I bet he used to hide textbooks in the seat of his motorcycle.'

'Flynn,' Levi said, and looked between Lee and me. 'Is that your brother?'

'My brother,' Lee explained. 'His name's Noah – our surname's Flynn – but everyone's always called him Flynn. He's dating Elle.'

'Oh. *Oh!* I – sorry, I thought you two were related or something. I mean, you don't look that much alike, but the way you guys act, I figured . . .'

'It's okay,' Lee said reassuringly. 'Easy mistake.'

Lee and I were twins in practically everything except

23

blood: we'd been born on the same day and had grown up together. We'd been best friends our entire lives. Sometimes people seemed to forget we weren't actually related.

'Lee and Flynn – Noah – God, I don't know what to call him now he's gone,' Cam muttered the last comment to himself, 'threw some epic parties over the last couple of years. There was one, a few months ago . . .' He started chuckling, chest heaving as he tried to suppress it to finish his story. 'And Elle got so drunk . . . she started dancing on the pool table, then tried to strip off to go skinny-dipping. Funniest. Thing. *Ever.*'

Levi raised his eyebrows at me. 'And here I was thinking you were a wholesome, all-American, average girl next door.'

'It was the single most humiliating experience ever,' I groaned, blushing over it. The guys were busy laughing at me. I had only vague memories of that night, and I hadn't had more than a few sips of beer at a party since. Although, the night *had* ended with Noah totally coming to my rescue, so . . . it hadn't been a total disaster. And I'd seen him in his underwear – Superman boxers, which I'd teased him about endlessly.

'Aw, come on, Shelly,' Lee said with a wicked gleam in his blue eyes, taking my mind off the image of Noah in his boxer shorts. 'I can think of far more embarrassing things you've done.'

'Shelly?' Levi asked.

'Short for Rochelle,' I explained.

'You should call her Shelly,' Warren told him. 'She totally loves it.'

'Do *not* call me Shelly.'

'But –' Looking lost and helpless, Levi glanced at Lee.

I might let Lee and Noah get away with calling me Shelly, but it wasn't exactly a nickname I loved. I narrowed my eyes now at Lee, who was shaking with silent laughter.

I pointed my fork at him, a french fry dangling off the end. 'You dare bring anything else up, and I will personally rummage through the photo albums in your attic to find those photos of you dressed up as Elvis to show Rachel. Or the Halloween we went as Sonny and Cher.'

Lee sobered up at that, and mimed zipping his lips shut. Then he stole the fry off the end of my fork and ate it, ignoring the mock-glare I gave him.

'Speaking of parties . . .' Dixon, playing peacemaker as usual, asked who we thought was most likely to host the first party of the year, and then tried persuading Lee or Warren to host, but they both seemed apprehensive.

I looked over at Lee, who was holding hands with Rachel on top of the table and talking to her in a low voice, looking at her like she lit up his entire world.

Noah looked at me like that sometimes.

The thought sent a pang through my stomach. Not just because I missed Noah, but because seeing Lee so wrapped up in his girlfriend made me worry again a little that I might lose him. I mean, of course I wanted my best friend to be happy, and I was thrilled that he was so in love with Rachel. But, now that Noah wasn't around, I was starting to notice how little time Lee and I spent just the two of us, since he had Rachel. Not that I was jealous.

Alright, so maybe I was a *little* jealous. Just a teeny tiny bit.

I glanced over at Levi again. Levi, who wanted to fit in and make friends. Sure, the other guys seemed to like him well enough, and they'd hang out with him – but without Lee attached to my hip, it looked like I might be hanging out with the new kid this year.

And weirdly enough, the idea didn't sound so bad.

Chapter 3

'Jesus, Lee,' I mumbled. 'Some of these guys are huge.'

Lee was bulked out with pads and a helmet, and he wasn't exactly small: shorter and leaner than Noah, still kinda tall, and strong. But some of the guys out on the field looked three times the size of him, psyching themselves up for tryouts. Some of them had already been on the team last year.

And, up until then, I'd thought Lee would be a shoo-in for the team.

'Sure,' he replied, bouncing on his toes, 'but I'm fast, and you know I can catch the ball. That wide receiver shirt has my name on it.'

'Actually, I think the quarterback shirt does.'

He pulled a face at me. Lee had always been into football – and pretty good at it – but he'd never wanted to be on the team before now. Not when Noah had been the shining star as the quarterback. I kind of couldn't blame him.

Lee started whistling, and it took me a minute to recognize the song.

'Is that that song? "I Hope I Get It", or whatever it's called?'

'Yu-huh. From *Chorus Line*.'

'You what now?'

'Hey. I watched a lot of musicals online with Rachel this summer so she could prep for drama club. She's going for a leading role this year. I'm a good supportive boyfriend, you know. Ask me to sing you Fiyero's part from "As Long as You're Mine". I rock that.'

First he picked a desk next to Rachel instead of me, and now I was finding out that he'd been spending time this summer singing musicals with her? What else wasn't he sharing with me?

But I rolled my eyes good-naturedly. 'Whatever you say, buddy.'

The coach's whistle shrilled across the field. 'Line up, boys! We're starting with running drills!'

'Guess you'd better go.'

'Wish me luck.'

'Hey.' I put my hand on Lee's shoulder so he looked me in the eye. I nodded at him. 'You've got this.'

'And you've got a zit on your chin.'

'Love you too!' I yelled after him, watching him run out on to the field to join the rest of the hopefuls. I took a spot in the bleachers to watch, and couldn't help comparing him to how Noah had once played. Lee wasn't *as* good, but he was still a strong player.

When they were done, Lee started toward me in the bleachers rather than following the rest of the guys to the locker room. I hopped down a few rows, grinning at him, but Coach Pearson got to him first, clapping him on the shoulder.

'You did good, Little Flynn. Maybe you'll live up to your name yet.'

'I made the team?'

'I'll post the sheet tomorrow morning, but it's looking good. Your brother help you with some of those passes?'

'Yes, sir.'

'He did a damn fine job. Now, go on – hit the showers. You can celebrate with your girlfriend later.'

'Oh, no, she's not –'

Coach Pearson was already gone.

I'd made my way down to the field, and did a little dance. 'You did it! You did it, you made the team!'

Lee stared at me blankly for a second before breaking into a grin, and throwing his arms round me before I could protest. I gagged. 'Did you even put deodorant on?'

'Why? Can't handle my manly man stink?'

He wrestled my head into his armpit before I squirmed away, shoving him back.

'I'm so proud of you, Lee. This is awesome.'

'Guess I've just gotta be as good as Noah now,' he mumbled. 'Keep up the Flynn reputation.'

'Oh, come on. Don't worry about that. Pearson's a jackass sometimes. That was a stupid thing to say. Now go shower before I actually vomit from your manly man stink.'

Lee saluted me before practically skipping off to the locker room. I cheered after him, whooping, and it turned to giggles as I watched him jump up, clicking his heels together and throwing his arms out.

Sitting back down to wait for Lee, I got my phone out to video-call Noah.

It was only after he picked up that I realized this was something Lee would probably want to tell his brother himself.

'Hey, one sec,' Noah yelled at the phone, holding it half against his chest as he walked. There was a lot of background noise. It sounded kind of like a party. I saw blurred figures in the background as he moved around, saying 'excuse me' and then, finally, 'Right. Hi. I'm back.' He grinned at me, showing off the dimple in his left cheek. His cheeks were flushed and his long, dark hair stuck to his forehead a little.

My heart stuttered to see him, and I found myself smiling back.

'Where are you?'

'The library, can't you tell?' He laughed. 'I'm at a party. Well, outside the party, now. We started early. So, what's up? Or did you just call 'cause you miss me?' He winked, then looked more closely at the video. 'Are you on the football field? Oh, shit! Trials! How did Lee do?'

As I stammered, 'He, uh, I probably shouldn't . . .' Noah whooped, punching the air and jostling the camera around. I sighed at him when he focused his phone back on himself. 'You so didn't hear that from me, though.'

'Hear what, Shelly?'

'Right answer.' I tucked a piece of hair that had fallen out of my ponytail behind my ear. 'Ugh, today could not have been over soon enough. Do you know how much homework I have after just one day? It's crazy. And all those résumés I handed out the last couple of weeks for part-time work? None of them have got back to me. Please, please tell me senior year isn't all like this.'

Noah raised an eyebrow at me. 'You don't even wanna know how many chapters my professors recommended I read this week. I have zero sympathy right now.'

'Speaking of, I wasn't sure if you'd answer. I thought you'd be studying.'

Noah shrugged, scratching behind his ear, eyes drifting away from the screen. 'I was, and now I'm at a frat house. Steve scored us invites. I swear to God, he knows everyone here, and I don't even know how.'

'That's cool. So how is college going? The classes, I mean. Obviously the parties are great.'

Obviously they were, because he'd been to a bunch since the semester had started.

I just kind of wished he'd tell me less about the parties and all his new friends and tell me more about how the rest of college was going.

'You know, it's just class. It's fine. So, get this, this guy just now was doing a keg stand, and –'

'Noah . . .' I couldn't hide the disappointed look on my face, but he was doing a pretty good job of trying to look upbeat and change the subject.

'What's up?'

'How'd that assignment you had go?'

'I, uh, I don't get a grade back on that for a while. Anyway, so –'

He cut off when someone shouted for him in the background, calling something I couldn't quite make out. Noah shouted back, 'One sec,' leaning away from the phone before bringing it back in front of his face.

He bit his lip – looking utterly cute and annoyingly apologetic. My stomach sank.

'Listen, Elle, is it cool if I call you later? I'm sorry, I really wanna talk, this is just . . .'

Do you? I thought, because he seemed to be doing a really great job of avoiding talking.

But it was no big deal. All the parties and stuff, it was just . . . part of the experience, right? When he'd started college, he'd sounded so excited about his classes. But the last few days . . . he he'd hardly mentioned them.

So I smiled, and said, 'Don't even worry about it. We can talk tomorrow. Have a fun night.'

'I love you,' he told me, blowing a loud kiss down the phone at me to make me laugh.

'Love you too.'

I didn't have long to dwell on whether or not Noah was avoiding talking to me or if I was just overthinking it, because Lee was out of the locker room soon enough. He waved his phone at me, a big smile on his face as he told me how the drama club would be doing *Les Mis* this year and that Rachel was planning to audition for Fantine.

Back at the parking lot, I caught his arm before we got into his Mustang. 'Hey, listen. I'm really proud of you for making the team, you know that?'

'This is our year, Elle. This is *our year.*'

Chapter 4

'What do you mean, *you're bailing on me*? You knew I was babysitting Brad tonight while my dad's upstate on a conference. You *promised* you'd stay over!'

Lee sighed into the phone, and I knew he was tugging at his hair. 'I know, Shelly. I'm sorry. I am a pathetic excuse for a best friend.'

'Oh, come on, Lee, please? Rachel will survive without you for one evening.'

I knew I sounded whiny and bratty, but it really felt like *ages* since Lee and I had properly spent any time together, just the two of us hanging out. We were only a week into school, but between Rachel and his new spot on the football team (and actual schoolwork, too, of course) I felt like he was slowly drifting away from me.

I was trying hard not to be mad at him about it. He was totally head over heels in love with Rachel. He was busy. I understood that. I was happy for him.

But – *what about me?*

Lee still hadn't replied. He was feeling bad, and I knew he was probably trying to figure out a way to say 'I'd rather spend my evening with my girlfriend than you' without sounding like a jackass.

'I just miss you,' I said, my voice sounding small. I cringed; I sounded so pathetic. Honestly, how crazy did I sound? *I miss you.* I saw him practically every day. 'We just don't hang out so much any more.'

'I know, Shelly. I'm sorry.'

'Can't you come over at least for a *little* while?'

'I can't.'

I sighed.

'I'll make it up to you, I promise. We'll go shopping tomorrow. Shoe shopping. I'm buying lunch.'

'Hmm . . .'

It didn't make up for it at all, but I knew how hard he was trying. I felt myself caving quickly. I always did, when it came to Lee.

'And I'll find you a replacement co-babysitter?' he offered.

'Is dessert included in this lunch?'

'Dessert *or* a starter. Not both.'

'Sold.'

He laughed, but then said quietly, 'I'm really sorry. It's just . . . You know?'

'I get it. It's okay.' It wasn't, but it had to be. 'Have fun. Say hi to Rachel for me.'

'I'll see you tomorrow. Thanks, Elle! You're the best.'

Hanging up, I fell back on to my bed. Brad would be home from soccer practice in about twenty minutes, so I decided to relish the peace and quiet while it lasted.

Soon enough, I heard Brad yell goodbye to the boys piled into the back of the minivan that dropped him off, and the sound of his footsteps as he ran toward the house. I went down to meet him.

'I scored a goal!'

I ruffled his hair. 'Awesome!' Then I pushed him away at arm's length before he stepped inside. 'Okay, little guy. Cleats off. Straight in the shower. Try not to get mud everywhere.'

'But –'

'Cleats, shower. Go, go, go!'

I knocked the dried mud off his shoes before following the trail of muddy laundry up to the bathroom door. On the other side, Brad was belting out some rap song I kind of recognized from the radio, but with most of the lyrics wrong. (I was sure that whatever the words were, they didn't mention grilled cheese.)

I was right by the front door, at the bottom of the staircase, holding the filthy bundle of Brad's laundry, when the doorbell rang.

It was probably Cam or Dixon, sent in Lee's stead to make my evening of babysitting more bearable. It was definitely too late for Girl Scout cookies. I fumbled at the latch with my shoulder, pressing my elbow down on the door handle, and once it was unlocked, I nudged the door open with my foot.

'What are *you* doing here?'

Levi raised his eyebrows. 'Nice to see you, too.'

I blushed. 'Sorry, I just – I wasn't expecting you.'

'Lee called me and said you wanted some company babysitting your brother. So, here I am. I did text you to say I was heading over?'

'Oh. Sorry, I didn't hear my phone.'

A couple of seconds passed in silence. Levi took in the bundle of muddy clothes in my arms, then looked back at me expectantly. He was wearing a thin water-proof coat with the collar turned up against the fine drizzle that was falling. His hair was damp, the curls flat. It was a cute look on him.

Noah always managed to look hot whenever he got caught in the rain. I, however, usually looked like a frizzy mess.

'Can I come in?'

'Oh, right! Yes – of – of course. Sure.' I stepped aside, making way for him. He brushed his sneakers off on the welcome mat before coming inside. I gestured with

37

Brad's soccer clothes. 'I'll be right back – I need to sort these out. The lounge is just there. Make yourself at home.'

'Thanks.'

It was amazing how Levi had integrated into our group so easily already. He shared a lot of the same interests and had the same sense of humor as the rest of us – it really didn't feel like we'd only known him a week.

Levi was charismatic. He was even getting to be kind of popular. But we still didn't know that much about him. His social media was pretty devoid of information, so most of what people had to say about him seemed more like rumor than fact – which only made people talk about him even more. He didn't talk about himself too much, either. The mystery only added to the novelty of him being a new kid at school. (And an attractive one, too. Objectively speaking.)

But he was easy to hang out with, and he made for a decent study partner when Lee ditched me for Rachel.

When I got back from doing the laundry, Levi was stretched across the couch, flipping through TV channels.

'We've got ravioli for dinner,' I told him.

'Sounds good! Thanks, Elle. Here, did you want –' He

held the remote out to me but I shook my head, telling him to go ahead and pick something to watch.

I put dinner on and fetched us both drinks. Levi had settled on *The Lego Movie*. I put our drinks down on the coffee table and sat at the other end of the couch.

Brad came downstairs soon after, and did a double take upon seeing some strange guy there. He looked at me uncertainly, and I pulled a face at him to warn him to be nice.

'Uh, hi.'

Levi turned to look at my younger brother hovering in the doorway, and smiled easily. 'Hey. You must be Brad.'

'Yeah. You aren't Lee, though.'

'Brad! That's not polite.'

But Levi was laughing. 'I'm Levi.'

'The new guy?'

'I may have mentioned you a couple of times,' I said, by way of explanation to Levi. 'Lee couldn't make it tonight, Brad. Sorry, bud, I know you were looking forward to seeing him.'

'What about the other guys? Like Cam. Or Warren. Warren's fun. He taught me how to swear in French. *Merde*. See?'

'*Brad!*'

'What? I'm just *asking*.' Brad started to take a seat and

39

then realized we were watching a movie. He scowled at me. 'You promised me this morning I could play video games.'

'I know, but now we're watching a movie. C'mon, you like this movie. You know, with Batman and stuff. "It's really awesome",' I sang.

'Those aren't the lyrics, Elle.'

'You know what I mean.'

'This is so unfair. You *promised*.'

He sounded just like I had earlier, whining to Lee on the phone. I only felt a little guilty, though. I mean, Levi didn't want to sit here watching my brother play games; at least a movie was better entertainment. Or so I thought.

'What video games?' Levi asked my brother.

Brad's face lit up, and I could see him wondering if he could win Levi over to his side. 'My dad says I'm not "mature enough" for any of the games with guns and stuff – you know, like *Grand Theft Auto* – but I've got some really cool racing games.' He started naming some of his favorites, meaning the ones he was best at. 'And *Zelda*. I have *Zelda*.'

'I don't mind playing with you. As – as long as your sister says that's okay?' Levi turned to me, waiting for approval, eyebrows knitted together. 'I mean, if you've got homework to do . . .'

'You honestly don't have to,' I muttered, so Brad wouldn't hear.

'Better than painting nails,' he said. 'My sister loves giving me a manicure.'

'Elle, can we play? *Please?*'

My eyebrows shot up; I couldn't help it. If Brad was saying please to me, his big sister, then he must've taken a liking to Levi. I made a mental note that he would always be my babysitting buddy from now on if Lee wasn't free.

'Uh, well, I . . . I don't see why not. Good luck trying to beat my high score, though. Even Lee hasn't managed that.'

So, while Brad set up his console and loaded a game, I left them to it, deciding to finish redrafting my essay on the Cold War that was due in on Monday. After that, I opened up the Word document titled 'College Application Essay' – but after staring at the blank page for a few minutes and not being able to think of something to fill it, I closed the lid of my computer. College was all anyone seemed to talk about at school, and even though I knew I wanted to go I had no idea what I wanted to major in or what I really wanted to do afterwards. At least Lee and I had decided long ago that we wanted to go to UC Berkeley together, so I didn't have to worry about *where* to go.

But everyone else seemed to know what they wanted to do at college, which wasn't really helping me deal with the stress of *not* knowing. I felt sure that once I'd written my essay, everything else would fall into place. I'd figure it out. It'd be fine. It had to be.

This evening, though, I gave up on my essay, too distracted by listening to Levi cracking jokes and Brad getting competitive. Levi glanced over his shoulder at one point to flash a grin at me – and I found myself thinking how unlike Noah's crooked smile it was. There was something less daring, less exciting in Levi's smile. It was more like . . . like he knew a secret, and I knew it too. I'd heard girls at school talking about his smile. It was pretty charming, I guessed.

Even if my brother had been looking forward to hanging out with Lee, he quickly became a fan of Levi, just like the rest of us had. Brad didn't even complain when I snuck some vegetables on to his plate with his ravioli; he was too busy chatting with Levi about soccer, and asking him about lacrosse.

He even went to bed more or less on time – after ten minutes spent arguing with me to stay up longer because Dad wasn't home yet and it wasn't even a school night.

'I've already let you stay up half an hour longer than Dad would've!' I exclaimed for the billionth time.

'Dad won't be home for another hour, though! Come on, Elle, don't be so uptight!'

'Lee taught you that word, didn't he?'

'This is *so* unfair. Tell her, Levi. Tell her to stop being so uptight,' he said, trying to rope his new best friend on to his side.

'Sorry, but I'm with your sister on this one.'

Brad scowled, but grumbled in defeat. 'Fine. Thanks for playing video games with me,' he added, then mumbled goodnight and started stomping up the stairs to bed.

'Don't forget to floss,' I called after him, even though I knew he wouldn't floss at all. Then, I sunk back down on to the couch next to Levi. 'Thanks for that. For all of tonight. I really appreciate the help.'

'I thought you said he was a total nightmare when you were talking about him in school. Let me tell you – you haven't even *seen* nightmare children. You should see my sister when she's hungry and tired. She gets so shrill and it's totally insufferable, I'm telling you. I'd switch any day.'

'Wait till her PMS kicks in, too. But you'll be in college by then, right?'

'Right,' he mumbled.

'Thanks, though. Really. The only people Brad really listens to are Lee and Noah, and that's only because he completely idolizes them from growing up with them around.'

Levi nodded, and after a pause said, 'So . . . you and Noah. Were you guys friends before dating? I know you and Lee are close.'

I scrunched my face up. 'Not . . . exactly. I mean, kind of. We were when we were all little kids, but then we drifted apart when he went to middle school.'

'How did you end up together, then? Stop me if I'm being rude. I'm trying for *politely inquisitive*.' He grinned. 'Just, nobody's really talked about what happened with you two. It seems kind of taboo or something.'

'Not taboo,' I said. 'It's just that not everyone knows the whole story. It's kind of complicated.'

He shrugged. 'I've got all night. Or, at least until your dad gets back and you kick me out.'

I smiled and tucked my feet up on the couch underneath me. 'Well, it all started with a kissing booth . . .'

And when I was done, Levi simply said, 'It's nice that Lee forgave you, and that you two are still such good friends. I never had a best friend like that. I mean, I had best friends, sure, but not like you've got Lee.'

I nodded, because I wasn't sure what to say. Times like tonight, I felt like I didn't 'have' Lee much at all. We both turned back to the TV – some documentary on the History Channel. And after a few minutes, my cell phone rang.

Noah.

I answered, mouthing 'one sec' to Levi.

'Hey!'

'I just got in from a party. I wish you were here. I've got this bed all to myself and it's *incredibly* lonely. I miss you.' He was slurring his words a little, and yawned, long and loud. I blushed a little.

'Much as I'd like to be there and, um . . . cuddle up with you, can I call you back in a second?'

'Everything okay?'

'Yeah, I just . . . have company.'

But Levi was standing up. 'It's okay, I should probably head off now anyway. I promised my mom I wouldn't be home too late.'

I nodded, and told Noah to hang on just a sec, as I walked Levi to the door. He slipped on his coat and picked up his car keys. 'I'll see you at school on Monday?'

'Yeah. Thanks again for tonight. I'll repay the favor sometime.'

He smiled brightly. 'I'll hold you to that.'

Back in the lounge, falling across the couch with my feet dangling over the armrest, I clicked to turn the call into a video one. Noah appeared on the screen, lying on his side with his handsome face half-smooshed into a pillow. I couldn't help but smile, seeing him – it made my heart swell.

'Hey. Sorry.'

'Who was that?' Noah's voice was more awake now, but still a little less than sober.

'Levi.'

'The new guy Levi?'

'No, the old Levi.' I rolled my eyes. 'Remember I said I had to babysit Brad tonight, because my dad's not back till late? And Lee was supposed to hang out with me?'

Noah propped himself up on one elbow so I could see him better. He wasn't wearing a shirt. I wished he was here, or I was there. His mouth twisted to one side. 'Let me guess – he ditched you for Rachel.'

'Yup. But he's taking me shopping tomorrow as penance, and buying lunch. Anyway, he sent Levi as a replacement co-babysitter to keep me company. Which was okay, actually. He's a pretty nice guy. Funny. Easy to talk to, you know? Everyone seems to like him.' I smirked. 'The girls definitely seem to like him. He's got a lot of admirers, the way I hear it.'

'Should I worry I've got competition, Shelly?' Even though his voice was slow, his tone was unmistakably teasing. His blue eyes glittered even through the phone screen.

'Oh, totally.'

He laughed.

'How was the party?'

'Alright, I guess.' Then, 'I miss you.'

'I miss you more.'

'Nuh-uh.'

'What're you gonna do about it? You can't tickle me into submission from all the way in Massachusetts.'

'Oh, believe me, when I see you next I'll have to pack in *weeks* of tickling you're owed.'

I grinned, laughing softly. We carried on talking a little about college, school, our friends – though Noah seemed to ask more questions than he answered. I got the feeling he was avoiding talking to me about something, but it was such a small, silly, nagging thought I chose to ignore it. I was too happy seeing him, talking to him. I thought about confiding in him how it felt like Lee and I were drifting apart, but I didn't want to risk it getting back to Lee and upsetting him, so I decided it was better to keep that to myself.

As we spoke, in hushed voices, I felt an ache somewhere inside. Not exactly in my chest, or my stomach, but just a deep-rooted all-over kind of ache. I missed him so much. More than anything, I wished I could be curled up next to him with his arms round me, the rise and fall of his chest beneath my head, his fingers teasing my hair. I watched his lips moving as he talked, thinking about how much I wanted to kiss him. Noah's voice got slower, heavier, as we spoke, and he sank back down into the pillow.

A car drew up outside – Dad was home.

'I should go,' I said, just as Noah yawned again. 'My dad's back. I'll talk to you tomorrow. I love you.'

'I love you too,' he mumbled, half asleep. 'Sweet dreams.'

He hung up then, and left me smiling and feeling fuzzy inside, and I walked out into the hallway just as my dad was hanging up his coat.

'Oh, bud, you didn't have to wait for me to get in.'

'You know I always do. How was the conference?'

He just pulled a face.

'Sounds like you guys had a wild time.'

He smiled tiredly. 'As always. How was Brad?'

'An angel,' I said, with no hint of sarcasm, and quickly explained that Levi had come to keep me company. 'Brad loved him.'

'I think this Levi guy is gonna have to be my new go-to babysitter. Come on, it's late. Way past *your* bed-time, bud.'

Chapter 5

I plucked the pickle out of my burger, dropping it on to Lee's plate with a look of disgust. Now that was disposed of, I dug into my cheeseburger with extra bacon, and gave a moan of appreciation, grease dribbling down my fingers.

'I should hope you're enjoying it, for fifteen dollars,' Lee muttered, but when I looked up he was grinning. We were at the food court in the mall, and he'd picked the restaurant. It was more expensive than our usual haunt; he was trying to soften me up and apologize for yesterday.

'It's worth every dime,' I assured him, wiping some rogue mayo from the corner of my mouth. Lee asked me how hanging out with Levi had been, faking horror that he might have been replaced as Brad's new favorite person.

'I should've known Brad would like him,' Lee said. 'Everyone seems to like the guy.'

'I heard he was nominated for prom king at his last school. I'm telling you, Lee. You keep bailing on me, you've got some serious competition.'

It was a joke, but he at least had the decency to look abashed.

We were both too stuffed from our meals to order dessert, so we spent some time wandering around the mall and window-shopping. Lee pointed to a couple of signs in windows declaring HELP WANTED – ENQUIRE WITHIN but I told him it was useless. I'd already applied to every one he noticed. The few times I did get a reply, it was only to say that I 'wasn't the right fit' or that they were looking for someone with more experience.

It sucked, but I wasn't especially surprised: Dixon and Warren had been having the same problem. I didn't take the rejections too personally after I found that out.

Once we'd walked off our lunch, Lee bought us both ice-cream cones from a stand in the food court.

'You know,' Lee said, as we ate our ice creams, 'we'll probably have to come shopping again in a couple of weeks for the Sadie Hawkins dance. I need a new suit jacket. My old one's too small across the shoulders.'

'Oh yeah?'

He flexed his muscles. 'You know, since I'm the next star of the football team, now.'

'Yeah, yeah, you have guns, I get it. So, Sadie Hawkins – that's not just a rumor, then?' I asked, but I was scrutinizing Lee. He'd been going to the gym with Dixon over the summer vacation, and practicing more football with Noah. I hadn't really noticed, but he *was* bulking up. He wasn't as big as Noah, but he was getting there. His arms were larger, for sure – the newly toned muscles in his arms were straining the sleeves of his T-shirt.

'Ethan Jenkins told me yesterday,' Lee answered, not seeing me staring at his shoulders and arms. Ethan was the new head of the school council, since Tyrone had left for college. We hadn't had a meeting yet this year. Just as I thought it, Lee said, 'And before I forget, there's a meeting Wednesday at lunch. Ethan told me that, too.'

'Sure, whatever. Now, focus on the major new development here: Sadie Hawkins dance. Did Ethan mention a date? Theme? Do you have *any* more information for me? You know I'm a sucker for a school dance.'

'Oh, crap, now you're freaking out. I shouldn't have told you.'

'I'm not freaking out!' I protested, maybe a little too vehemently. More calmly, I said, 'I'm *not* freaking out.'

'I think it's, like, the first weekend of November or

something? I wasn't really listening. But I *do* remember he said it was only gonna be in the school gym. Nowhere fancy. He said they've cut the budget this year, like, a lot, so they're doing Sadie Hawkins instead of the usual Winter Dance, and they're gonna save most of the budget and the profits from fundraisers for the Summer Dance.'

'That makes sense, I guess.'

Lee started telling me about some new football play Coach Pearson was making them learn, but my eyes drifted, assessing dresses in store windows. My mind was half on the dance and half on the fact that, actually, I could really do with a job after school to help pay for a new dress.

'Shelly?'

'Huh?'

'Are you even listening to me?'

'Sure. One of the juniors fumbled the ball too many times and Coach had him run laps.'

'You were thinking about the dance, weren't you?'

I hung my head slightly in confession. I didn't want to bring up the job thing again right now; Lee knew I'd been trying to get something, but I didn't think I could handle yet another pitying smile over it. 'Maybe.'

'Thinking about who you're gonna ask?' he guessed, and I could have sworn I felt all the blood drain from my face. I'd forgotten that about the Sadie Hawkins dance: the girls asked the boys.

Crap.

'Wanna go to the Sadie Hawkins together?'

I knew what his answer would be, but I remained hopeful. Lee was my best friend, after all. We'd been to tons of dances together, before – well, before Rachel.

Predictably, his face fell, before scrunching up with apology. 'I'm sorry, Shelly. You know I would, but . . .'

'No, no, it's fine. Totally. I shouldn't have asked. Of course you'll go with Rachel.'

'I'm sorry.'

I shrugged. *She's more important to you.* I didn't say it out loud, because I knew it would sound spiteful and jealous; and I *was* feeling kind of spiteful and jealous. Instead, I said, 'You can't ditch your girlfriend to go to a dance with me. I'm sure that's overstepping some kind of boundary. Rachel's nice and all, but even she'd hate that.'

'I'm sure Dixon would go with you, as friends, if you asked him.'

I shrugged. Dixon would probably have offers from other girls. He might not have been conventionally attractive, but he was charismatic and funny and sweet.

'Maybe Noah will be home the weekend of the dance?' Lee suggested brightly – a little too brightly.

Neither of us actually expected that to happen, and I wasn't going to hold out hope. Besides, Noah didn't even like school dances. He'd gone to them before because that was what the whole football team did, but he didn't enjoy them so much. He'd made a big display of asking me to the last Summer Dance and asking me to be his girlfriend in front of everyone, but . . .

'He's a college boy now,' I said, trying to joke about it. 'Way too cool for some stupid high school dance.'

Would he laugh at me, if I asked him? Would he come home for a weekend and go with me? Was it even fair of me to ask him to come all the way back here just for some dance?

Lee reached over and slipped his fingers through mine, squeezing my hand. I squeezed back before letting go.

We wandered around a couple of stores and, while I was still busy wondering how I could bring up the dance to Noah, I noticed Lee checking his phone, and getting agitated. He kept almost saying something.

I kept waiting for him to say something. I wasn't sure what, but *something*.

Eventually, I grabbed his arm, yanking him to a stop near the fountain.

'What the hell is going on with you? You're acting weird.'

'I have to talk to you.'

The words sent a pang of dread through me. I forced out a laugh and said, 'Lee, are you – are you breaking up with me?'

He rolled his eyes, but the grim look stayed on his face – eyebrows pulled low and close together, eyes downcast, mouth twisted, nostrils flared.

'Okay, now you're scaring me. What's wrong? Is it Noah? Did something happen with Rachel last night? Lee?'

'I didn't see Rachel last night.'

'Huh?'

'You assumed that's where I was, and I didn't tell you otherwise, but . . . I let you think I was with Rachel. I didn't bail on you last night to see Rachel.'

'Then . . . Then where were you?'

The only time I'd kept anything from Lee was when I was sneaking around with Noah; I'd kept it from Lee because I didn't want to hurt him or ruin our friendship. But it wasn't like I had a sister Lee was sneaking around with, so what secrets did he have to keep from me?

'Football.'

'Wait, hang on, you . . . lied to me, because you were at football practice? None of this makes sense.'

'It wasn't practice.' Lee hooked his hands behind his

head, leaning back. 'It was initiation. A bunch of guys who were on the team last year organized it. They said we couldn't tell anyone, so when I bailed on you, and you assumed it was because I was hanging out with Rachel . . .'

'Why couldn't you tell anyone?'

'I don't know, it was just a *thing*. It wasn't like they threatened to kidnap someone we cared about if we told,' he added, lightening up a little and flashing me a fleeting grin, 'but I just . . . I guess I wanted to be part of the team, you know?'

'How come you didn't just tell me earlier?'

'I don't know. But someone just posted a photo on Instagram, and I wanted you to know before you thought I was lying to you. For the record, I never lied.'

He gave me a steady look.

'Oh, come on! This is so not the same thing.'

'I'm just saying. I didn't lie. I just let you think it.'

I chewed on my lip for a moment. 'No, it's – it's fine, Lee. It's no big deal. Initiation. I get it.'

'It sounds so stupid now I'm saying it, but it seemed really important last night. Being part of the team, you know? And they were pretty intimidating about it. Like, they take this shit *really* seriously.'

'Yeah. I get it. Hey, stop looking so worried.' I patted his cheek, smiling. Although, keeping secrets from me – and over *football*, no less – was very un-Lee-like behavior. 'So, can you tell me what the initiation involved or, if you tell me, does that mean you'll have to kill me?'

Relaxing, Lee laughed, and after swearing me to secrecy, he told me how they'd all snuck into the school, and the new guys on the team had had to get through this kind of obstacle course to the locker room, and the first guy to make it there won . . .

'Well, they never said what the prize was, but I get the feeling it's just winning the respect of the rest of the team.'

'Obstacle course?' I wanted to know.

'Oh, yeah. Not like, hurdles and shit, though. So, the rest of the team hid on the way to the lockers with pies and Nerf guns and stuff, and they set up trip wires, and they'd put butter in one of the hallways so we were all sliding everywhere, falling on our asses . . . That's what the photo is of.' He laughed.

'Oh my God.' I snorted, reaching for my phone. 'I cannot wait to see this. You're in it, right?'

'Only a little, and not on my ass.'

'Did you win?'

'Of course. C'mon, Shelly, it's like you don't even know me. Yeah, I won.'

I found the photo, on Jon Fletcher's profile, and

giggled so loudly a few people looked over. 'Oh my God. I hope this makes the yearbook. The janitor is going to lose his shit on Monday when he sees this.'

'Oh, no. The rest of the newbies on the team, they had to clean up because they didn't win.' He paused. 'I'm sorry I didn't tell you last night.'

'No, Lee, don't – you can stop apologizing. I totally get it. I mean, I don't have to like it, so much, but I'm not mad at you, or anything. I swear.'

'Pinky promise?'

'Always.'

Before we left the mall, Lee insisted on going into the video-game store to find something. 'I need to win your brother back somehow. I can't risk losing both of you to Levi from Detroit.'

Chapter 6

It was Tuesday afternoon, and once again, Lee was not spending time with me.

Much as I tried, it was hard not to feel bitter about it. I kept telling myself I was happy for him, and I liked Rachel. But it stung every time Lee would come up to me with that spanked-puppy look on his face and take a deep breath, and I'd know he was about to blow off whatever plans we might have had before he even got a syllable out. I'd suggested hanging out as a trio a few times, but even I knew they wanted some space, and that I needed to step back.

So I asked Dixon for a ride home (again) and now I sat on the couch waiting for Brad to get home from Boy Scouts and Dad to get home from work, scrolling through my Twitter feed in case anything interesting was going on. Nothing was.

I tried calling Noah, but he didn't answer. Maybe he

was studying, I thought. If he was, he probably didn't want to be interrupted.

It wasn't long after that my cell trilled, and I jumped to answer it, not even pausing to check who was calling. 'Hey.'

'Hey, Elle.'

My heart sank; it wasn't Noah. I got a heavy, sick sort of feeling in my stomach, like after you watch a sad movie. Maybe he'd call me later. 'Hi, Levi.'

'You sound disappointed. I guess you were hoping for somebody else?'

'Kind of. No offense.'

'None taken.' Then, 'Noah?'

'Yeah.'

'Well, if you're not too busy sitting around waiting for your boyfriend to call you, do you wanna come over to my house for dinner?'

I was a little taken aback, until something clicked into place. 'Is this payback for helping me babysit Brad?'

'Yes, indeed.'

I sighed heavily, like it was a total hardship to stop doing nothing and hang out with a friend for the evening. (And hey, it'd take my mind off Noah and Lee a little, too.) 'I'm on my way.'

Twenty minutes later, I walked up the driveway and rang the doorbell. Levi's house was small but sweet-looking, with a tidy front lawn and peeling paint around the windows. A wonky brass 209 was nailed to the bright green door. Levi opened it seconds later wearing a floral apron, his hair sprinkled with flour. He was wearing the shirt he'd worn to school, with the sleeves rolled up to his elbows, but the pants from his school uniform had been switched for skinny jeans.

'Hey!'

'I like the apron. It's the epitome of masculinity and macho-ness.'

He laughed. 'That's the look I was going for. Come on in. We're baking brownies.'

'Sounds yummy.'

'I'm not sure about that,' he admitted, as I stepped inside and slipped off my shoes, placing them neatly on the rack by the door, and hanging my purse from a hook. 'I'm aiming for *not poisonous.*'

Now it was my turn to laugh. 'Just don't ask me to help. I've sworn off baking ever since my Home Ec disaster back in eighth grade.'

'Ooh, an embarrassing story? Tell me everything.'

'I may have used baking soda instead of salt and my cupcakes may have . . . exploded in the oven. Just a little. It was messy, but there was no fire extinguisher required.'

'Damn,' Levi muttered. 'All the best stories have a fire extinguisher. But if that's the case – maybe just . . . don't touch anything in the kitchen.'

I held up my hand. 'Scout's honor.'

As we walked through to the kitchen, I couldn't help but look around. It was pretty much the same lay-out as Cam's house, except a little more worn-in – I guess the previous owners didn't care to refurbish much before selling. The dark hardwood floors in the hallway were scuffed and slightly scratched, maybe from moving furniture in and out.

In the kitchen, there was a rack above a counter with spatulas and serving spoons and ladles hang-ing from it, scrawled pencil drawings and report cards and certificates on the refrigerator were held in place by brightly colored magnetic letters, and school books and papers were splayed out on the break-fast bar.

The messiest thing in the kitchen by a mile was the eight-year-old girl who stood on a small, sturdy plastic stool so that she could reach the counter. Her frizzy brown hair was falling out of its pigtails, and she wore one of those easy-clean aprons – again, floral, like Levi's, and pink. She turned round when we walked in, and the entire lower half of her face was covered in chocolate goop.

'Becca!' Levi cried, exasperated. 'I *told* you not to eat any more, you're gonna make yourself sick.'

'Who're you?' she asked me, completely ignoring her brother, in the same way Brad ignored me if Lee was around. She had wide hazel eyes, and right now they were fixed on me.

'I'm Elle. I'm one of Levi's friends from school. He asked me to come help babysit.'

'Are you his girlfriend?' She turned her attention to her big brother. 'I liked your old girlfriend better. She had freckles.'

'Becca,' he snapped.

But I smiled. 'No, I'm not his girlfriend. I'm just here for the brownies.'

I let them direct me to greasing a cake pan while they finished off the brownie mixture. Becca talked at both of us about the drama from recess that day. I held the pan toward Levi, ready to say, 'Hey, is this okay?'

Except I barely got out 'Hey' before he threw a healthy sprinkling of flour in my face.

I gasped, coughing and spluttering, flour flying from my mouth and nose and obscuring my vision. I blinked some bits of flour out of my eyes to see both of them laughing at me.

'Did you just . . . throw *flour* . . . in my *face*?'

'Becca did it.'

'No I didn't! I didn't, Elle, I didn't. Levi did it. You *saw* him.'

'I'm going to kill you,' I assured him, glaring.

'I'm sorry, I don't know why I did it,' he said, grinning maniacally.

I set the pan down on the counter and wiped my hands over my face, shaking flour on to the floor and the front of my clothes. While Levi had his back to Becca, I noticed her sneak another finger into the bowl and lick the mixture off before her brother could turn round again.

'If you do that again, I'm going to unfriend you. Officially. I'll unfollow you on Instagram and everything.'

Levi held a hand to his heart, pouting. 'In that case, you have my sincerest apologies.'

I grabbed some flour and threw it right back at him.

The brownies turned out great. Levi cut one in half and we shared it before dinner, away from Becca's prying eyes. After dinner, he refused my help with the dishes, so I sat in the lounge with Becca while she did some homework.

She stopped writing to look up at me from the floor, tongue poking between the gap in her two front teeth.

'I liked Levi's old girlfriend a lot, but I like you, too.'

'That's okay. You can like lots of people.'

'His old girlfriend was called Julie. Has he told you about her?'

'No, he hasn't.'

'Well, I'm going to tell you all about her,' she announced, lowering her voice to a conspiratorial whisper. She abandoned her notebook to sit next to me on the sofa and she told me gravely, 'They were *in love*.'

I leaned in, dropping my voice, too. 'Really.'

'*Really*. But she broke up with Levi just before we moved. He cried a lot, but whenever I told him I knew he was crying he said he wasn't. She had freckles and orange hair, and she played violin and piano. And she bought me nail polish for my birthday.'

'She sounds very nice.'

'I miss her.'

'I'm sure Levi misses her, too.'

Becca pursed her lips. 'I think he still cries about her sometimes.'

If I'd wanted to say anything else, I couldn't: the front door opened. I hadn't even heard a car pull up outside. Keys jangled and bags rustled and a voice called, 'I'm home! Whose car is that outside, Levi? Have you got a friend over?'

A woman I assumed could only be their mother walked into the lounge, dropping down some Publix bags filled with groceries. She wore a pantsuit and didn't have a hair out of place; but despite the stern appearance she had a kind face, which softened her whole demeanor.

'Hello.'

'Hi. You must be Mrs Monroe.' I stood up quickly, putting on my most parent-pleasing smile. 'I'm Elle, a friend of Levi's from school. It's so nice to meet you.'

She smiled back. 'I'm Nicole. Lovely to meet you, too. Levi's told me a lot about you.'

'Mom.' He'd just appeared in the doorway behind her. Catching my eye, he shot me an apologetic smile.

'Oh, Levi, go put the groceries away, will you? Have you had a bath yet, Becca?'

'No, but we made brownies.'

'I hope you saved me some.'

Before Becca let her mom usher her upstairs, she poked my arm and said very politely, 'Thank you for babysitting me.'

I suppressed a giggle, but smiled. 'You're very welcome, Becca.'

She babbled away to her mom as they went upstairs, and I collected the two remaining Publix bags and took them to the kitchen.

'Oh, thanks.' Levi took them from me. 'I was just about to come back for those.'

'Your sister's not half as bad as you made her out to be, you know.'

'I could say the same for your brother. Maybe we should switch.'

'That might not be such a bad idea.' I looked past him at the clock hanging on the wall. 'I guess I should probably head home . . .'

'You don't have to leave,' Levi said quickly, then blushed. 'I mean, you're welcome to stay a little longer, if you want, but obviously you don't have to.'

'I don't mind staying.' And then I heard myself saying, 'So, um, your sister was telling me about Julie.'

Levi's whole body seemed to sigh.

'You never mentioned her at school, to any of us.'

And I hadn't seen anything on his social media about her. Rachel and I had snooped, one lunchtime.

'She broke up with me when we found out we were moving here. We'd been together since freshman year. It was . . .'

'Whoa.'

And I'd thought a few months felt like a long time to be dating.

'When I broke the news about the move, she broke up with me there and then. She said that senior year was really important – and it is, obviously – and that a relationship on top of all that was hard enough, but a long-distance relationship was something she didn't think she could handle. She said . . . she said it was better this way for both of us. A clean break. And that was that.'

'You didn't fight for her?'

'She didn't want me to. I tried, but not much. It was killing her, I could see. She didn't want to break up, but she didn't want a boyfriend she'd probably not see unless we ended up at the same college. And honestly?' He shrugged, giving me a smile. 'I have no plans to go to college. So that was never gonna happen.'

I blinked, surprised. We'd all been talking a lot about college lately, and now that I thought about it, Levi had never shown much enthusiasm, or talked about where he wanted to apply or what he wanted to major in.

'I'm kind of jealous of you, you know. Because you and Noah – you guys are trying, at least. I wish she'd given us a shot. Even if it didn't work out.'

'Maybe it was for the best, though. Like she said.'

'Yeah, but . . .'

'But you loved her,' I finished gently, my voice soft.

Levi sighed again, and went back to putting away groceries.

I didn't know what to tell him. It wasn't like I had any experience to speak from, and I wasn't sure that the stuff I'd read in romance novels really counted. I settled on asking, 'Do you still talk to her?'

'No.'

'Oh.'

'I'm just trying to move on, you know? That's why I haven't kept in touch. And I guess that's why she hasn't messaged me either. I even deleted all the photos of us off my Instagram and stuff. It felt weird, keeping them up, seeing them, whenever I went on my profile. Now I'm just waiting to find that girl who I look at and who makes me forget all about Julie. Or maybe it'll only ever be Julie.'

'I can't tell if you're a romantic or not.'

He just laughed. Then said, 'Sorry, you probably don't want to listen to me pining after some girl who's states away from me and not even my girlfriend any more.'

'I don't mind. I mean, I've only ever been with Noah, so I'm not sure I'm best placed to give you any advice, but I don't mind listening, if you want to talk about it. I know the guys might not seem like the best audience for pining to. They goof around a lot, but they're delicate, sensitive little flowers underneath it all. You know, Cam cried once because he thought Lisa was ignoring his texts. But you didn't hear that one from me.'

His smile was small, and shy, but he looked touched. 'Thanks, Elle. I appreciate it.'

'Any time.'

Levi grabbed the plate of brownies, the groceries all put away now, and brought them over to the breakfast bar. I took a seat next to him and grabbed a brownie.

'So,' he said, tossing his curls back from his face, 'now you know all about my ex and the fact I'm not actually going to college . . . What else do I need to tell you about me? I feel like we're really unraveling the mystery of Levi Monroe tonight.'

I laughed. 'Oh, come on. Like you don't love being all mysterious.'

'One girl asked me last week if I really did cameo in *Riverdale*. That one was kind of cool.'

I smiled, but found that I did have a question to ask now he'd mentioned it. 'Where's your dad tonight?'

Levi shifted, a little uncomfortable. 'He's, uh, he's . . .'

'I'm sorry, you don't have to answer that.'

Levi didn't talk about his dad much at school, but as far as I could tell his parents were still together. There was even a photo of them on their wedding day in pride of place in the lounge, I'd noticed. But Levi's unease made me feel like I'd poked a hole in something I shouldn't have.

'No, it's okay.' Levi sipped his scalding-hot coffee, then said firmly, 'He's at a support group. He goes after work. He's in remission from prostate cancer. That hit him hard, and then he lost his job, and . . . Things kind of spiraled. That's why we moved. Fresh start, you know? He's been doing better since he got a new job, even if it's only part-time.'

'Oh my God.'

Because, honestly, I didn't know what else to say.

'I know, right? Talk about a bit of a bombshell. I'm sorry, I shouldn't have said anything. Just – forget about it, alright?' He started to get up, cheeks blotchy, unable to meet my eyes.

'No, I – I just . . . Well, I've never known anyone with cancer before, so I'm not really sure what to say, that's all. I hope everything's okay for your dad.'

'It will be.'

Levi sounded so convinced I didn't dare try and suggest things might be otherwise or that I was there for him if that was the case.

'Don't tell the others, though, will you? I just don't want them to treat me weird or anything because of it. Everyone at my old school did, except Julie. She was the only person who didn't look at me like I was some sad, stray puppy after my dad first got diagnosed.'

'You said he's in remission,' I said, then, 'and that's – that's good, right?'

'Well, he lost his balls, so no more surprise siblings – oh, shit, you didn't hear that either. Becca was *totally* planned.' He shot me a crooked smile. Cracking jokes because that was his way of dealing with things. Not wanting to open up too much about the hard stuff. I got that. I *really* got that.

In that moment, I really felt for Levi. The poor guy had lost his girlfriend, moved away from all of his friends, his parents had lost their jobs, his dad had been *really* sick . . . No wonder he hadn't opened up much. I had the urge to hug him tight.

'But yeah, otherwise, it's good,' he went on, before I could. 'They caught it right in the first stages and it was all resolved really quickly.'

'And I guess it's good he's got support groups to go to.'

Levi nodded, but was quiet.

'You know, my mom died. Years ago, when I was little. She was driving and it was icy, and she didn't make it home.'

Now it was his turn: 'Oh my God.'

'It's weird, though, because I'm just used to it now. Like, I've spent nearly half my life without a mom, and sometimes I really, really miss her, and then I feel guilty for not missing her all the rest of the time, too, which makes things worse.'

'Didn't your dad ever remarry?'

'No. Sometimes I think he's still not over my mom

72

dying. Or maybe being a single dad and having a full-time job doesn't leave a lot of time for dating.'

'But you're . . . over it? Okay with it?'

I gave Levi a wan smile. 'I don't think it's something you get over. You just go on anyway. But I get it, you know? People looking at you weird because of something like that. I think the guys would all be okay with you about it, but . . . I don't know. If you want a shoulder to cry on, or someone to vent to . . .'

Levi gulped, eyes shining. 'Thanks, Elle.'

'Anyway,' I said briskly, 'I totally forgot to ask you earlier – are you going to Jon Fletcher's party in a couple of weeks?'

After my heart-to-heart with Levi, when I got home later that night, I took one of the old family photo albums out of the small cabinet in Dad's office. He walked past the open door on his way to the kitchen, and stopped when he saw me sitting cross-legged on the floor flicking through pages of photos from before Brad was even born.

'What're you doing, Elle?'

I shrugged, not quite trusting my voice.

Last time I did this was in February. I'd had a complete breakdown because I'd forgotten it was Mom's birthday until Dad mentioned going to get some flowers to take to the cemetery. I'd spent the entire afternoon and evening studying photos of my mom and wondering what she would look like now. I did that when I missed her badly. I tried so hard to think if I remembered her looking like she did in the photos because I really did remember her, or just because I'd seen her photos around the house so many times.

'Missing your mom, huh?' Dad's knees creaked as he sat down on the floor beside me.

'A little.'

I didn't want him to stay; I didn't want him to talk to me about it, or talk about her, or tell me stories, because that was only going to make me cry, and I didn't want to cry right now. Crying wasn't going to bring her back, I told myself, just like I'd told myself a hundred times before.

I closed the photo album, but didn't put it back just yet.

'She'd be proud of you, you know.'

I just shrugged again. *For what?* For still not having written my college application essay? For almost losing my best friend a few months ago because I decided to date his brother behind his back? For not being able to get a part-time job despite the number of applications I'd sent out?

'Don't wanna talk about her, I take it?'

I shook my head, and Dad took the photo album from me and slid it back into its home in the cabinet.

'How was Levi?'

Now this was a conversation I could handle.

'Good. His sister was cute. We made brownies.'

'I hope when you say "we", you mean "they", because we all know you can't bake, bud.'

'I mean "they".' I smiled. 'But yeah, anyway, it was all really good. Becca – that's Levi's sister – she was telling me all about his ex-girlfriend. And then Levi told me that his dad had prostate cancer.'

'Oh, Christ. Is he okay now?'

'Levi said he's in remission, but his dad lost his job and stuff, too.'

'That's gotta be tough on them.'

'Yeah.'

'I'm guessing this is why you're thinking about your mom a lot, then.'

I nodded, and Dad said, 'Sounds like you two are becoming good friends. I'm glad to hear it, though – Lee hasn't been around much lately.'

There was a note of reproach in his voice I didn't fail to notice.

'He's got Rachel now. And football.'

'And Noah's not around either.'

I was never really sure if my dad completely approved

of Noah as my boyfriend. But he never said too much about it – he said he was just happy I was happy.

Although, I'm not sure 'happy' was exactly how I felt right now. I'd still barely heard from Noah all day. I was trying not to think about the missed call and texts he'd not returned, telling myself he had to be asleep: it was three hours later on the East Coast, after all.

Dad sighed heavily, with a concerned frown behind his glasses. 'Is everything okay, bud?'

Not really.

But I couldn't handle thinking about that right now. Things with Lee were – well, they'd go back to normal, or this would start to feel normal, at some point. Noah would be home for Thanksgiving soon, and maybe even for the Sadie Hawkins dance, if I could work up the courage to ask him. College would work itself out, and so would a job. It'd all be totally fine.

'Sure it is. I'm just tired. I'd better get to bed. Night, Dad.'

'Goodnight, Elle.'

Instead of hearing him leave the office, though, I heard the cabinet door opening and the rustle of pages as he took the old photo album back out. And I was pretty sure I heard him sniffle.

Chapter 7

I was willing it to be the Thanksgiving holidays already.
The days seemed to be dragging by. It wasn't just that
I was desperate to see Noah; I felt like I already needed
a break from school and my homeroom teacher asking
me every other day if I'd worked on my college application essay yet (*did* I have a first draft I wanted him to
give me a second opinion on? Not exactly . . .) and the
mountains of homework that never seemed to get any
smaller.

Lee had been spending a lot of time at football practice, or hanging out with the guys from the team. And
when he wasn't doing that, he was usually with Rachel.
And if Rachel wasn't with Lee, she was pouring herself
into studying – she wanted to make sure she got into
Brown – and rehearsing for the drama club. (She got
the part of Fantine in the end.)

So I found myself hanging out with Levi a lot. After
talking about his past and his dad, and my mom,

I could tell there was a shift between us. We'd bonded over something the others wouldn't really understand.

And, honestly, he was maybe the only person who made me feel at least a bit less stressed about college. He worked hard at school, but he was pretty blasé when it came to college. He had no desire to go. It wasn't for him, he said. It was as simple as that. But he did try to help with my application essay.

The less Lee was around, the more I found myself missing Noah. One study hall, Levi and Dixon jokingly threw Skittles at me each time I mentioned Noah's name. They ran out of candy after ten minutes.

'So sue me,' I'd snapped at them. 'I miss my boyfriend.'

Sometimes it just made me feel cold and empty, like he should've been there with me, arms wrapped round me. Sometimes it was an ache so strong it hurt. All the phone calls in the world couldn't make up for it. And the Uber Eats of my favorite takeout he had sent to me one evening he knew I was trying to work on my college application essay had totally made me cry.

'You're such a sap, Elle Evans,' he'd laughed at me when I'd FaceTimed him to say thanks, my eyes teary and voice thick.

'Speak for yourself. You're the one who sent your stressed-out girlfriend cheesy fries.'

He grinned at me, blue eyes sparkling, the dimple in his left cheek showing. And damn, I missed him *so* much in that moment. He was just the sweetest.

'I should let you go, so you can work on your essay,' he said – looking as reluctant to go as he sounded. I ended up putting off the essay for another hour while we talked.

We had some school council meetings about the Sadie Hawkins dance, too, which kind of helped distract me and kind of didn't.

It didn't help because I hadn't worked up the courage to ask Noah, not sure I could handle the rejection when I was already missing him so much; and it did help because, duh, it was a school dance, and planning was a welcome distraction. Even if it was being held in the gym. (That just made the challenge of decorating on a low budget all the more fun.)

Lee was getting just as antsy about everything as I was. Rachel had her college application for Brown all ready to go, and it seemed like most of our friends were on their way to completing applications or at least their essays, while Lee and I were trailing behind.

Not that we talked about it much.

Actually, we didn't really talk about much of anything any more.

It felt like Lee was avoiding seeing me as much as

Noah was avoiding talking to me about Harvard – the more time that passed, the less he seemed to talk about classes and his friends. I kept telling myself it was no big deal, and that, obviously, there was nothing to tell, but . . . I couldn't help but wonder, sometimes, if there was something he was hiding from me.

Luckily, there was a brief respite from everything I was stressing over with Jon Fletcher's party. It was the first party of the year, aside from a few we knew the juniors had thrown, but none of us had bothered to go to those.

Maybe, I realized, when we'd thrown parties last year and all the seniors hadn't come, it wasn't necessarily because they thought they were too cool; it was probably because they didn't have the time.

Levi offered to give me a ride.

'You don't wanna drink?' I asked as we sat down on a patch of grass in the shade off the side of the football field at lunch on Friday. We'd got out of our last class a little early, so still had to wait for the others to turn up.

He shrugged, focusing on taking his lunch out of his backpack. 'It's not really my thing. When we all started going to parties and drinking beer and stuff last year, all this stuff started happening with my dad, and I wasn't really in the mood to party. It wasn't really Julie's scene either.'

'So, what, you've never really been to a party?'

'I went to one at New Year's, and one at the end of the summer, but I didn't stick around too long. Showed up late and left early.'

'Oh. Well, I'm sure you're gonna love this one. You can let your hair down now, right?'

Levi tugged at the ends of his hair. He'd had it cut a couple of days ago, and you could hardly see his curls any more. 'Yeah, you know, this pigtail I've had in for the past ten months has *really* been bugging me.'

I rolled my eyes, and tore the crust off my sandwich. 'How is your dad?'

'He's good. Finally found a therapist he likes.'

'That's good.'

Then Cam and Lisa showed up hand in hand, and Dixon wasn't far behind, engrossed in his phone, so we dropped the conversation and all started talking about the party instead.

Now, standing in front of my closet with clothes on the floor all around me, I huffed for the millionth time. I had *nothing* to wear.

'For Christ's sake, Shelly.' Lee sighed. 'Just pick something. Levi's going to be here soon.'

Rachel had declined going to the party because she was staying in to revise for the SATs she was sitting next week. She was praying for early admission to Brown, and we all knew she'd get in, even if it was just through regular admission. Her GPA was good, and she was going to kick ass in the SATs.

I sighed again, and picked out a black skater skirt that went to my knees, and stepped into it. That was half an outfit, so I deemed it good progress.

My cell phone rang, and Lee answered it before I could ask him to. 'Hey, Levi . . .' After saying 'mm-hmm' a few times, Lee hung up. 'Levi will be here in fifteen minutes.'

I picked out a pale blue silky cami and a cute yellow wraparound top I'd bought in an end-of-summer sale. 'Which one?'

'Uh . . . the yellow one.'

'Are you sure?'

Lee sat up and gave me a flat look, silencing me. Not that he was very convincing – I was just surprised at how pissed he looked. I knew he wasn't really happy that Rachel wasn't going to be there tonight, but he hadn't told her that – he understood that she wanted to stay home to study. But now he was taking his grouchi-ness out on me. And I felt grouchy enough on my own without his attitude.

'You know what? I'll wear this white one.' I picked a plain white cropped T-shirt instead, turning away before I rolled my eyes at him. 'I know it sucks Rachel's not coming with us tonight, but this is going to be fun! Hanging out, us and the guys, like it used to be. And it'll totally be worth it for her when she gets into Brown.'

Lee was quiet – so quiet it startled me. When I glanced back, he had his hands knotted together in his lap, scowling at them.

'What? What's up?'

'I was thinking,' he said slowly, not looking at me, 'about applying to Brown. With Rachel.'

Brown?

He was . . . applying to *Brown?*

It was like a punch to the gut, knocking the breath out of me for a few seconds.

'You are? But what about Berkeley? We . . . We always talked about it.'

'Yeah, and now I'm talking about Brown, with Rachel. I could do it, maybe. My grades are good enough. Like you always said, school council looks good on college applications.'

I stared at him for a long while, not sure what to say.

Lee and I had always done everything together. Whenever we talked about college, it was always together, and it was always UC Berkeley.

'I might not even get in,' he said eventually. 'But . . . you know. It might be nice. Hasn't Noah talked to you about applying to somewhere in Boston, so you guys can be closer together?'

He hadn't, and I'd never even thought about it before.

And I wasn't thinking about it now: I could only think, *Lee's picking her over me. Again.*

'Levi's gonna be here soon,' he said, avoiding my gaze and hunching his shoulders. 'I'm gonna go wait downstairs.'

I watched him go, not sure I'd ever felt like Lee was such a stranger to me.

By the time Lee and I were climbing into the back of Levi's green Toyota, he was still quiet, withdrawn, nothing at all like his usual upbeat self. Cam was riding shotgun, and I was squashed between Dixon and Lee in the back seat.

'Who's excited?' Dixon yelled as I wrestled with the seatbelt.

'Sure,' Lee muttered.

'Wow, look who's got a stick up their ass tonight. What's your problem, dude?'

'Nothing, alright?'

I turned to Dixon, pulling a face, and he shrugged in response. Was this all about college? Rachel? Or was it something else entirely?

Lee started to liven up once we were actually at the party, and once he'd gotten a few beers down him.

I watched him refill from the keg for the third time warily, but decided not to nag him about it. He was a responsible drinker. He always got tipsy, but rarely ever got completely wasted. I tended to be the irresponsible one.

When Rachel told us she wasn't going to come tonight, I'd been way more thrilled than I'd ever let on. But now we were here, I was starting to wish Rachel had turned up after all. I couldn't help but think Lee's bad mood had something to do with me, and that she would have helped.

Lee seemed more interested in hanging out with the guys from the football team than any of us. A few of them walked past, yelling, 'Hey, hey, Little Flynn! How's it going, man?'

'It's not just me, right?' I said, clutching on to Cam's sleeve, looking around the guys. 'He's being weird.'

'He's being a dick,' Warren agreed, and walked off.

By the time Lee was on beer refill number thirteen, he was acting as if I wasn't even there. He refilled his cup from the keg, swaying a little as he stood, laughing at something Jon Fletcher had just said.

'Lee,' I said, 'don't you think you've had enough for now? It's not even eleven o'clock . . .' I hiccupped. I'd only had a couple beers, but it was enough to make me feel less than sober.

'Shut up, Shelly.'

When Lee told me to shut up, he was usually smiling. Now, though, he was rolling his eyes at me, grinning at Jon like it was some big joke. Jon didn't look like he found it so funny though, and looked at me awkwardly while I gawped helplessly at Lee, hurt and confused.

'Lee –'

'Stop trailing around after me like a lost puppy. It's just *sad*. Just because Noah's not around any more doesn't mean you have to moon over him around me.'

Then he barged past me, leaving me with my jaw somewhere on the kitchen floor. The words were a slap in the face, but Lee *never* got angry with me like this for no reason. I just didn't understand. I bit my lip, feeling tears prick at the back of my eyes.

'He's just drunk,' Jon said apologetically. 'He's . . .'

I gulped, taking a second to gather myself and blink my eyes clear before whispering, 'Sure.'

'I'm gonna . . .' He patted my shoulder before making his way out of the kitchen and calling out to someone. I was glad he didn't try and talk to me any more about it: I didn't think I could manage to speak right now.

I was still standing there when some of the guys from the basketball team barged through, holding a bottle of tequila aloft, shouting, 'Shots! Shots! Shots!' and, for some reason, I followed them.

Out in the hallway of Jon Fletcher's house, the party intensified. The music was louder, different songs pouring from different open doors, and people leaning against the walls or draped round plant pots and the banister.

It was a lot hotter out here, too, and harder to move.

I walked right into someone, and stumbled back into someone else, staggering unsteadily as I tried to find my footing again. The first person I'd bumped into caught my elbow.

'Hey,' I cried, seeing it was Levi. 'They're doing shots. You up for it?'

'I'm driving.'

'Oh, yeah, of course. Well, you can come watch the rest of us do shots.'

'Lee told me to keep an eye on you if you got drunk –'

'I'm not drunk!' I protested. 'Kind of offended, a little tipsy, but not drunk.'

'– and he told me to stop you doing shots. The guys said you don't handle your drink well, and, much as I don't mind keeping an eye on you, I am *not* going to stand there holding your hair back while you puke into a toilet bowl.'

I argued that I wouldn't puke, but I was still too angry about Lee's attitude tonight to take much notice of what Levi was saying. I'd lost sight of the arm holding the tequila bottle up in the air above the crowd like a neon orange flag held by a tour guide. If Lee was that concerned for me, then why did he push me away? Why wasn't he looking out for me himself if he thought I was so much of a problem?

Why hadn't he told me he didn't want to go to college with me any more?

And I started to cry.

'Oh, Jesus Christ,' Levi said.

I sniffled, but now I'd started, I couldn't stop. I saw a few people glaring at Levi, like he'd done something to upset me, and I half expected him to walk away and leave me for someone else to look after.

But he took my sweaty hand and said gently that maybe some fresh air would help, and pushed through the crowds to the front door, tugging me along behind him. Outside, we went to sit on the sidewalk in front of the house, and after a couple of minutes I calmed down. It was mild, but after how hot it was inside the house with so many people in there, I shivered, rubbing my arms.

'Feel better now?' Levi asked me.

I wiped my fingertips under my eyes to try and get

rid of any rogue mascara, then wiped my nose with the back of my hand. My purse was inside somewhere. It had Kleenex in it, but that was no good to me right now.

'Wanna talk about it?'

'Lee's just being so mean to me,' I whined, sounding pathetic even to my own ears. 'We hardly get to spend any time together now, just the two of us, and tonight was supposed to be a chance for us to hang out without Rachel or anything, and instead he's just ignored me and I don't know what I did to make him hate me!'

'Lee doesn't hate you.'

'Then why's he being so mean?'

'He's probably just stressing out about college, like everyone else.'

'Then why isn't he talking to me about it? You know he told me tonight he's gonna apply to Brown, with Rachel. Like, out of *nowhere*. We used to spend all our time together. And now, if we make plans, he almost *always* cancels to spend time with Rachel, or he's too busy with football. He's even canceling our college plans for her.'

'Maybe it's because of Rachel that he's not spending much time with you, when he has free time outside of football practice. Don't take this the wrong way, but it's gotta be weird for her when her boyfriend's best friend is a girl. And a very pretty girl, at that. Objectively speaking, of course. And, like, don't lots of people want to go to college with their other half?'

'I'm supposed to be his other half.'

'You know what I mean.' Levi sighed. 'I don't know. I'm just trying to say that maybe there's a good reason for it. I can't see him being a dick just because he *is* a dick. He's not. He's a good guy.'

'Yeah, he is.'

Somehow, that only made me feel even worse.

'I think I want to go home,' I said, folding my hands over my knees. 'I'm not really in the party mood any more.'

I stood up.

'Wait, you're not gonna walk home, are you? A) you're not sober so that's not a good idea, b) you don't exactly live nearby, and c) that's just not safe at this time of night.'

'Thanks for your concern, but I was actually only going to go find my purse. I'll call my dad for a ride home.'

'Oh,' Levi said, and stood up too. 'I don't mind taking you home if you want. Then I'll come back here for an hour or whatever till the others are ready to go.'

'Are we paying you to be our personal chauffeur or something?'

'Nah, this is just me building up some good karma.'

'I'm not sure you get the karma if you're trying that hard.'

'Worth a shot, right?'

'I guess. Just a shame we're not talking a shot of tequila.'

At home, the light was on in the lounge and the drapes were shut. Levi put the car in park and pulled up the hand brake.

'Thanks. Are you sure I can't give you some gas money?'

'It's fine, Elle, really.' He smiled. 'But I may call in another babysitting favor in payment.'

'Ah, I knew there was a catch.' I unbuckled my seat-belt and climbed out. 'Well, thanks. Again. I appreciate it.'

I shut the door and walked up the path to my front door, but only got halfway to the porch before I heard him call out to me. I turned back.

'Yeah?'

'I'm sure Lee will come round. You guys will figure out the college thing. If you two are best friends, you'll work things out.'

'I hope so.'

Then he smiled again, waved, and drove off. I was fumbling around in my purse for my house key, when my dad opened the door.

'I wasn't expecting you back for a while.'

I just shrugged. 'I got bored. Wasn't a great party.'

'That doesn't mean you got so drunk you threw up, does it?' He frowned like he was already trying to decide how long I deserved to be grounded for.

'No, it means it was a crappy night. I just wasn't feeling it. Levi gave me a ride home.'

'Did anyone else leave early? What about Lee?'

'No, only me. I'm just gonna go up to bed.'

'Are you sure? Me and Brad are watching the new Tom Cruise film. There's not long left, but you can come watch it with us. It's not exactly a difficult plot to pick up on . . .'

Brad didn't usually stay up this late, but I guessed it didn't matter as a one-off. And I *was* kind of tempted, because I felt so crappy that maybe being around my family with a not-too-crappy movie would make me feel at least a little bit better.

But I was way more tempted to go crawl under my comforter and stay there forever.

'No, thanks. I'm just going to go to bed.'

'Okay.' My dad had never known me to leave a party early; if anything, he'd tell me off the next day for getting home too late. So, right now, I wasn't surprised that he was looking at me with concern knitting his eyebrows together behind his glasses.

I got halfway up the stairs before he called after me. 'Are you sure everything's okay? Did something happen?'

I gave him a smile, seeing the worry turning to panic. 'No, Dad, really. It's fine. It was just a really sucky party, and I'm beat.'

'You know you can tell me anything, right, bud?'

'I know, Dad.'

'And there's nothing you want to tell me about?'

'No. God, everything's fine!' I huffed, and carried on up the stairs, and that was the end of that.

Once I was wrapped up inside the cocoon of my comforter and wearing one of Noah's T-shirts he'd left behind, and my makeup was all washed off, I looked at the screen on my cell phone, and pulled up my contacts.

June Flynn. Lee Flynn. Matthew Flynn. Noah Flynn.

My thumb hovered. I knew I needed to talk to one of the Flynn brothers – I just couldn't decide which.

Call Lee. Talk to him. Sort this out. He might be home already.

No, call Noah. You haven't had a chance to talk to him properly since Monday, and that was only a little. Call him. Tell him about Lee and see what he has to say. It's a Friday night and he's probably just getting in from a party, too.

93

I called Noah, even though he would be fast asleep by now.

It rang, and rang, and . . . rang, and . . .

'Hey, it's Noah. Leave me a message and I'll get back to you.'

Instead of hanging up as the beep sounded, I held the phone at my ear as the beep sounded. When had he changed his voicemail message? It used to be shorter: 'Hey, it's Flynn. You know what to do.'

I realized that, by now, he'd have ten seconds of me breathing down the line, and I figured I should probably say something. 'Hey. It's me. Um, Elle. I wanted to talk but I guess you're asleep. I'll call you tomorrow. Um . . . Love you.'

Tonight, more than ever, I wished Noah was here with me. Between his voicemail and Lee's attitude at the party, I'd never felt so lonely.

Chapter 8

I expected Lee to ring me and apologize the next day.

He didn't.

By late morning, though, I gave up waiting for him to talk to me and I text him, asking if he was with Rachel. He wasn't; he was at home. So I went straight over there, psyching myself up to argue with my best friend if necessary, and demand an explanation for why he'd been such a jerk at the party last night. And we really, really needed to talk about this whole college thing.

I was losing faith in myself by the time I walked up to the front door.

I didn't really like fighting with anybody (except squabbling with Noah over petty things, but that was different). I hated the idea of fighting with my best friend most of all.

Maybe it'd be better to forget all about it, and just pretend it didn't happen.

The door opened.

'Why are you standing out here?'

I looked up, and Lee was smiling at me, but looking confused because I stood about a yard away from the door, hands clenched in fists down by my sides, and I guessed I must've been there for a few minutes if he'd noticed.

There were purple bags under Lee's eyes, which were bloodshot, like he hadn't slept and had drunk way too much last night. His dark hair was damp – still wet from a shower, I guessed.

I pressed my lips tight together. I had to talk to him, and I had to do it now, before I chickened out.

My stomach flipped.

My mouth fell open, and I blurted, 'Why were you such a jerk to me last night? Are you doing this on purpose, pushing me away? Why don't you want to go to college with me any more? Is it because of Rachel? Is it something I've done? Is it to do with Noah?'

'Whoa, slow down,' Lee said, as I gasped for breath. 'Look, come inside, and we'll talk, okay?'

I nodded, and walked the rest of the way up to the door. Inside, I could smell June's cooking – spicy, and good enough that it made my mouth water – and the TV was on in the lounge, where I guessed Matthew, Lee's dad, was. June yelled hi to me, and I shouted back, trying not to sound as anxious as I felt.

We headed upstairs to Lee's room. He had a little balcony, and the doors were wide open, the thin drapes billowing outward with the breeze, and there was music playing on his MacBook, which Lee turned down. I perched on the end of his bed.

Usually, I'd treat Lee's room like my own, but now I felt nervous. Now wasn't the time to throw myself down on the bouncy mattress.

It had been a while since I'd been over here. The room was tidier than I'd ever seen it. 'You got rid of your drum kit,' I said, noticing the empty space in the room.

He shrugged. 'It wasn't like I played it any more. I sold it.' He took a seat in the spinning chair at his desk, straddling it backward. His toes pressed into the floor, and he swiveled from side to side very slightly. I waited for him to say something, say *anything*, but he was quiet. And just like that, my patience snapped.

'You know,' I said – and it came out short, angry. Sharp and fierce. It sounded wrong but I couldn't stop it. 'It's bad enough that I barely get to speak to Noah lately, but I can't stand you pushing me away as well. And I don't just mean because of the college thing. We never talk, not like we used to, we hardly ever hang out, and I – I – It feels like you're pushing me away,' I finished lamely, trailing off. I was wringing my hands,

I realized, and stopped, sitting on them instead. At least that way they wouldn't shake.

'I'm not pushing you away.' Lee sighed.

'Yes, you are.'

He rolled his eyes.

'You are,' I insisted, my voice growing louder with conviction. I wasn't going to let Lee brush this off, now that we were finally addressing it. Or, at least, now that I was. 'It's like you don't even want to make time for me. Last night you told me to shut up.'

Lee's shoulders sagged, and he looked down at where his hands were clasped round the back of the chair. He knew I had a point.

He was quiet for a while, which made me more nervous, and I stopped sitting on my hands so that I could fidget again. My heart thudded, and there was a lump in the back of my throat that tasted like bile.

'I know. I'm a bad best friend,' was what he finally said.

'Thanks for admitting it and all, but I'd kind of like an explanation.'

Lee ran his hands through his hair. He hadn't cut it for a while, and now it was almost as long as Noah's.

'I didn't mean to be such a dick. I'm sorry.'

'I don't want you to say sorry, Lee! I want you to tell me why. I want to know what's going on.'

'Nothing's going on. So what, I drank too much, and I was a little bitch to you. I don't know what you want me to say, Elle. I'm sorry. I shouldn't have done it. I get it if you're mad at me.'

I pushed my knuckles into my forehead, then scraped my fingers back through my hair and sighed. 'Jesus, Lee, I'm . . .' I stood up, shaking my head and feeling sick. I couldn't stay here if he was going to brush me off like this. 'Fine. You know what? Keep it up. Keep acting this way. You might lose us all that way. All the guys said you were acting weird last night. But I don't have to stand here and take this bullshit from someone who's supposed to be my best friend. If you're not going to talk to me –'

Lee shot to his feet, knocking the chair over, and blocking my way.

'They call me Little Flynn.'

'Huh?'

'The guys on the football team. They call me Little Flynn. And Coach keeps talking about Noah, how he was faster, or throws better, or whatever. They're all expecting me to be like him. I'm the new Flynn, you know?'

'So what, that means you have to act like I don't exist?'

'It means I'm trying to . . . be cool.'

I scoffed. 'And acting like this? Being mean to all of us, telling me to shut up? This is being cool?'

He didn't have anything to say to that. He just looked down at his feet.

'I thought you were already cool because you won the initiation thing.'

'They said Noah won when it was his initiation to the team, and he was still a sophomore at that point. They're expecting me to be as good as Noah was.'

I sat back down, and Lee let out a rush of breath, eyebrows relaxing before carrying on. He picked up the chair, setting it back upright. He leaned against his desk, hands braced behind him. I'd heard a couple of the guys call Lee 'Little Flynn', but I'd never realized he felt like *this* about it. It made my temper flare on his behalf – but it also made me feel even more sad about this entire argument. He could've talked to me. And why hadn't he?

'It just really gets to me, you know? The way they treat me. Like, even though I've impressed them, and I'm part of the team, I'm still not good enough. I like being part of the team, Elle, and I'm . . .'

'Noah never told me to shut up at a party.'

'See? He's literally better than me at everything.'

'No, Lee, I'm not . . . You're . . .' What the hell did I say to that?

'I get how stupid it sounds,' he told me, eyes wide and wet. 'I get how pathetic and whiny I sound, okay? I know. If it helps, I haven't even told Rachel about this. I wanted to handle it myself, you know? Just . . . figure it out.'

'You don't need to be Noah, Lee. And it's not pathetic. You're amazing just like you are. Besides, you're not even the same position as him on the field. Pitch? It's a field, right?'

He smiled, meeting my eyes again. 'Field.'

'Right, that. They can't even compare you guys if you're not playing the same position.'

'Yeah, I guess.'

'Plus, you're not even that little. There are smaller guys than you on the team.'

'Yeah . . .'

'And I will one hundred percent quit defending you and giving you an ego boost if you tell me to shut up like that ever again.'

'If I ever do that to you again, feel free to throw a whole keg of beer over me.'

'Can I get that in writing?'

Lee laughed, and moved across the room, stopping in front of me. 'Are we good? Am I allowed to hug you now? I feel like things aren't good until we hug it out.'

I raised a finger at him. 'Swear to God, Lee, this

never happens again. You can talk to me about any of this, you know that, but don't be like you were last night.'

'Cross my heart.'

I stood up, and Lee was hugging me tight, practically tackling me, before I was even standing straight. All the weeks of not really seeing him and all the tension that had built up between us evaporated, and he clung to me just as tightly as I clung to him. He sniffed.

'Are you smelling my hair?'

'No, I'm trying not to cry.'

I laughed, burying my head in his shoulder in return. I was still kind of mad, but at least he'd talked to me. And he was sorry. That counted for something.

Besides, if you couldn't forgive your best friend when they were trying not to cry, could you really consider yourselves best friends?

'Did you have a good time at the party, at least?' I asked him, when we finally broke apart. 'Aside from pissing all of us off?'

'It wasn't my finest hour. I broke a vase, missed my curfew and almost ruined my friendship with you. And I threw up on someone's car.'

'Wow.'

'Yeah ... And I'm sorry I ruined your night, too. I know you left early because of me.'

'Did Levi tell you that?'

Lee nodded, then changed the subject, clearly done with talking about himself now. 'You two seem pretty friendly. It's good. You know, as long as he's not trying to take my position as best friend, then it's good,' he added with an imitation of the impish grin that made him look much more like the Lee I knew. 'I just mean, because I haven't been spending time with you and because Noah's not here, and it's good that you've got someone. I worry about you sometimes, Shelly. Like, Rachel's got drama club, but you're like . . .'

'Not talented enough to join in with any extra-curriculars like drama club?'

'That's not what I was gonna say.'

'True, though.'

'You could join track. Maybe not volleyball, but you'd be decent at track.'

'Sure, maybe. Wouldn't hurt to put something else on my college application.'

Lee rolled his eyes. 'You and those goddamn college applications. Speaking of . . . Look, Brown isn't just about Rachel. It's where my dad went, too. And you could apply. Your grades are even better than mine. We could all go to Brown.'

'Maybe.'

'And I'm not . . . I'm not picking her, you know?

I don't mean to, anyway. But all the guys said how she must find it weird, with me being so close with you, and that I should make more of an effort with Rachel, and . . .'

'Did Warren tell you that?'

Lee pulled a face.

'Warren is single and an idiot. But . . . I get it.' I hated to admit it, but I *did* get why he was worried about that. 'If you don't figure it out, though, Lee, I will. I'll make a damn roster for you if I have to. We'll share custody of you on the weekends. I'll see you every Tuesday night.'

He laughed. 'I'll figure it out.'

Then there was a shout up the staircase: 'Kids! Lunch is on the table!' And the conversation was over. But another one started up just as quickly, less serious and more like old times, both of us joking and teasing each other, and his arm bumped against mine as we walked downstairs.

It was good to have Lee back.

Chapter 9

I tried calling Noah again when I got home from lunch with the Flynns. We'd texted a little during the day – the usual *Hey / How are you / What're you up to today / Miss you* – but I *really* wanted to *talk* to him. Hell, I texted Levi more than I texted Noah these days.

It sucked that Noah had to go to college on the other side of the country. Why did Harvard have to be so damn far away?

I hated not being able to walk to his house to be with him.

I hated not being able to take a nap wrapped up in his arms next to him on the couch.

I hated not being able to argue with him about what to watch on TV, even though we'd end up not paying that much attention to it anyway.

I hated that he wasn't here to make me laugh and

kiss my nose and look at me like I was the only thing that mattered in that moment.

I hated that I missed him so bad and I couldn't do anything about it.

Sure, I'd had plenty of things to take my mind off how badly I missed Noah, but times like this, it felt like there was a chunk of me missing – specifically, a Noah-sized-and-shaped chunk. It was like an ache in my chest, or something heavy pressing down on my lungs, and a kind of sadness that not even cute pictures of kittens or funny memes could alleviate. ('Alleviate' was one of the SAT words on my list to learn this week.)

The longer I waited for Noah to pick up, the closer I got to the edge of my bed, and I started biting my thumbnail.

Why wasn't he answering? He hardly ever answered me lately when I called.

Was he studying? He was probably studying and had his cell on silent, or maybe even turned off so he wouldn't be disturbed.

Was he out with friends?

Why wasn't he picking up?

Was he ignoring me?

Finally, Noah answered. The video of his face filled the screen. His beaming smile, his crooked nose, the dimple in his cheek, his bright blue eyes. His hair was shorter than usual and – was that a beard? Was he actually growing a beard? I hadn't been able to video-call him for a few days and suddenly he'd cut his hair and was growing a beard?

Damn, if it didn't suit him. He looked so much older. There were trees in the background, a low sun, blue skies. He was sitting down somewhere with his head-phones in and the breeze stirred his hair.

'Hey, you.'

And he sounded so happy to talk to me that I stopped biting my nail, flopped on to my stomach on my bed, propped myself up on my elbows, and smiled back at him. 'Hey. How are you?'

'I'm good. Yeah, everything's good. What about you? You look stressed. Did you get wasted last night and grounded?' He chuckled, giving me a look of mock-disappointment.

'No, I'm good. The party was okay. I've just come back from lunch with Lee and your parents.'

Noah knew Lee had been blowing me off for Rachel a lot lately, and we'd argued for, like, twenty minutes a couple of weeks ago, until he swore not to talk to Lee about it on my behalf. I got the feeling telling him *everything* about the party last night would only cause a fight between them.

'Elle, c'mon. What's up?'

I sighed, biting the inside of my cheek. I shouldn't have video-called him. 'Lee was kind of a jerk last night, at the party. To everyone, not just me. That's why I went over to your place, actually, to talk to him.'

'And?'

'We're good. He's gonna try not to ditch me for Rachel so much.' And then, before I could stop myself, I frowned and blurted, 'Did you know he wants to go to Brown?'

'What, like Dad did?'

'Like with Rachel,' I clarified.

I watched it dawn on Noah. His eyes drifted away from the screen and I watched his eyebrows draw together and his lips press into a line. I waited for him to start on some kind of rant about how Lee was out of order, how that was too far, and what about me, and Berkeley?

But when he finally opened his mouth, what he said was, 'You know, there's plenty of good schools in Boston.'

It knocked the breath out of my lungs for a second, and we stared through the phone at each other. I drew a breath through my nose – it sounded loud, sharp, uneven. Lee had made a throwaway comment about it yesterday, but hearing *Noah* suggest it . . .

He really wanted me there with him?

I must've been quiet for too long because Noah shuffled, uncomfortable, his cheeks faintly pink. His eyes looked anywhere but at his phone and he ran a hand back and forth through his hair.

'Maybe I can look,' I said. 'Or something.'

'So Lee's looking at Brown,' he said. 'That must've been weird for you. Is that why he's been such an ass to you lately?'

I tried hard not to look as relieved as I felt that he'd changed the subject from going to college in Boston with him. I was flattered he wanted me to be nearer to him, but . . . I couldn't choose a school just because my boyfriend was there, could I? And what about Lee? And there was my dad and Brad to think about – Berkeley was close. That was always a factor. I couldn't just *leave them*.

It just didn't feel like the kind of conversation to have on a whim, over the phone.

'Actually . . .' I said, and explained that Lee's attitude had less to do with Rachel, like I'd thought, and more about him feeling he had to live up to Noah's reputation. I watched Noah's expression cloud over as I told him about it, torn between guilt and annoyance.

'Maybe I should talk to him. Tell him to cool it, or something. I don't know.'

'Seriously, don't – he was pretty upset about it. He'll probably just feel worse if you try and talk to him.'

'Yeah, I guess you're right.'

'Damn straight I'm right. I'm always right.'

'Sure, Shelly. Always right.' He flashed me his trademark smirk, turning my insides to goo . . . and making me miss him. *So. Damn. Much.* I wanted to reach through the screen to grab his face and kiss him.

'I can't believe you're growing a beard,' I told him.

He tilted his head back, rubbing a hand over his jaw and giving me a better view of it. 'You don't like it?'

'It's hot.'

'Right again, Shelly.' He winked, making me laugh. 'Honestly, I broke my razor and haven't got a new one yet.'

'Classes keeping you busy?'

'Something like that,' he said, expression stiffening.

I felt my stomach knot. What had I said? He'd stopped talking to me so much about his classes and stuff. Honestly, I was kind of worried about him. He *always* seemed to change the topic when I asked about how he was doing in his classes or asked him about that essay he'd been working on lately. Sure, maybe he just didn't have much to say, or thought I'd find it boring or wouldn't really get it, but I could *tell* he was holding back.

But I asked, 'So . . . how are you finding college? Are you handling everything?'

He gave a blasé half smile, shrugging one shoulder. 'Sure I am. I'm not top of the class or anything but I'm coping, you know?'

My voice was quiet when I responded. 'No, not really. You don't talk to me much about college.'

Apparently, it was my day for brutal honesty with the Flynn brothers.

'Sure I do –'

'Not really. You tell me about people, and stuff that's going on socially, or about football, but you don't ever talk to me about your classes.'

'I'm doing fine, Elle.' There was an edge to his voice. A muscle jumped in his jaw, which only solidified my impression that something was up.

'It's okay if you're finding it hard. You know, I was reading some articles on this lifestyle blog by a college sophomore about how a lot of students struggle to settle in at college, you know, with the workload and stuff, and –'

'Elle!' Noah didn't exactly *shout* my name, but he raised his voice. He didn't seem mad, just . . . tired. He lowered the phone to his lap and I saw him rub a hand over his face. 'Would you *please* stop hounding me about this? I'm *fine*. Alright?'

Maybe I *should* just let it go.

He'd talk to me when he was ready, right?

(How long was that going to take though?)

I could've pushed him on it, but I wanted to be able to trust him. I wanted him to be able to trust me. I didn't want to be a nag, and I hated having *actual* arguments with him now, when we couldn't kiss and make up. He obviously didn't want to talk about this, and I knew the easiest thing to do right now was drop it.

So I did.

'Alright.'

'So,' he said, smile stiff, and I could hear the effort he made to sound casual, 'you got any plans for later?'

'Not really. Have another go at my college essay. Maybe watch a movie. Lee was going to stay in and do some reading for English class. He needs to keep his grades up for football – and Brown now too, I guess – so I figured I'd leave him to it.'

'Fair enough.'

'What about you?'

'There's a party at one of the frat houses. Steve managed to get us an invite. His girlfriend knows one of the guys there or something.'

'Oh. Um, cool.'

There was a lapse, one I didn't know how to fill.

Over the summer, we'd fall into silence sometimes,

but it never mattered – we didn't *need* to fill the quiet, because it was comfortable. I told myself that it was only awkward right now because we were on the phone, and that was different from going quiet when we were together in person.

I considered bringing up the Sadie Hawkins dance. Asking him if he'd come home for the weekend to go with me. But I had a feeling he'd say no, and I didn't want to hear that right now. Especially after we'd just avoided an argument.

And when the silence just got worse and more uncomfortable, so much so that Noah cleared his throat but didn't bother to say anything, I said, 'I'd better let you go, then. To get ready or whatever.'

He was visibly relieved for the out.

I tried not to appear so obviously disappointed.

'Yeah. Yeah, I promised Am– I promised Steve I'd get there a little early with him. The frat said they're not taking any more new pledges this year, but he's still trying to get in.'

'Okay.' I sucked in a deep breath, but it was hard. It was hard to sound genuine when I said, 'Well, have fun.'

We hung up together, and I sat up, leaning back on my elbows, and trying to draw in deep breaths through my mouth, past the lump in my throat. I blinked hard. Nothing was wrong and there was no reason to cry.

Nothing *was* wrong. Things were just ... *strained* ... because we were so far apart and it had been over a month since we'd seen each other. That was all. Yeah. Yeah, that was it. Everything was fine.

I hoped.

The awkward silence, the almost-argument, and my unconvinced response to his suggestion that I apply to schools in Boston gnawed at me. I lay on my bed for a while, feeling queasy, scowling at the dark screen of my phone. It lit back up – another text from Levi, begging me to check out a vlogger.

When had things stopped being so easy with Noah?

Chapter 10

By the time Monday morning rolled round, I was actually glad of it for once. Noah and I had talked on the phone again on Sunday, but it had been worse than usual: stilted and full of pauses and so not like it normally was. I just couldn't figure out exactly what had gone so wrong to know how to fix it.

I was being stupid, right? There was nothing wrong, and I was getting paranoid for absolutely no reason, and things were fine. We'd just been away from each other for a while and that was why things were weird. *I was being stupid.*

Lee was running a little late in picking me up for school – it was his turn to drive this week – so we arrived just as everybody started pouring from the student parking lot to homeroom.

'Is it just me, or are people staring at me?' I asked him, dropping my voice and looking around furtively.

Maybe it was leftover paranoia from thinking about Noah, but I was *sure* that people were looking at me. And not glancing over my way and smiling, like they might on any other day, but staring at me and muttering to their friends.

I looked down at myself. Had I dropped peanut butter down the front of my uniform? Had one of my buttons popped off? Was my fly open? Was there toilet paper stuck to my shoe?

Nope.

'Is there something on my face?'

Lee gave me a quick once-over. 'No, you're good.'

'People are staring, aren't they?'

'Maybe it's me. I mean, now Noah's gone, maybe they realize that I'm a hot piece of ass myself.' He tossed his head to get the hair out of his eyes. He'd been growing it out – now I realized, probably to look more like Noah (or at least how Noah had looked up until recently). 'Noah does take after me in his good looks, after all.'

'Ha-ha.' I rolled my eyes. I'd have laughed, except my heart was pounding and my palms were starting to sweat. I hated this feeling. Either I was the center of attention, or I was missing out on something big. Whichever one it was, I hated it.

'Seriously. Please tell me I'm imagining things.'

'No, I think they're staring. Yeah, see? That guy pointed.'

'Why? What did I do?'

I racked my brain, trying to think if I'd done anything at the party on Friday night that people would be talking about. Sure, I'd been crying, but so what? A sobbing, tipsy girl wasn't unusual for a high school party. And I had a clear memory of the whole night and knew I hadn't done anything *really* stupid.

We merged into the throng, not bothering to try and find the others – there was no point in trying to catch up with them now; it wasn't long until homeroom. We'd just see them later. Lee started talking about this book passage he was writing an essay on for English class and how brilliant one of the metaphors in it was, but I wasn't really listening.

I was too busy concentrating on what everybody else was saying.

'I feel so sorry for her.'

'Did you see her at Jon Fletcher's? She left with that new guy, Levi Monroe. I bet they went home together. Slut.'

'You saw her leave with that Levi guy, right?'

'I heard they broke up.'

'She doesn't even *look* upset. If that were me, I'd be devastated.'

'I can't believe he'd do that to her.'

'He's *such* a dick. I mean, she's such a sweetie. How could he?'

'I heard she hooked up with Levi Monroe. I know, right? He could *totally* do better ... Do you think they broke up?'

It was only when Lee pushed me in front of him into homeroom that I realized he'd had his hand on my back and had been guiding me along the whole time, and I'd totally zoned out. Now, I froze, and he pushed me again, gently. I stumbled, feeling like Bambi on ice.

When we took our usual seats, Rachel leaned forward immediately. 'What the hell, right?'

'Huh?'

'All these rumors going around. They're crazy.'

'What rumors?' My brain felt fuzzy. Maybe they weren't even rumors about *me*. Maybe someone else had pulled some crazy shit over the weekend. Maybe someone else had gone home with Levi, when he'd gone back to the party. I blinked a few times, but it didn't help clear my head.

'*Everyone's* talking about it,' Lisa pitched in, and even though she gave me a pitiful, sympathetic look, her tone was laced with the excitement that accompanied any kind of gossip. 'How you left the party early. With Levi.' She glanced at his empty seat.

'But we know you didn't actually, you know, *go home* with Levi,' Rachel added, cutting Lisa a glance that clearly said 'shut up'.

Then I caught on, gaping at them, and Lee said what I was thinking before I could recover from my speechlessness.

'Wait, people think *Elle* hooked up with *Levi*?'

The girls exchanged a look. Lisa said, 'Yeah. Everyone's talking about it.'

'That's ridiculous,' Lee and I chorused. We exchanged a look, Lee pulling his best 'WTF?' face. I carried on, 'Why would they think that? Just because I left early and he took me home? Like that never happens to anyone else?'

The girls looked at each other again, more apprehensively now. My stomach was already tied up in knots, and now those knots pulled tight and I squirmed in my seat. My nails dug into my palms.

'What? What aren't you telling me?'

'People are also saying,' Rachel said slowly, looking down at her fingertip tracing a pen mark on her desk, 'that . . . that you and Noah broke up.'

That threw me even more than the rumors that I'd slept with Levi. 'Wait, *what*? Where did that come from?'

'Well . . . *did* you?' Lisa asked, obviously unable to help herself. My eyes narrowed.

'No, we're . . . we're still together.' If a little rocky . . . *'Why?* What are people saying?'

Rachel suddenly hauled her huge Mary Poppins-esque purse up on to her desk, pawing through books and files and sheets of paper for her cell phone. 'It's less what people are saying . . .' She tapped on her phone a few times, before holding it out. 'And more what they're seeing.'

Lee got up and moved to Levi's empty chair, then leaned over so his head was next to mine. He sucked in a sharp breath. I was pretty sure I'd forgotten how to breathe.

Blown up on Rachel's cell-phone screen in crisp, high definition, was a photo uploaded to Instagram by someone called Amanda Johnson.

Noah was tagged in it.

The caption read: *Such a fab night!xxxx – @nflynn.*

The picture had sixty-two likes. It had seventeen comments. Eighteen – someone else commented while I was looking.

The photo showed Noah, wearing a white shirt lined with blue under the collar and with blue thread; I remembered him buying it just before he left for college. There was an extra button undone. There was a huge grin on his face, and he looked like he was laughing at something.

He had his arm round a girl, holding her in close.

The girl was blonde and beautiful, and her dress (at least, I guessed it was a dress) was strapless and very low-cut, sitting flat against her slim frame.

And she was pressed right up against my boyfriend, and she looked like she was giggling, her eyes half closed and crinkled around the edges.

And she was kissing his cheek.

And he was grinning.

I felt sick.

Lee took Rachel's phone out of my hands – which was lucky, because I probably would've dropped it a second or two later. My shoulders slumped before it hit me; I tensed up completely, even my toes curling in anger.

'This is some kind of sick joke, right?'

Rachel leaned away from me slightly, and slowly took her cell back from Lee, dropping it into her cavernous purse. 'Um . . .'

'Oh my God.' I ran my hands hard over my face and up into my hair, shaking it out just for something to occupy my agitated hands. Was this why he'd been weird when we talked yesterday? Not because of our conversation on Saturday, but because something had happened with this girl? 'Tell me this is some kind of joke.'

'Shelly . . .'

'Please.' My voice broke on the word, but somehow, miraculously, I managed not to start crying.

Rachel and Lisa looked at each other yet again, and something in me snapped. I shot out of my chair, almost knocking it over, and stormed out – ignoring Mr Shane calling for me to sit back down – and I heard Lee chasing after me.

I stormed down the hallway, taking a few turns until I was in the staircase, where it was silent, and Lee grabbed my hand from behind, stopping me from running away any further.

He jerked my arm, tugging me round, and I let him wrap his arms round me.

I took a few shaky breaths, more angry than upset.

No, I wasn't angry – I was *furious*. Livid. In a rage. Irate.

And even more than that: I was confused. How could Noah do this to me? There had to be some kind of explanation for that photo, but . . . but even if it was totally innocent, why was some random girl kissing his cheek? Wouldn't he have told me about it, if it was no big deal? And why did he look so damn happy about it? Things between us had felt so distant lately . . . What if . . . ?

I drew in another ragged breath and then stepped

back from Lee, and he let me. I blinked the tears out of my eyes, to see Lee smiling sadly.

'I'm sure it doesn't mean anything, Elle. Noah loves you. You know that. I know that. Everyone knows that, after he went all out at the Summer Dance to win you back. He was probably drunk and even if some girl kissed him on the cheek, it's not like it was a proper kiss, you know? It doesn't mean anything. Cam kissed you on the cheek at Jon's party, and Lisa didn't go crazy.'

'That's . . . Everyone's looking at me like it *does* mean something, though. And what if it does? What if they're right, Lee?' Without meaning to, I'd raised my voice, so that it echoed throughout the stairwell. My chest heaved with shallow breaths. 'What if it does mean something? I haven't seen him for weeks and what if he's forgotten all about me and met other girls – better, smarter, prettier, funnier girls, who are there, with him, and not on the other side of the country, and in a totally different time zone, too? Things were so weird between us when we spoke this weekend. What if he's met someone and he's just waiting until Thanksgiving when he sees me in person to break up with me, because he's trying to be nice?'

Lee shook his head, but the way he bit his lip made me wonder if I was right.

'Has he said something to you?' I asked, my voice a hesitant murmur and totally pathetic. 'Lee? Please, tell me.'

'He just said that he's finding it hard to be away from you.' Lee sighed, looking me in the eye from under his thick eyelashes. 'But I didn't think he meant that he'd met someone else and that he didn't want to be with you.'

'And what if he did?'

'Then . . . I guess you'll have to call him later and talk about it, and find out. But, Shelly, listen – Noah can be kind of a butthead sometimes, but he wouldn't cheat. That's not him.'

I knew he was right, but it made me feel nauseous all over again, just to *think* about making that phone call. And, if I was wrong, how much worse I'd make things by accusing him of something like that. Sure, maybe it was totally innocent and everything would be fine, but . . .

But this was the same guy who couldn't tell me something as simple as the fact that he was finding college hard.

So, what if it wasn't fine?

For the rest of the day, I had to listen to people gossip about me.

The general idea everyone had decided to go with was that Noah and I had broken up, and I'd hooked up with Levi at the party (I heard the terms 'revenge sex' and 'rebound' getting thrown around a lot) and Noah had, in turn, hooked up with this preppy girl Amanda from college, the (so-called) evidence now all over Instagram.

Levi had showed up to school late – he'd had a doctor's appointment first thing – and we'd told him about the rumors over lunch. He'd just laughed.

'People should mind their own goddamn business,' Rachel had muttered, taking an angry bite out of her apple. I didn't think I'd ever heard her so irritated.

'It's high school,' Dixon responded, deadpan. 'What else do you expect?'

When I finally did get home, I barged up to my room, slamming the door so my dad and brother got the message not to try and talk to me, and I called my boyfriend.

If I could call him that any more.

My hands were trembling so hard that I could feel my cell phone shaking against my face. I stopped pacing around and sat down on the floor, my back against my bed, and I brought my knees up to my chest, wrapping my free arm round them.

I crossed my fingers that he wouldn't pick up.

And closed my eyes and wished he would.

Any second now, it would go to voicemail.

Pick up. Don't. Pick up. Don't. Pick –

It went to voicemail. I hung up.

And before I could decide whether to just toss my cell on to my bed out of the way or whether I should try calling again, he was calling back.

I jumped when my phone started buzzing in my hands, and fumbled to answer it.

'Hi,' I croaked, my voice sounding weirdly raw. I coughed to clear my throat, but it didn't do anything to clear my head and order my mess of thoughts.

'You rang?'

'Yeah.'

There was a pause. 'Um, was there anything in particular you wanted to talk about, Shelly? Or are you just calling because you miss my dulcet tones?'

I wanted to laugh.

I couldn't manage a smile.

'Elle? What's up? Is everything okay?'

'I saw it.'

'What?'

'I saw the photo.'

Another pause. 'I'm really not following. What're you talking about?'

'The photo on Instagram!' I yelled, my frustration

bursting out of me. 'The photo of you and that *girl* –'
I spat the word, like it was some kind of insult – 'at the
party you went to on Saturday night. With your arms
round each other and her kissing your cheek, and –'

'Oh, that.'

I bristled. How dare he sound so flippant?

'Did you think I wouldn't see it? That I wouldn't
find out?'

I heard him wince. Maybe I was a little shrill, but I
couldn't help it. 'Elle, please, stop freaking out on me.
Take a deep breath. Let's talk.'

'Talk? You want to talk? You had all of yesterday to
talk to me about this, but you didn't. Do you have any
idea how humiliated I was when I went into school
today and everybody else had seen that photo and
everybody else knew, and gossiped about it behind my
back? Do you have any idea what that felt like?'

'Elle, I'm sorry. I didn't think it was a big deal. It's
just a photo from a party.'

'Oh, so if I go on your Facebook profile, I'll find a
whole album of you cuddling random girls at parties
with them kissing you?'

I knew I was being overly dramatic as soon as I said
it, but I couldn't stop myself. I was spiraling. I just kept
thinking if he couldn't talk to me about something as
normal as how he was *actually* doing in college, then

what else couldn't he talk to me about? Was he finding our relationship hard too? Was the distance too much – was that why he'd suggested I apply for colleges in Boston? Did he regret trying long-distance, and was just waiting for the right time to tell me?

Definitely dramatic, but . . .

But I was so scared of losing him.

'Amanda's not some random girl.'

Those were the last words I wanted to hear from him, and I sucked in a sharp breath through my nose, and clenched my jaw. 'What are you trying to say – she *means something* to you? Are you trying to tell me something?'

'That's not what I meant and you know it. I meant, she's a friend. She's my lab partner. We hang out, we study together. That's all I meant by it. Seriously, Elle, just calm down.'

'If she's such a good friend, why is this the first I'm hearing about her?'

Noah sighed, agitated. 'Okay. So, Elle, there's a girl I've been hanging out with a lot. We have classes together and she's my lab partner, and we study to-gether a lot. We have mutual friends and hang out and go to parties together. You think I don't know how that sounds?'

I bit my tongue, hard, before snapping back, 'Is that your way of telling me you think I'm some psycho, jealous person who won't let you hang out with other girls?'

He was quiet for a moment. His voice came out cold and steady. 'You just called me to yell at me about a photo, Elle.'

I was *so* ready to snap at him again but caught myself, seething quietly instead. There was a bitter tang in my mouth and I was flushed, heart hammering. I'd broken out in a cold sweat.

So he was right. But it still felt like he'd been *lying* to me.

I started to understand, for a moment, just how shitty Lee must have felt when he found out I'd been dating Noah behind his back. The realization was like barbed wire round me.

When Noah realized he had a chance to say something, I heard him sigh heavily. 'Listen, Elle. I know how bad things look, and that maybe I should've mentioned Amanda before, and I know that wasn't exactly the sort of photo you wanted to see of me, but I swear, nothing happened. It was totally innocent. She's a hugger. She kisses people on the cheek. It's just her thing. That was *all*. It wasn't a romantic thing, and she's not even interested in me like that. And I'm not interested in her like that either, okay?'

'Okay,' I said quietly. *But . . .*

'I want you,' he went on, 'to be able to trust me.'

I didn't answer. Instead, I pursed my lips, because I was afraid of what I might say. Because much as I wanted to say yes, of course I trusted him, this whole thing made me second-guess that.

'I'm sorry you were so humiliated by it at school. But it's no big deal, what *actually* happened. You know? I get that you're mad right now but you'll see it wasn't. And you know I love you, and we're good, right? It's just gossip. You know how much people used to gossip about me. Trust me – it never means anything.'

'It feels like it means something,' I murmured. 'It's not nice to hear people calling me a slut in the hallways between classes. Or to think you're keeping secrets.'

'Why were they doing that?' he asked, a protective edge sharpening his words.

'Because I left the party on Friday early with Levi. And with that photo of you and . . . Amanda . . .' God, I hated saying her name. I hated her. I didn't even know her but I hated her. Talk about irrational. '. . . everyone jumped to conclusions. They thought we'd broken up and that we were both on the rebound. Or whatever.'

'Oh.'

'You can say all the gossip doesn't matter, and maybe it doesn't in the long run, but right now it's pretty damn hurtful. Not to mention embarrassing.'

'This guy Levi . . .'

'Yeah?'

'You and 7 For All Mankind seem pretty close now.'

His tone was neutral, but like he was trying to make it so – and I couldn't tell if he was jealous or not.

And he had *no* damn right to be. My temper flared.

'We are. And his name is Levi. Don't be mean.'

There was a long pause. In a weird sort of way, I was glad if he was jealous – like it was payback for Amanda.

I hated myself for even thinking it.

This whole long-distance thing was *such* a breeze.

'Shelly?' Noah's voice was startlingly soft and quiet; not irritable and full of jealousy like I'd expected. 'We're good, right?'

'Of course we are,' I said, though if I was being honest with myself, I really didn't know any more.

I wanted us to be good. I wanted everything to go back to normal. I didn't want to fight – or be petty. I took a deep breath.

'I'm – I'm sorry I got so angry.'

'That's okay. You had every right to be.'

Part of me wondered where this calm, cool, collected Noah had suddenly come from – he would usually yell just as much as I would; we could both get fired up when we argued. But he was rarely ever the voice of reason like this.

Had college really changed him so much?

'I have to go,' he said, sighing. 'I'm sorry, I really am, but I promised some of the football guys I'd meet them for dinner to hang out . . . but I'll try call you later?'

We both hesitated, listening to each other's breathing, and then I pulled the phone away from my ear and hung up.

My eyes slid shut and I tilted my head back against my bed, taking a deep breath. If things were supposed to be so great with me and Noah, why did I feel like my heart was breaking?

Chapter 11

The rumors about me and Noah, and me and Levi, died down after a couple of days when people decided they probably weren't true and, since everyone was busting their asses with SATs or midterms or regular homework, no new rumors came to replace the ones about me.

Noah's birthday came and went on October third (I sent him a movie collection on iTunes and a card), and neither of us talked about the photo. He seemed to be making an effort to talk a lot more, make plans for when he was home over Thanksgiving . . . I appreciated it, but something still felt . . . off.

The rumor mill might have already forgotten about Noah and Amanda, but I sure as hell hadn't. And I absolutely had *not* been compulsively checking Amanda's Twitter and Instagram for more cutesy pictures of her and my boyfriend. Absolutely *not*.

It's not like I'd spent hours tracking her down. She had the same handle on Twitter as on Instagram.

Lee told me it was weird to keep checking her social media.

Rachel said she'd be doing the same in my shoes.

Levi just commented on the 'metric shit ton' of photos she posted every day, saying she couldn't possibly be drinking so many coffees with her friends.

I was just opening up Instagram, when Ethan Jenkins, head of student council, knocked his fist on the table, like he was a judge calling a court to order. I looked at Lee, who crossed his eyes and pulled a face at me. We hadn't been due to have a student council meeting this week, but Ethan had made it sound like there was some kind of emergency.

'Alright, everyone! Thanks for showing up. I know we're all busy with SATs and stuff right now, but it's time for a progress check with the Sadie Hawkins dance. Where are we on catering?'

'Oh, man, does he have to talk about food right now? We're giving up our lunch break for this,' Lee muttered to me, his stomach growling as if to back him up. I stifled a giggle, pressing my hand to my mouth.

Even though the dance was shaping up to be pretty awesome, I didn't feel like I shared everyone else's excitement for it. I hadn't picked out a dress yet, and

I hadn't asked anybody. Specifically: Noah. Things felt so delicate between us lately; I got the feeling that asking him to come home to go to the dance with me would just lead to another fight and make things even worse than they already were. I kept finding excuses not to ask him. As people gave updates on whatever they were responsible for, excited whispers filled the room.

'And we're still not doing a theme?' Faith wanted to know, interrupting the update on decorations.

'It's just a dance.' Ethan sighed. 'It doesn't need a theme.'

'Tyrone understood how important a theme was,' Faith muttered.

'Tyrone also blew the whole budget on dances, and that's why we had to hold extra fundraisers,' Ethan shot back. 'Excuse me for thinking about keeping the Summer Dance a huge event.'

'Still need a theme,' Kaitlin said under her breath, pouting.

'Jeez! Fine, you guys want a theme? Here's a theme: *high school dance.* Can we get back to the update on decorations now? On kind of a tight schedule here, if anyone wants to eat this lunchtime.'

'Decorations, please,' Lee cried.

When it got to the music, Lee looked at me desperately. Music had been our responsibility, but Lee hadn't been involved at all so far. He'd been so busy with football and keeping his grades up, and making time for Rachel, that I'd said I'd handle it. I was on the track team now, but it wasn't like that took up massive amounts of my time. I wasn't going to compete or anything – I was mostly just doing it to have on my college application, especially since I'd given up on the whole 'get a job' thing.

Plus, since Lee had to keep his grades up for the football team and if he wanted to get into Brown, he was focusing a lot of his spare time on schoolwork. I knew I couldn't hold that against him. (Though I kind of did.)

'We were thinking,' I said, 'about asking around the school if anybody has a band who wants to perform at the dance. Free entertainment, you know? Remember there were a couple of bands who performed at the Spring Carnival last year? And I'm not talking about the marching band, or the guy who wouldn't stop playing "We Are Family" on his tuba.'

'That's actually a great idea,' Ethan said. 'What's the plan?'

'Put up some posters around school, ask people to send us a video submission. That way we can show you who we pick, and we don't have to find somewhere to sit and listen to them for, like, eight hours after school.'

'Perfect. Get on it, guys. Now, chaperones ... I've been told we need chaperones since it's being held in the school gym. Where are we on chaperones?' As Ethan spoke, he flipped over the handwritten list in front of him, revealing ... another full-page list.

'We're not getting out of here before the end of lunch, are we?' Lee mumbled.

I dug a hand into my backpack, passing him a packet of beef jerky under the table.

'You're my hero.'

'Just call me Wonder Woman.'

Friday afternoon after school, my dad had taken Brad to a soccer tournament and wouldn't be back until later on in the evening; Lee was going to the movies and dinner with Rachel – after checking I was cool with it first; the rest of the guys were having a guys' night in (playing video games, eating too much pizza and drinking a few cans of beer they'd managed to persuade someone's dad to buy for them) ... and I was relishing some me time.

I'd been invited to the guys' night in, but said I'd give it a miss.

My 'me time' involved me pasting on a thick green tea tree-oil face mask, painting my toenails and waxing my legs, while lying across the couch watching an old season of *RuPaul's Drag Race* that was being marathoned on one of the TV channels.

I had my laptop out in front of me, too, a YouTube page open with a video of some guys from school playing a Mumford & Sons cover. Actually, they weren't too bad. One of the best I'd seen so far. I forwarded the link on to Ethan with the message '/10?'

That done, I closed my laptop. I was determined to put the stress of school and college and even my doubts about my relationship with Noah out of my mind and relax properly for the first time in weeks.

Until the doorbell rang.

I froze. No way could I answer the door like this! My hair was scraped back. Green goop covered my whole face. There were waxing strips still on my legs (just three minutes until they came off) and I had toe dividers in to stop my nail polish smudging.

And, I was in Winnie the Pooh pajama pants rolled up to my knees and the T-shirt of Noah's I wore to bed.

Crap.

I figured I should probably see who it was, though, in case it was important. Or Lee. Lee had seen me like this too often to find it funny any more. He'd join me in the face mask and pedicure fun, sometimes. If it was Levi, I got the feeling he'd take a picture to send to all the guys.

I waddled to the window, pulling back the corner of the drapes to look out and see who it was. They were mostly hidden from view, but it couldn't be anyone other than Lee. Maybe his movie night got canceled? Maybe Rachel got sick.

I was way too happy at the thought of something happening to spoil his evening with Rachel, and hanging out with him for the night.

So I waddled a little further out to the doorway, desperate not to ruin my carefully applied nail polish, and opened the door, saying, 'Hey, dude, what happened to –'

And slammed it back shut again.

A hand caught it, laughter drifting in through the crack in the door. I stumbled back a few steps as it opened, and Noah walked in, laughing, a smile splitting his face. He was in the leather jacket and big black boots I knew so well, a white T-shirt hugging his torso.

'What are you doing here?' I cried. If it weren't for the mask all round them, I'd have rubbed my eyes. I had to be seeing things. All the fumes from the nail polish were making me hallucinate.

Because Noah couldn't be here, inside my house. He was across the country at college.

And yet here he was, laughing at me, practically doubled over.

'It's nice to see you too,' he said, when he managed to stop laughing.

'What are you doing here?' I repeated, too shocked to say anything else.

He grinned, the dimple in his left cheek showing. 'After weeks of not seeing me, *that's* how you greet me? I mean, come on, Elle. Where's the *Fifty Shades* lingerie? Where are the rose petals on the floor, the candlelit dinner?'

'I –'

And then his arms were wrapped round me and his lips were on mine, and I melted. The tension, the anxiety about *us*, it all vanished. Instinctively, my arms curled round his shoulders, fingers toying with the ends of his hair, not used to it this short. He tasted like coffee. His body against mine felt exactly like I remembered. He kissed just the same.

And God, he kissed so *good*.

'That,' he said, breaking the kiss but not moving away, noticeably breathless, 'is how you should've said hello.'

I drew back, my hands still on his shoulders. 'You have stuff all over your face now,' I said, running a fingertip over his cheek, just below where my face mask had smeared. It was in his stubble, too. He hadn't shaved in a couple of days. He looked so cute like this – way more so in real life than he had on camera.

He just smiled again. 'God, I missed you.'

In reply, I pulled myself closer and kissed him.

Once I was a little more presentable – still in pajamas but without the various skincare and beauty products – we lay down facing each other on the couch in the lounge, my back to the TV and my nose touching Noah's, his arms holding me in close, and I was right where I wanted to be. I liked his new beard, even though it was a little itchy against my cheek and neck. His eyes were impossibly bright, and even more electric blue than I remembered, and he didn't take them off mine for a second as we lay there with *Brooklyn Nine-Nine* playing in the background.

I still couldn't believe he was here! Actually *here*. I felt so dizzy; it completely overwhelmed all the nervousness I'd felt around our relationship lately.

Noah had talked to me through the bathroom door – his classes on Monday were canceled, so he'd decided to come home for the weekend and surprise me (which, he gloated, he'd done a damn good job of).

He said that after our (admittedly mostly one-sided) argument about the incident with the photo he'd decided to come visit, because he missed me, and said that things were probably so tense between us because we hadn't seen each other in so long.

'You could've picked a more opportune moment to show up. Like, five minutes later would've been great,' I'd called through the bathroom door, tearing off the last waxing strip. 'Seriously. I'm mortified.'

'Because I saw you looking a little bit like Princess Fiona from *Shrek*?'

'Because I'm trying to maintain the illusion that I achieve this flawless beauty with absolutely no effort,' I'd joked, opening the door back up to him. 'And now you know my secret.'

He bent his head to kiss me again. 'You always look beautiful, Elle. Even with hairy legs and zits.'

Now, I ran my fingertips over his cheek – he'd washed the face mask off – and over his nose, along the edge of his two-day beard, up round the shape of his eyebrows.

'What are you doing?'

'Just admiring my gorgeous boyfriend.' I kissed him. I'd forgotten how good it felt. Had kissing him always been like this? 'I've missed you so much. Like, words could not *describe*.'

'I missed you more,' he protested, smirking a little. I shook my head and kissed him again, slowly and softly, trying to memorize how his tongue moved with mine. Who knew how long it'd be until I got to do this again? I was going to make every minute with him count.

When we did stop kissing, it was because a car pulled up outside: my dad and brother were back. We sat up. I straightened my shirt, and Noah stole another brief kiss before the door opened.

'We're back,' my dad called out.

'In here.'

Brad was already running upstairs, yelling, 'Hey, Elle! Hey, Levi!' He was probably under instructions to change out of his muddy soccer gear straight away (he *always* got muddy, and I was sure he did it on purpose) but my dad came into the lounge – not before Noah raised an eyebrow at me for Brad yelling hi to Levi. I shrugged. He'd hung out here a lot over the last few weeks . . . more than Lee, actually.

Dad did a double take, staring at Noah with his mouth slack and eyes squinting. Noah's arm was slung round me and he lifted it to wave. 'Hey, Mr Evans.'

Then he cleared his throat, composed his face. 'Good to see you, Noah. Home for the weekend?'

'Yep. I haven't got any classes on Monday so figured I'd come see Elle for a couple of days.' He punctuated it with a smile at me – with an expression so eerily like the soppy look I caught on Lee's face when he was looking at Rachel that it made me blush.

Dad nodded. 'And how is college? Your mom said you seem to have settled in well.'

Noah answered quickly, enthusiastically, and not at all like himself. 'Yeah, it's great. I've made some really good friends, and the football team is great, and my classes are really interesting. The only downside is having to do my own laundry,' he added, and they both laughed.

We stuck around for a while, and when my dad was out making himself some decaf coffee and Brad was in bed, Noah's lips brushed over my neck and his hand slid under my shirt. Warm and heavy and familiar and making my heart flip. He said softly, 'Do you wanna stay at mine tonight?'

'Your parents won't mind?'

'Have they ever? You have a toothbrush and deodorant in our bathroom. You have a drawer full of clothes in Lee's room.'

'Yeah, but . . . I dunno, I feel like I have to check. It's different now.'

He kissed my cheek, lips grazing over my skin toward my ear. 'Hey, if you want to stay here instead, all by yourself . . .' He kissed my neck, just below my ear.

'Give me two minutes.'

I hurried upstairs to put on some appropriate clothes to leave the house in, and threw some essentials in an oversized purse – namely, clean (and cute) underwear and my cell-phone charger – before putting on some shoes and heading back downstairs.

'I'm gonna stay over at Lee's house,' I said to my dad. Then, seeing he was about to make some cringe-inducing comment about 'being careful', I added, 'In the spare room.'

I had exactly zero intention of staying in the spare room; the box of condoms in my purse was a testament to that.

He nodded, like he didn't want to hear more about it, but I didn't miss the mildly disapproving look he cast me over the top of his glasses. 'What time are you coming home?'

I shrugged. 'Sunday, I guess. Maybe after dinner?'

Dad nodded. 'Alright. Text me tomorrow and let me know. Do you have a key?'

'Yup.'

'Got your pill?'

My cheeks flamed. I should've known I wouldn't get away that easy. I'd been on the pill for over a year – not so much because I'd needed the contraception at that point, but more to balance out my irregular periods – but it looked like my dad was treating the situation like alcohol at parties: he knew it was gonna happen, and he knew he couldn't stop me, so he just wanted me to be safe about it.

Even so, I hissed, *'Yes*, Dad. *God*. I'm a responsible adult.'

'Yesterday you were playing Disney soundtracks. And singing along.'

'Responsible adult. I'm going now.'

The Flynn house was silent, save for the distant, steady rumble of the washing machine. Noah said his parents had gone to their friends' twentieth-anniversary party and wouldn't be back until the next day. Lee was still out with Rachel.

Neither of us was complaining.

Later, we were curled up in his bed, wrapped under the comforter even though it was a warm night, our legs tangled together and my head resting on Noah's chest. I splayed my fingers out across it slowly.

'You smell different,' I said to him. He still smelled of the citrus body wash and shampoo he used, and of his aftershave, but there was something different about it I couldn't place.

When I told him as much, he said, 'Well, I haven't smoked a cigarette for a few months, so maybe that's it.'

I pushed myself up on an elbow to look at his face. 'I never understood that habit. It wasn't even a *habit*. You just did it to look cool in front of everyone else, didn't you?'

His mouth twitched, and he glanced away for a second. 'Kind of.'

'Why's it so important for you to be seen as a bad boy?'

Now I'd asked, I wondered why I hadn't before. Noah sighed, and trailed his fingers through my hair. His fingers snagged in a knot, so he stroked the top of my hair down to the roots instead. It was the kind of absentminded, soothing gesture that I'd missed so much when he'd been gone.

'What, you don't think I'm a bad boy?' He was trying to be playful, mock-dismay on his face now. 'I'm wounded. Maybe I need to go punch a wall and light up a cigarette to prove it to you. Race off on my motorbike and pick a fight with someone. Go . . . I don't know, go kick all the potted plants outside over. My mom would hate that. Seriously badass.'

I rolled my eyes. '*Funny*. Seriously, though. You're a big softy around me, and you're a closet geek, but you put up this front for everyone else, like nobody can touch you. Sometimes you act like you're just asking for a fight. Don't think I hadn't noticed it's just a front.'

Noah held my gaze for a moment; I thought he was trying to decide if I was bluffing or not. He must've realized not. His fingers moved to trace circles on my back, and I pressed a kiss into his shoulder blade.

'You were too little to remember it, you and Lee, but in grade school I used to get bullied. A lot. I wasn't as big as some of the other kids, and I was this weedy little guy.'

'I've seen pictures. I kinda remember.'

'I was smart, too. And you know what some assholes like to do to geeks and nerds – the bigger, not-so-smart kids like to pick on them because it makes them feel better about themselves. Happens all over the world, right? Textbook situation.'

'Right . . .' I said slowly, drawing the word out and my eyebrows together. How had I been so close to Noah all these years and never known he used to get bullied? Did Lee know? His parents never mentioned it . . . Had he asked them not to?

'I hated it, because I just wanted to shove them back – but, you know, if you fought back, you got in more trouble . . . And I wasn't a snitch. I never tattled on a bigger kid when they pushed me off the swing or stole my cookies at lunch. It just made me so . . . *angry.*'

Noah drew in a shaky breath, and I reached over to take his other hand in mine, locking our fingers together. He didn't return the hold, but he didn't pull away, either.

'I couldn't take my frustration out on them, and I didn't want to tell my parents. You know what they're

148

like – they'd have called the school and made a lot of fuss and it would've made me an even bigger loser.'

'So you took your frustration out on everything else,' I said, thinking about the time he told me he'd gone to anger-management classes a few years back, but they hadn't helped.

He carried on as if I hadn't said anything. 'Middle school wasn't so bad. I had my growth spurt that summer, and my parents had signed me up for kickboxing –'

'Oh, yeah, I remember that.'

'Because they thought I just needed an outlet, so I wasn't a weedy little guy any more.'

'But you were still a geek,' I said, trying to fill in some of the gaps. This conversation was like a jigsaw puzzle – and I was trying to fill in the middle without having the edges to work from first. I couldn't believe we'd never talked about this until now. 'You're smart. You've always been smart. Hell, you got into an Ivy League college, Noah. Not just anybody can do that.'

'I remember,' he said, a wry smile on his face, 'this one time in eighth-grade Spanish class. We had a test, and I got a C in it. I'd never had anything below a B-plus, even on a bad day in my worst subject. I was smart, I knew that, but I didn't slack. My parents weren't mad about the C – they said it was just one little test, no big deal. But they were disappointed in me. Even if they didn't say it, I could see it in their faces. And I was harder on myself for it than they ever could've been.'

'So . . .' I sat up a little more, snuggling further into the crook of Noah's arm, which tightened round me in response. He hadn't been looking at me during the conversation, fixing his gaze on the wall in front of him instead. I pulled my hand out of his and titled his chin toward me so he'd have to look at me.

'So,' he said, 'I decided that I'd had enough.'

'Of what?'

'Hating everything and not doing anything about it. I started pushing back. I got into fights sometimes, I cut class once in a while. My parents and teachers thought it was just a phase. Give it a year, and I'd stop rebelling and take school seriously again, right?'

'But you didn't.'

He shook his head. 'I was already taking school seriously. I just made people think that I wasn't. At high school, to stay on the football team, you have to keep up an A-grade average, right? Or, you're supposed to. Coach cut some slack for a couple of kids. But I kept my grades up, and because the other jocks did too, I wasn't called out on it. And, to be honest . . . I *liked* being called the bad boy. It was fun to cut class and know my teachers would just roll their eyes if I sauntered in late and without my homework, because they'd come to expect that of me. I think they expected to fail me by the end of the year.'

'And you . . . what, you liked to surprise them by doing really well and finishing with the third-best grades in your class?' I guessed.

'I did well at school for *myself*, not for anybody else. I didn't want to be valedictorian or whatever. I didn't need that; didn't want it, or the attention that came with it. I kept up the bad-boy reputation not just because I didn't want to be pushed around any more, or because it was kind of fun, or because sometimes I'm kind of an asshole, but because if people never expected anything of me, they'd never be disappointed.'

We were both quiet for a long time. At first, Noah's breathing was shallow and ragged, but it calmed down after a while. He'd always been kind of closed off to some degree, making comments about how he didn't deal well with emotional stuff. This was the most vulnerable I'd ever known him.

I realized that I didn't actually know who Noah was any more: not because of what he'd just told me, but because he seemed like a different person coming home from college. He was quicker to smile, more relaxed. Even when we'd argued about the photo – he'd been rational, way calmer than I was used to.

'And now? Now you got into Harvard and high school's over, you've dropped the whole rebellious act?'

'Who says I've dropped it? Here I was thinking that was the reason why you fell for me.'

I rolled my eyes, unable to keep a smile from my face. 'Yeah, because you're a badass who says he's gonna go kick over his mom's potted plants.'

'I could eat some ice, too,' he deadpanned. 'Whole cubes. Tell me that's not badass.'

I swatted at his chest gently, and he caught my fingers in his hand, kissing each fingertip. I giggled, happy he was being playful again instead of being so serious. Noah had never really dealt with his emotions well, for as long as I'd known him, so it didn't surprise me that after being bullied he'd wanted to lash out instead of cry. That was just who he was.

'I just mean –' I started, but he cut me off with a light kiss.

'I know what you mean. I just don't really know how else to be, is all. But I'm trying not to put up so much of a front now. Not argue with people so much. It's easier because everybody's new, and I can … reinvent myself – and everyone at Harvard is pretty smart, so it's okay to be a geek.' He smirked. 'But it's still hard to be anything else, because I've spent so long being like this.'

'I'll love you either way,' I told him sincerely. I think I loved him more in this moment than I ever had.

'Even if I start wearing pink polo shirts and tying sweaters round my neck, and trade my motorbike in for a golf buggy?'

'Okay, *now* you're just being totally ridiculous.'

'You started it.' But he was grinning at me.

'No, you did.'

'You definitely started this.' Then he pulled me on top of him, his fingers poking at my ribs and waist and neck, and I shrieked, trying to squirm away from him, but giggling too much to put up a fight. Noah chuckled in my ear. 'But I'm starting *this*.'

Chapter 12

I slept better that night than I had in weeks. When I woke up the next morning, sometime after ten, Noah was already awake, sitting up watching YouTube videos, and I was snuggled into his side.

It was a good way to wake up.

'Morning, sleepyhead,' he said, dipping his head toward mine as I went to kiss him. He tasted like toothpaste, so I guessed he'd already gotten out of bed, and I probably had morning breath, but neither of us really cared. I smiled against his lips.

'I've missed you –' I told him, then broke off to yawn. 'I missed *this*.'

'Watching videos in bed first thing on a Saturday?' he joked.

'Waking up with you.'

His smile stretched wider, and so did mine. Noah paused the video and set his phone aside, rolling on top of me and holding his weight on his elbows. I slipped my arms up his toned chest and over his muscular arms, pulling myself closer against him and pressing my lips to his. Whenever we kissed, it filled me with the same euphoria it had the first time.

Why did I ever doubt this relationship? I must've been crazy. I'd thought I'd missed Noah a lot over the last few weeks, but now I was here with him I realized just how lonely I'd been without him. There was *nothing* wrong between us. We weren't just good – we were *perfect*. We'd just needed some time together, that was all.

The rest of the morning was lazy, cozy and completely idyllic.

At some point, I worked up the courage to ask him about the dance.

'Noah . . .'

'Yeah?'

I gulped, wet my lips. My mouth had turned dry. 'It's . . . There's a dance, soon. At school. The Sadie Hawkins dance. And I was wondering if you'd come home for the weekend to go with me?'

Noah sighed, looking away from me. My stomach sank; he didn't need to answer me. The sigh was answer enough.

This was exactly why I'd been avoiding asking him. Because I'd been dreading this reaction.

'I would,' he told me, voice full of apology. 'You know

I would, Elle. But this weekend was a one-off. I can't keep coming back here, especially for a high school dance. It's too much time out of studying, and football, and it's not exactly cheap to keep flying back and forth.'

'But . . .' I took a breath and sat up slightly. 'I really want to go to the dance with you. And I hate going so long without seeing you. It's hard, you know?'

'I know,' he said, scowling. 'It's hard for me, too. I miss you. But I can't just come back every time you guys have some dance, or a party, or whatever. And Sadie Hawkins – it's in November, right? I'll be coming back just after that for Thanksgiving.'

I was about to argue again, but bit my tongue, and sank back on to the bed beside him. Both of us were stiff, the silence awkward, bordering on tense. It was just a dance, I tried to tell myself. It was no big deal. It made a lot of sense why Noah wouldn't come home for it.

But was it so bad of me to want to spend more time with him, or go to a dance with him?

Noah leaned over to kiss my temple, arm wrapping round me. 'Maybe I'll be home around the Summer Dance.'

It was a peace offering and I took it, nodding and turning to kiss him again. Even if all I wanted to do was wriggle out of his arms and pull on a hoodie to hide my face in, his rejection sitting like a stone in the pit of my stomach.

Lunchtime, we headed downstairs for something to eat, and Lee was in the kitchen making a sandwich.

'Hey,' he said. 'Did you know he was coming home this weekend?'

'No.'

'I'm right here, you know,' Noah said.

'Did you hear something, Shelly?' Lee looked around melodramatically, and I bit back a laugh.

'Just the wind. I think your mom left a window open . . .'

Noah sighed, walking past me and opening the fridge to peruse the contents. 'Where's the apple juice?'

'We don't have any.'

'But we always have apple juice.'

'You're the only one who drinks it, and Mom said there's no point in buying it if nobody's here to drink it.'

'So much for empty-nest syndrome.'

'I think that only kicks in when I leave, too.'

Noah took some orange juice (no pulp) from the refrigerator, gesturing with it to me in question. I nodded. 'There's no bacon, either.'

'Mom's got us on a new diet. We're all cutting down

on meat. Something to do with Dad's cholesterol, I think?'

'God, it's like a different place back here.'

'I think there's some turkey rashers.'

'That's *not* bacon.'

'Mom insists it's the same thing.'

'Lies, all of it.'

I couldn't help but smile at them. I'd forgotten how Lee and Noah got on almost as well as Lee and I did – if not better, in some ways.

Once we'd eaten, Noah announced that we were gonna go back upstairs and watch TV.

Lee snorted. '*Watch TV*. Right, sure. Don't forget to use protection. Don't do anything I wouldn't do. Et cetera.'

I blushed, ducking my head so my hair hid my reaction. Noah smacked Lee across the head and told him to mind his own damn business. Before Noah shut the kitchen door, I heard Lee making elaborate gagging noises.

I turned round on the stairs to stop Noah, shushed him, and then giggled loudly. 'Noah! Stop it! Not on the stairs!'

'You guys are so gross!' Lee yelled.

'Ooh, Noah.' I threw in an exaggerated moan.

'You're off my Christmas-card list, Shelly!'

'Love you too, man!'

'You guys are so goddamn weird,' Noah muttered, shaking his head.

I grinned at Noah before I walked up the stairs ahead of him, and he tapped my butt lightly. When I glanced over my shoulder, raising my eyebrows at him, his eyes were skirting the walls and he whistled, feigning innocence. I turned back, carrying on up the stairs – and he smacked my butt again.

I skipped up the next few steps, and felt Noah swipe at me again, but his fingertips only caught the edge of my shirt. He laughed, chasing after me up the stairs. I heard Lee yelling, 'You kids keep it down up there! You're disgusting! I hate you both!' but it only made me giggle, and I kept running just out of Noah's reach until he tackled me on to his bed, rolling me on to my back before lying on top of me to kiss me until I was sure that nothing in the world felt as blissful as this.

I went downstairs to make myself some coffee. Lee had gone to see Rachel – apparently, her parents were away at a relative's wedding, and she was planning a big evening in, complete with candles and takeout and a movie. (She'd told me this might be 'The Night'. As in, the night they finally had sex.) Lee and Noah's parents were still out, at their friends' anniversary celebration.

They'd stayed the night in a hotel up there, and weren't due back till later tonight.

On my way back upstairs, I was silent: I was walking slowly anyway because I'd filled the mug too much, but since I was barefoot on their carpet floors, Noah didn't hear me coming.

And maybe that was a good thing, in hindsight.

Or not.

I could hear Noah's voice drifting out into the hallway, low and tense.

His door was cracked open, and I paused just outside, listening. He was sitting on the edge of the bed facing the window, his back to me and the door, his cell phone pressed to his ear and his head bowed. I could see his hand knotted in his hair. His shoulders were tense.

Something was wrong. And I . . . stopped to listen.

Okay, so I probably shouldn't have been eavesdropping, and I knew that, but the urgency of his hushed voice intrigued me enough to stop and listen in.

'Yeah, I'm with her, she's downstairs . . . What? No, of course I haven't told her! . . . No, not yet. It's not the right time . . . No . . . Look, I'll tell her at some point, but not today . . . She doesn't need to know. Well – no, fine, okay, maybe she does, but . . .' He sighed, and I watched him run a hand through his hair again. 'What're you gonna ring her and tell her yourself if

I don't?' He scoffed. '*Right*. Listen, Amanda, it doesn't *mean* anything. Elle doesn't need to know.'

Amanda.

He was talking to *her*.

About *me*.

I heard blood rushing in my ears, and I was surprised I didn't drop the coffee when my heart plummeted. I felt cold all over. I'd known, hadn't I? That something was wrong? That things were weird between us? It wasn't just the distance. It was . . .

It doesn't mean anything. It's not the right time. She doesn't need to know. It doesn't mean anything.

I pushed the door open, knowing the creak of the hinges would let Noah know I was back. He twisted on the bed to look at me, a stiff smile on his face – but it dropped away in dismay when he saw my expression.

'Oh, shit,' he muttered into the cell phone, his voice clipped. 'I've gotta go. I'll talk to you later, or something.'

He hung up, tossing the phone on to his pillows. He stood up to face me. I walked over to the nightstand, my limbs stiff but not paralyzed, at least, and set down the coffee before I either dropped it, or threw it in his face.

'That was *her*, wasn't it?' I asked, my voice devoid of emotion, but shaking ever so slightly.

Noah bit his lip, looking more nervous than I'd ever seen him. 'Elle, how much of that did you hear?'

Wrong thing to say, buddy.

'Was that her? The girl from the photo?' I couldn't bring myself to say her name. I hated her too much right now.

'Yes, that was Amanda, but it's not what you think –'

'Oh? You sure about that?'

'Yes,' he said, almost snapping, but his voice was earnest and his hands were palm-up, held out toward me – begging me, pleading with me to listen, hear him out. My heart was pounding furiously and my hands shook. 'I know what you're thinking, and I already told you: nothing happened with Amanda, I swear. Nothing *is* happening.'

'How do you expect me to believe that?' I stumbled back a step, as though his words physically repulsed me, and my eyes filled with tears. I couldn't cry, not right now. I blinked, so hard that I saw stars against my eyelids, to clear the tears away. 'After what I just heard? I knew you were hiding something from me. You're on the other side of the country, Noah! For all I know, you've forgotten all about me and this visit is some – some last-ditch effort –'

'You're overreacting.'

'Am I? With the history you've got?'

It was a low blow, and not even fair – he'd had a reputation as a player that was mostly all talk, and as far as I knew, he'd never cheated on anyone. But I couldn't control the words coming out of my mouth.

His words kept punching me in the gut: *It doesn't mean anything. She doesn't need to know . . .*

What else could that even mean?

I put a hand on my stomach, even though I wasn't sure where I hurt – my head was spinning, my legs were probably going to give out any second, and it was like a mountain had been dropped over my chest. I needed to scream, or cry, or . . . I didn't know what.

The imploring expression on his face dropped away in an instant as my words hit home, and those blue eyes were suddenly ice, and narrowed at me.

'You don't trust me.'

I felt awful, in every way possible, but my voice was biting and I couldn't seem to stop talking. I was destroying everything and some voice in the back of my mind begged me to stop, but weeks of nervousness and strain bubbled to the surface, taking over.

'Like you're any better. You get jealous every time I mention that I'm hanging out with Levi, just the two of us, I know you do. Is it one rule for you and another for me? Like I'm not allowed to be cagey about hearing a conversation like that with some bitch you –'

'Amanda's not a bitch.'

'*Stop* defending her. Stop *talking* about her. I don't want to hear how nice she is.' I was practically screaming now, and I was *so* glad that nobody else was home. 'Do you have *any* idea how humiliating that was for me? *Everyone* saw that picture online. *Everyone* knew, and they assumed that we must've broken up.'

'I know, Elle, and I'm sorry, but you have to believe me when I tell you – *again* – that nothing happened. And nothing is happening or is going to happen. I don't know how else I can say it. Amanda doesn't mean anything to me like that; she's just a friend.'

'A friend you didn't tell me about!'

'You're the last person who should be getting jealous of a girl I'm friends with,' he snapped at me. 'Look at you and Lee!'

'That's different – you know it is.'

He scoffed, shaking his head. 'And Levi? Do you tell me every time you hang out with him?'

I grit my teeth. What did Levi have to do with any of this?

'We have lab together, classes together. It's intense. It's . . . You wouldn't understand.'

Maybe it was a fair comment, but it felt like a stab in the stomach. What, like I was too stupid? Like he was so much better now he was in college? Like I wouldn't get it, but *Amanda* would?

'Why were you on the phone to her just now?' I asked, suddenly quiet. The yelling had taken it out of me, and so had his last comment. 'What was that about? Because if it's not what it sounds like, then please, please, just tell me.'

Noah opened his mouth to answer, but words appeared to fail him, and he faltered, looking away. He closed his mouth, defiant, not answering me.

I shook my head. I wanted to believe him, but when I closed my eyes I could see that dumb photo: her arms round him, his round her, her lips on his cheek, leaving an imprint of ruby-red lipstick, the drunken grin on his face. *It's intense*, he'd said. What did that even mean?

Nothing good, judging by the way I felt right now.

'Please, Noah. Just tell me the truth.'

All I got was silence.

Then, he sucked his teeth, took a breath . . . and kept saying nothing.

I watched him. The way his shoulders sagged, the torn expression on his face, the fact that whatever the hell was going on, he couldn't talk to me about it – *wouldn't* talk to me about it. The longer I waited, the worse it got. My mind raced, picturing them in compromising positions, imagining them laughing together, cozied up in some cute little coffee shop or on the quad or in his dorm, or . . .

My whole body felt weak, and my head felt heavy. Noah closed his eyes, refusing to look at me.

And suddenly the rift between us wasn't just a small crack we could patch up with a surprise visit home or more video calls. It was a chasm so deep and so wide I didn't even know who I was looking at right now. This new, mature Noah, who refused to talk to me and kept secrets from me was a stranger, and seemed to have changed, exactly like I'd been scared he would.

I heard the next words come out of my mouth as if somebody else was talking. My voice was dead, flat.

'I don't think that this is working out.'

I counted four heartbeats of silence. Noah was holding his breath – I knew, because I was too, and it was so silent between us that I should've been able to hear him breathing. All the tension, the anger, even the pleading, had drained from his face, leaving his complexion ashen. I couldn't look him in the eye, so I focused instead on the frayed hem of his jeans where a loose thread brushed his bare foot.

'What?'

He sounded like he was being strangled. I winced.

'I can't do this any longer.'

'Do what?'

'This. *Us*. I can't do it. I hate being away from you all the time. And I hate knowing that you're at college with all these other girls – smarter, prettier girls, who are probably throwing themselves at you, and I – I just . . .'

'You don't trust me,' he filled in, every syllable carefully controlled.

'I want to trust you,' I tried to explain, my voice breaking. 'But if you can't tell me the truth about whatever's going on . . . what kind of relationship is this? It's . . . I can't deal with it any more. And – and neither of us should – should be tied down to something that's just dead weight.'

'So, what . . . what are you saying?'

I drew in a breath to try and steady myself, and dragged my eyes up to meet his, trying to ignore the fact that they were glistening and that his face was utterly disconsolate (another SAT word of Lee's).

Lee. Shit. How was Lee going to take this, when he found out? How would I even tell him? Would Noah tell him first? Would Lee have to take sides? Would I make him do that, after everything I put him through by lying to him when I first got together with Noah?

'Elle?'

I couldn't keep doing this. It hurt too much.

'I'm saying that this isn't working out. And we . . . we should break up.'

This time, I counted three heartbeats of silence.

'Don't do this, Elle,' he whispered.

'Tell me what's going on.'

'I – I just . . . can't . . . right now, okay? It's . . . complicated.'

I shook my head. It wasn't the right answer. It wasn't good enough. It wasn't enough to keep the tears out of my eyes.

'We can fix this. Elle. *Please.*'

'No, Noah, I don't think we can, otherwise you'd *talk* to me about something like this.'

He strode round the bed toward me and I moved back. If he held me right now, I'd want to forget about it, I'd want to forgive him, and I knew that was the wrong thing.

I fixed my eyes back on his feet, watching the way he shifted his weight from one foot to the other, before pressing down his toes firmly as he stood up straighter.

What other choice did I have? This was getting to be too painful – and better I got out now, before he realized there were girls at college much more worth his time than me. Right? He was clearly moving on with his life, and I was just one more string tying him down to his old life he didn't need – or want – any more. And

168

from the sound of things, he already had something going on with *that girl*.

And whatever was going on, he obviously didn't trust me enough to tell me.

'I'm sorry,' he murmured.

And something inside me shattered.

My breath caught in my throat and if I thought this was painful before, it was nothing compared to the sharp ache that spread through me now, the needles pressing into my skin and making me feel numb on the outside.

And now, when I was prepared to fight more tears down before getting out of here, none came. I simply stood there, my jaw a little slack, and my limbs too numb and leaden to run away.

Neither of us moved for a moment.

Until I couldn't bear to look at him any longer.

'I should get going,' I mumbled, picking up my sweater and purse from the bed, throwing in the book I'd been reading earlier that I'd left on the nightstand, and my cell phone. I ducked my head as low as I could, my hair acting as a curtain to block out Noah.

He made no move to follow me out, even just to walk me to the door.

I hesitated in his doorway, though. Should I say something? Even just a goodbye? A 'see you round'?

My mouth hung open for a few seconds, and I stole a glance over my shoulder. Noah had turned his back to me now, and I could see the muscles pulled taut in his back and arms, wrought with tension. His hands balled into fists for a second before hanging limp at his sides.

So I left, without saying anything.

It was only when I got in my car that the finality of what I'd just done hit me.

We'd broken up. *I'd* broken up with *him*. Everything outside blurred. I automatically put the wipers on, only to realize that I was crying, and it wasn't rain. I didn't want to risk Noah seeing me sitting in my car bawling my eyes out, so I tore off down the drive with jerky movements as I fumbled with the clutch. I was trembling all over, so I punched the heat on, but it didn't do any good.

I was crying too much and too hard to concentrate on driving, even just the short distance home, so I turned down the nearest side street and stalled to a stop, killing the engine. I collapsed forward on to the steering wheel, and let loose the tears.

Chapter 13

I called Lee.

I knew he was at Rachel's and I knew this was their big romantic evening in, and he'd told me about how excited he was about it, so I hesitated when my best friend's number was up on my cell-phone screen. I could barely see it from crying so hard. It would be so selfish to interrupt their night together, I knew that.

I clicked dial.

It went to voicemail, and by that point I was a mess – I'd used up the entire mini packet of Kleenex I kept in my car for emergencies, and the ones in my purse, and I was snotty and tearful and so distraught it was hard to breathe properly. I kept taking these huge, gasping breaths like I was drowning.

What the hell had I just done?

I could've called Levi. He and I were good friends

now, and I knew he'd be there for me. He'd understand, too – he'd had a rough breakup with Julie. I should call Levi, I told myself, and leave Lee be.

But much as I liked Levi, it was Lee I needed right now. My best friend.

Before I could tell myself to leave my best friend to have his night in with his girlfriend, I was already calling him again.

This time, he picked up on the first ring.

'I'm kind of in the middle of something here, Shelly. What's up?' Lee's voice was hushed and testy, but somehow, I couldn't bring myself to feel bad for disturbing him.

I sniffled, and before I could decide how to start this, he realized I was crying.

'What's wrong?' he asked, his voice gentle now. 'Elle? Talk to me.'

'I – I b-b-broke up with . . .' I hiccupped. 'With N-Noah.'

'What?'

'I b-broke up w-with him.' I sniffed, wiping the back of my hand across my cheek. 'I'm sorry to spoil your evening because I know how important this is to you guys, but I just – I needed to talk to you, that's all. Just spare me ten minutes, and then you can get back to wining and dining Rachel. Please.'

'I'll do more than give you ten minutes,' he said. 'You guys really broke up?'

'Oh, God, Lee . . . I don't . . .' *I don't know what I've done.*

'Where are you?'

'In my car. I'm . . . I'm sorry, Lee. I know I shouldn't have called but I didn't know what else to do.'

'Don't apologize.' Lee's voice was soft, calming. 'Where are you, exactly?' I looked around, blinking away enough tears to read out the street name on the nearby sign. 'Okay. I'll be there as soon as I can.'

Shit, I didn't expect him to *leave* Rachel. I mean, I should've guessed he would, but all I needed was to talk to him, for him to comfort me. I didn't intend for him to bail on Rachel, especially tonight.

'No – it's – honestly, please, don't –'

My protests were futile; from the sound of it, he'd taken the cell phone away from his ear, but I could hear him talking, even if his voice was a bit distant. There was rustling, like fabric.

'I'm sorry, Rach, I have to go.'

'What? What's happened?' Rachel's voice was faint, but I could still make out every word she said. And from the tone of her voice, she didn't sound remotely happy that their evening together was being disrupted.

'Elle needs me. I'm sorry. I'll be back soon, I promise. I can't just leave her. I swear, I won't be too long. Maybe an hour or two. I'm sorry.'

'What do you mean? You're *leaving*?'

'Well, yeah, I . . . I have to go. She's my best friend.'

'Lee, we've been waiting for tonight for *weeks*, and we just . . . And now you're just going to walk out on me?'

'I'm not walking out on you.' I heard the strain in his voice as he tried to keep it calm and cool and collected. It made me wince. 'I told you – I'll be back soon. I know this isn't exactly . . . ideal . . . She's in her car, upset, and she needs me. She's crying, Rach. I'm not leaving her like that.'

'No, but you're leaving *me*.' I'd never heard Rachel so snappy and blunt before. It made my stomach twist with guilt.

Lee didn't try to deny it. 'She's my best friend, Rachel.'

'And I'm your girlfriend!'

'You knew exactly what kind of relationship I had with Elle when we got together. She's a huge part of my life. Always has been. You knew all of that. And I've been neglecting her for months since I got together with you –'

'Are you seriously blaming me for the two of you drifting apart?' Her voice was getting borderline angry now. I cringed, hating myself. I shouldn't have called him.

'No! Did I say that? No. I just meant I've been putting you first for a long time, but right now, I need to put Elle first. I'm sorry if you can't respect that, but –'

'Respect that? Lee, we just had sex, and now you're running off to be with another girl! I know you guys are close, but this is just . . . Whatever you say, she's always going to come first, and I – I don't know if I can . . .'

Oh, shit. Shit, shit, shit. I *definitely* should not have called.

Way to go, Elle, wrecking two relationships in one night!

Lee sighed tersely. 'Rach, can we please not do this right now? Okay? I'm not going to leave her when she's this upset. I love you, but this is my best friend we're talking about. I'm sorry.'

I was sure that Lee had forgotten I was still on the line; or maybe he thought he'd hung up on me, because, from the rustling noises, it sounded like he'd put the cell phone in his pocket.

But I did hear, very clearly, Rachel crying, 'Lee Flynn, don't you dare!' and then the slamming of a car door. At that point, I punched the button to hang up, dropping my cell phone into my lap.

There was a thunderclap overhead, and it started to rain, hard and heavy.

Talk about pathetic fallacy, I thought dryly, choking out a laugh.

And I began to bawl even harder.

There was a rap on my window, and I jumped. For a moment, I thought it was Noah and he'd come to try and talk things through because he wasn't going to let me go so easily after all.

But as my eyes focused on the figure outside the window, I realized that it was Lee, not Noah, outside my car. I couldn't help it when my heart sank a little, any notion of a romantic declaration, Noah telling me what was going on, us fixing things, gone.

Lee had his arms hugged round himself, and he was bouncing on the balls of his feet, collar turned up against the rain. Not that it helped. He was already drenched.

I swept the used, snotty Kleenex off the passenger seat on to the floor, and climbed over, letting Lee take the driver's seat.

The first thing he did was lean in and hug me tight for a long time, letting me cry into his fancy black shirt and wrap my arms round his waist, underneath his coat. He didn't ask how I was, or what had happened. He just hugged me, and stroked my hair. He was wet all over, and it seeped into my own clothes, making them damp, but I didn't care. This was exactly what the breakup doctor ordered.

Maybe five or ten or twenty minutes later, I'd calmed down enough to talk.

'I'm so sorry. I shouldn't have called you. I – I should've just gone home, or called Dixon or Levi, or something. I didn't mean to make you and Rachel fight.'

Lee groaned. 'You heard that, huh?'

'You forgot to hang up. I thought you were coming back on the line to talk.'

'How much did you hear?'

I shifted my weight, pulling out of the hug to lean back in my seat, and grimaced. Lee just nodded with a grim sort of look on his face.

I opened my mouth to apologize again – one breakup was more than enough for one night, and Lee didn't need to deal with my relationship troubles as well as his own. I'd been totally selfish to call him. But he clamped a hand over my mouth before I could utter so much as a syllable.

'Don't. I'm not going to leave you sobbing in your car after a breakup and just console you for a couple of minutes over the phone.'

'You did just have sex with Rachel and then run out on her.'

He winced, running a hand through his hair. 'Yeah . . .

177

But she'll understand. You needed me. If I didn't want to be here, I wouldn't be here, Shelly. Listen, how about this: I'll drive, go get us some ice cream, and we'll go back to your place. Watch some movies. One with Noah Centineo, or something. Huh? How about that?'

I could only nod and sniffle. Lee dug around in his pockets before starting the engine to hand me a crumpled (and, he swore, unused) tissue.

I stayed in the car when he got to the store, and when he came back, he thrust a plastic bag with two large tubs of Ben & Jerry's, marshmallows, some nail polish, and a couple of sheet masks and a large box of extra-soft Kleenex.

'What's all this for?'

He just smiled brightly at me. 'Shelly, over the years, you've made me watch enough chick flicks to know exactly what to do when someone goes through a bad breakup.'

'I think you're confusing a breakup with a slumber party.'

He just laughed.

The house was empty.

'Hello?' Lee called, as I poked my head around the lounge door and then into the kitchen.

'Nobody's home,' I said, stating the obvious.

'Huh. Where'd they go?'

I shrugged. 'I guess they're out somewhere.' It wasn't that late yet. Maybe they'd gone to see a movie, or they were at the mall, or Brad was over at a friend's and my dad had gone to pick him up. Lee brushed past me into the kitchen, and dug a bag of popcorn out of the back of a cupboard and set it in the microwave.

I stood there, clutching my bag of slumber-party/ breakup goodies, and watched Lee set out a tray with some empty bowls ready for ice cream with two spoons, make two mugs of coffee, pour two glasses of water, and then retrieve the popcorn and pour it into a huge bowl, hot and delicious and ready to be eaten.

He picked up the tray, the spoons rattling against the mugs as they were displaced. 'C'mon. Upstairs.'

I led the way, pushing open my bedroom door and holding it open for Lee. He set the tray on my desk, and took the bag from me. I stood there again, watching as he spooned out huge helpings of ice cream, set up Netflix with the first *Bridget Jones* movie and opened the marshmallows. He picked up my comforter from the bed, spreading it out on the floor, and then went out into the hallway, returning with piles of knitted afghans and fleece blankets from the linen closet, piling them at the foot of the comforter ready to be snuggled up in. He threw my pillows and many decorative cushions down there too, for us to lean against. Then, finally, he sat down, and patted the space next to him.

I had to have the best friend in the entire world. Who else would drop everything to do this for me?

Noah wouldn't. Noah didn't care. Noah had *her* to go back to.

I wondered if he'd cried over the end of our relationship. Some part of me that was still angry with him doubted it. Noah wasn't the kind of guy who cried much. He hit inanimate objects instead. Had he cared enough to do that? Or was he grateful, because now he was free to be with *her* and didn't have to explain to me that there was someone else he'd rather be with instead.

I looked back at Lee. He still wasn't pushing me with questions about what had happened and why his older brother and I had broken up. He wasn't acting like it was weird between us now, or even pretending it wasn't. He was here in his capacity as my best friend, and right now, he was smiling at me and putting his arm round me. It was all the comfort I needed.

'Come on. Let the breakup therapy begin.'

Chapter 14

At some point, when I was stuffed full of ice cream, marshmallows, coffee and popcorn, and I'd cried so much that my eyes were practically swollen shut they were so puffy, I snuggled into Lee's side like he was my favorite oversized teddy bear and I was six years old. We hadn't shared a bed since we were thirteen – after I'd gotten my first period, it seemed like suddenly it was only the kind of thing little kids did and we weren't little kids any more – but Lee didn't object when I fell asleep against him on the floor, under our mountain of blankets.

We'd heard my dad and brother arrive home, not long after Lee and I had gotten back, and I sent Lee out to talk to them. I'd heard his voice floating through my open door from downstairs as he talked to my dad.

'Elle's just having a rough day, so we're watching movies and pigging out on ice cream,' he said, not explaining any further to my dad – but then, it had taken me the entire first *Bridget Jones* movie to feel like I could tell Lee everything that had happened without breaking down; and when my dad and brother got back, we were only thirty minutes in.

'Sounds more like a slumber party.' Dad had laughed, but no more had been said, and Lee came back upstairs to me, shutting the door.

Now, though, I stirred from sleep when my bedroom door was pushed open, and my brother said, 'Hey, Elle, do you – OH MY GOD!'

The door was slammed shut so hard it made the photo frames on my desk rattle and, combined with the noise Brad made barreling downstairs, woke both of us up.

'Dad!' he was yelling. 'There's a boy in Elle's room! She's totally gotta be grounded!'

Lee groaned, untangled himself from me, and stretched, his neck cracking. 'Ugh, I ache everywhere. I knew I should've stolen some of the blankets and slept on your bed instead of on the floor.'

'Sorry.' I yawned, rubbing my eyes.

I heard footsteps up the stairs – my dad, from the sound of it – that came to an abrupt stop outside my door. A pause, then a tentative knock.

'You can come in,' I called, trying to work the stiffness out of my body. 'It's just Lee.'

The door opened, my dad not doing a great job of hiding his confusion. 'Oh. I thought you'd gone home last night, Lee.'

There was an edge to my dad's voice, and the way he looked between us was obviously suspicious – if only a little.

'I thought Brad meant you had Noah up here,' he added.

'Well, that would be something,' Lee said, keeping his tone cheerful and blasé. He hopped to his feet. 'Considering they broke up yesterday. Sorry, did I not mention that when I talked to you? I didn't mean to fall asleep in here, but Elle seemed like she needed a friend.'

'You guys broke up?'

I watched emotions play over my dad's face. Shock, first, then confusion, finally settling on pity.

'What happened?' he asked.

'I really don't wanna talk about it,' I groaned, burying my head in my hands for a moment.

'At least give me *some* details. I'm your dad. I need to know these things. Why did he break up with you? Was it the distance – was it too much for you, did he say? Did he meet someone else, or –'

'*I* broke up with *him*, Dad.' I was a little offended that he thought Noah must've broken up with me, but

I didn't feel like this was the time to point it out. 'It just . . . wasn't working.'

'Oh. Well.' My dad cleared his throat. 'You holding up okay, bud?'

I shrugged.

'Do you want pancakes for breakfast?'

I managed a small smile at that.

Lee stayed for breakfast, and as we sat waiting for the pancakes to cook, he turned his cell back on to check it. I vaguely remembered it ringing last night, and him looking at the screen before sighing and shutting it off.

Now, as it came to life, I saw him wince. Guilt coiled in my own stomach, remembering how hurt and angry Rachel had sounded when he'd left her last night. I'd started to talk to him about it, but he shut me down quickly, so I hadn't pushed it. I knew how torn he must've been between us. It was horrible but honestly, I was glad he'd picked me last night when I'd needed him.

'What's the damage?'

'Three – no, four – missed calls from her, and a couple of texts.'

'What's she said?'

He tapped at the screen. ' "Please call me back when you have five minutes. Hope Elle's okay" and . . .'

I watched his face fall. ' "I think we need to talk. Please call me tomorrow." '

Ouch.

'She didn't even put any kisses or anything. Or say goodnight. We always say goodnight.'

'I'm sorry.'

'It's not your fault.'

It was, because I didn't have to call him; I could've just as easily called Dixon or Cam or Levi. And we both knew that, but Lee smiled at me, not blaming me in the slightest. He understood, and I was so damn grateful.

'What're you gonna do?' I asked. 'Do you want me to talk to her for you?'

'No offense, Elle, but I really don't think that's gonna help right now. I guess I'll buy her some flowers, go over there, beg forgiveness. Isn't that what I'm supposed to do?'

'You can't get all your life advice from the chick flicks and rom-coms I make you watch.'

'They've served me well enough so far.'

I laughed, for the first time since before the breakup. I shivered thinking about it, before pulling the shutters down in my mind over yesterday afternoon. I didn't want to think about the breakup, or Noah, or how much more I'd miss him, or that phone call . . .

My hands clenched into fists.

Stop thinking about it! Stop thinking about him talking to her and hiding things from you. Stop thinking about that photo and how close they looked . . . Stop picturing them kissing.

I clenched my jaw, squeezing my eyes tight shut like that might block the mental image. It didn't go away though. Noah and Amanda. Amanda and Noah. Kissing.

Nothing else could explain that phone call – he was hiding something from me, something Amanda knew enough about that she'd called him *while he was with me* to see if he'd told me. There had to be something more going on – maybe they had kissed, maybe at that party . . . I didn't want to even think about the possibility that it was more concrete than just a hookup, and that there was something serious between them. It hurt too much.

I opened my eyes to see Lee looking at me.

'You okay?'

I shook my head.

'You wanna talk about it?'

Part of me did, but right now I couldn't bear to. I'd told Lee everything I could last night – including every word that I could remember of the phone call I'd overheard. And he hadn't said much of anything in response. I knew Lee well enough to know that he didn't want to say anything about it because he shared the same suspicions I did. Maybe he knew a little more about it than he was letting on, but didn't want to hurt me.

If I talked about it now, I had a feeling he'd tell me something I didn't want to hear.

Then my dad said, 'Alright! Pancakes are ready!' and I was saved.

Lee went home to change after breakfast, before going to see Rachel ('I probably shouldn't show up in last night's clothes, right?') and I was surprised when he called me only a few minutes after leaving my house.

'He's gone.'

'What do you mean?'

'I mean he's not here. There's a note on the kitchen counter – says he has stuff to do back at college so he got an earlier flight back. Shall I break the news to my parents?'

I bit my lip. Had Noah told them already himself? Had he gone back early because he didn't want to risk bumping in to me again, or was he going back to share the good news with *her* that now he was a free, single, available guy?

So I said, 'Yeah, sure. Someone has to, I guess.'

'Do you want me to tell the guys, as well?'

I thought about it; I found I wanted to talk to Levi

about it all. I didn't want him to hear from some group text from Lee, or through someone else. 'No, it's okay. I'll get round to it.'

'Have you told your dad everything?'

'No. He already didn't like Noah enough because he was dating me,' I said. As if my dad had needed any reason to dislike my boyfriend other than the fact that the guy was dating his only daughter – it didn't matter that he'd known Noah for almost eighteen years; as long as we were dating, he had his reservations about him. 'He doesn't need any more reason to. It'll just make Thanksgiving more awkward than it already will be. Let me know how things go with Rachel, yeah? Tell her I'm sorry.'

Since yesterday, I'd thought about the repercussions – how awkward everything would be now if I went to Lee's house and Noah was there, and so on . . . the biggest deal, though, was Thanksgiving. Lee had even been helpful enough to point out last night, 'Thanksgiving is gonna be so weird now this year.'

Every year we spent Thanksgiving with the Flynns. My parents didn't have many siblings, so I only had a small handful of cousins, all on the other side of the country, and we only saw each other at the summer family reunion one of my great-aunts held every couple of years. Lee was more like family than any of them were, so it only made sense to have Thanksgiving with the Flynns.

And now, what with the breakup, I was so not looking forward to sitting round the table with my ex after such an intense breakup.

I put it out of my mind, deciding to try and focus on my college application essay for the day instead. I needed to work on it, and I needed *some* way to channel all this energy without screaming – so once Lee hung up, I sat down at my computer and pulled up the Word document, rereading the three hundred and forty-eight words I'd managed to write earlier in the week. I needed to focus on something that wasn't my breakup, or Noah, or the state of Lee's relationship, which I was most definitely responsible for. This was as good as anything.

I did do one more thing before I started work, though – I opened up my browser, clicked on the Facebook tab, and changed my profile picture from one of me and Noah at the beach this summer to a picture of me and Lee from our birthday party. Then, I changed my relationship status to 'single'.

Chapter 15

If I'd thought people had talked about the photo a few weeks ago, it was *nothing* compared to all the talk now. Lee bumped his shoulder against mine, letting me know he was there, as I ducked my head and made my way over to where the guys were hanging out by Warren's car. Levi gave me an encouraging smile, and the guys looked at each other like they didn't know whether to ask me all about it, or leave me be and get the details off Lee later.

Levi already knew everything, of course.

After working on my college application essay for an hour yesterday, I'd had enough, and called him.

'Let me guess,' he said. 'You're babysitting and want some company?'

'I broke up with Noah.'

He was quiet for a while, then: 'How're you holding up?'

'You don't wanna know all the gory details?' I asked

instead, thinking of the various texts and Facebook messages I'd had from some of the girls at school, eager for the gossip, asking what had happened, they'd seen I'd changed my profile picture, what did it mean?

'You can tell me if you want,' Levi said, 'but you don't have to.'

It was an oddly comforting response.

'I'm . . . not okay. But I will be. I think.'

'You will be,' he said confidently. 'I was a mess for *weeks* after the breakup with Julie, and look at me now.'

'Oh, God,' I deadpanned. 'I'm doomed.'

Levi laughed and, rather than being offended, said cheerfully, 'See? You're already cracking jokes.'

'I think he's seeing someone else,' I'd told Levi, my voice little more than a whisper, like saying it louder would make it true. I explained about the phone call, how he was hiding something from me, how we'd argued about Amanda and how he'd defended her.

'Defended her?' he interrupted me to ask.

'I said she was a bitch and he said she wasn't. It was a big deal,' I snapped, firm, when I realized how petty that sounded now.

Glad when he didn't tell me how stupid that sounded, I carried on, until –

'Wait, so *you* broke up with *him*?'

'Why is everyone so shocked about that?' I sighed, testy. Seriously, was Noah really in a league that far above me that it was such a shocking notion that I'd been the one to instigate the breakup, and not the other way around? *If people keep saying that to me in school on Monday,* I thought, *I'm gonna scream.*

Talking it through with Levi helped – and was so emotionally draining, I decided to spin a slightly different story in school. One that, hopefully, would involve a lot less questioning and a lot less gossip.

'The whole long-distance thing just wasn't working out for us,' I said calmly to the guys in the parking lot before we went into homeroom on Monday morning, when Cam cautiously broached the subject and asked what had happened.

And word spread pretty quickly.

Even so, the rumors were flying around just like the photo incident.

'Did you hear? He caught her with *Levi*. Yeah, from English class. I know, right? She's such a slut. Totally deserves it for screwing him around. Or, you know, screwing someone else.'

'She found out that he's been boning that blonde chick from the photo – you remember the photo, right? – behind her back. He's such an asshole. How could he do that to her? I bet she's heartbroken.'

'I told you it wasn't gonna work out. These things never do, not that long distance. Hey, you think I should give her my number? Now she's single again?'

'Well, my cousin was on the football team with Noah last year, and *he* said they've been on the rocks since Noah went to college. I mean, he can do *so* much better than Elle Evans.'

I grit my teeth as the rumors carried on spreading around me.

It made me feel two inches tall and vulnerable. It felt like they were tearing my personal life apart at the seams just for kicks, and I hated it. I'd never been gossiped about so maliciously before.

The day felt endless. Especially when Lee kept a little distance from me, at my own insistence – Rachel was sympathetic about the breakup, but it was clear when she hugged me that she still held it against me that Lee had run out on her on Saturday. I felt shitty enough already without completely destroying their relationship too. I stuck with Levi as much as I could instead, although that only seemed to make the rumors worse.

It was exhausting.

Now, tucked up in bed, the glare of the cell-phone screen was giving me a headache. I rubbed my eyes again, and yawned. It was past midnight, and despite it all, I was still awake.

I'd picked up my cell over an hour ago to check my notifications and, like every night, to check my texts from Noah. We never went more than a couple of hours without talking, even if it was sporadic. We always texted each other goodnight – even if we were in different time zones.

We hadn't spoken in two days.

Now my eyes were filling with tears, and I pressed the heels of my hands into my eyes and willed myself not to break down again.

This was my decision. This was my choice, I reminded myself. I mean, I'd been the one getting hurt. I was the one who couldn't handle him hiding things from me. I was the one who decided we should break up. This was all for the best, ultimately. It had to be.

Somewhere around three a.m., I fell asleep.

'You look like shit,' Levi told me on the way out of homeroom a couple of days later. I'd spent the whole time reading the text for English Lit, trying to ignore him and Lee so they wouldn't ask me how I was doing after the breakup and tell me I looked like shit. (Rachel was still a little cool toward me, and Lisa had clearly picked her side – and it was not mine.)

I glared at him. 'Don't. Even. Go there.'

'Sorry. Um . . . You look . . .' He bit his lip, trying to

think of a different word. Something a little less harsh. And a little less true.

I knew I looked like shit. I had huge bags under my eyes from another night of not being able to sleep, I had some pretty horrendous zits (probably from all the stressing out and getting upset), my hair wasn't doing *anything* right today and, even though I'd put it in a ponytail, there were strands frizzing around my face, and I was pretty sure the scowl on my face was semi-permanent.

'Um . . .'

'You can stop trying to not offend me,' I told Levi. 'I *know* I look like shit. I just don't need you to remind me.'

His expression turned wounded. 'I'm sorry.'

I sighed. 'Whatever. Look, I'm not in the mood for anything today, okay?'

'Is this to do with Noah?'

'Sort of.'

'Only sort of? What's up?'

'Will you leave me alone already?' I snapped so loudly that a few heads turned our way. A couple of people started whispering. *Great, I bet that'll set the rumor mill going again . . .* God, why did everything have to be so stressful in high school?

Screw being the best time of our lives.

This was hell.

I tried to ignore it, but it was hard to block the judgy looks and whispered comments out completely. And it was really getting me down. Couldn't everyone just mind their own goddamn business already? Why did they have to keep talking about mine?

I couldn't even walk down the corridor with Levi without people looking at us like they were waiting for us to launch into a crazy make-out session right there in the hallway.

It was just making me so *mad*.

And, with everyone talking more and more about colleges and asking for second and third and fourth opinions on their application essays, I only seemed to be falling further and further behind. Lee had mentioned Brown a couple more times to me, and I knew I had to work that much harder if I wanted to get in there – but after the events of the weekend, I got the feeling Rachel would never forgive either of us if I suddenly rocked up at Brown with the pair of them. She'd probably react badly if she even knew I was applying – and I was still a long way off even being accepted.

It wasn't like I could talk to Lee about it. He was spending all his time with the football team, while Rachel was busy with drama club rehearsals, and they were still patching things up. If I asked him about college again, it'd just be another rift in their relationship – because of me.

I knew how much Rachel meant to Lee.

I didn't want to be a burden.

Right now, though, I felt like I could scream. Or cry. Maybe both.

'Elle? You okay?'

'I'm fine,' I snapped. 'God, Levi, why don't you find somebody else to follow around like a lost puppy for a change?'

I regretted it as soon as I said it.

I had a flashback to Jon Fletcher's party a couple of weeks back, when Lee had said more or less the same thing to me, and how upset it had made me.

I didn't mean it. I just needed to vent somehow, and Levi was just . . . just *there*.

We'd both stopped walking, and I stared at the hurt look on his face for a fraction of a second, then I turned on my heel and stormed away before I could feel any worse about myself than I did right then.

I was starting to understand why Noah felt like punching walls and doors and lockers sometimes.

In our next class, I pretended not to even notice when Levi took a seat at the other end of the classroom instead of his usual one next to me. And when the bell rang, he left class first, and didn't wait for me.

First Noah, then Lee, and now Levi.

Was I going to push every guy in my life that I cared about away from me?

When lunch finally rolled round, I went to buy a sandwich, and looked over at our lunch table.

There was Lee, sat with his arm round Rachel. She was laughing at something Dixon had said, and Lee was talking over her head to Cam and Levi, and two of Rachel's friends sat at the table, too. Warren and Oliver took a seat then, and they all stopped their conversations to say hi to them. Lisa sat down with her bagged lunch as I watched.

I stood watching them for a moment, wondering if they were waiting for me. Maybe they hadn't even noticed I wasn't there with them.

I stepped up to pay for my sandwich, and then stood looking around the rest of the cafeteria. There were so many people I would normally be happy to sit with and talk to, but none I felt like I could confide in, the way I would with Lee, or Cam, or Dixon – or Levi.

A few people looked my way, and turned to talk to their friends.

They probably weren't talking about me, but – but what if they were? They'd been talking about me all week, so why stop now? Why *wouldn't* they talk about me when I was just standing there clutching my tuna sandwich and looking like a lost, lonely freshman on my first day.

I looked back at my friends at our lunch table, willing one of them to look over and see me, wave and gesture for me to hurry up already, to come sit with them.

No one did.

Rationally, I knew they just hadn't noticed me yet. The same way I knew people probably weren't talking about me, because the reality was that I was throwing myself a huge pity party. But it's hard to be rational when it feels like you're drowning.

I took a few shallow breaths, tossed my sandwich in the nearest trash can, and walked back out of the cafeteria.

Lee smiled easily at me as I dragged my feet over to where he'd parked his car that morning. 'Hey.'

'Hi.' I got in the car and shut the door, waiting for him to get in, too.

He did, after what felt like five minutes waiting for him, and he frowned across at me. 'What's up with you today? You didn't show up to lunch, didn't talk to me in class, Levi said you yelled at him –'

'Lee, can we just go home? Please?'

There must've been something in my tone or my face that made him decide to give up trying, because he shook his head at me, sighing through his nose, totally exasperated, and threw the car into drive before pulling out of the parking lot.

The drive home was silent.

I wasn't in the mood to talk. I wasn't in the mood for anything.

I was overtired – I kept lying awake at night and playing back my last conversation with Noah, and all the times I thought he'd been hiding something from me, how I should've known something was going on. It made it impossible to focus – which only made me more stressed about the schoolwork I knew I needed to be focusing on. I was upset and wanted a hug, but I was so mad about everything and at everyone that I didn't want to even give them the chance to ask me what was wrong.

Lee knew something was up. He was my best friend, after all.

He stopped the car a few blocks away from both our houses. 'Right. What the hell is going on with you? I know the breakup was tough on you, but let's face it – you were the one who broke up with him, and I thought we agreed that it was for the best if he's keeping secrets from you and might have something going on with that Amanda chick. And I know you loved him, but you can't take it out on us.'

'It's not about Noah, okay? Jesus.'

'Then why are you acting like this?'

I huffed, sucking my cheeks in. 'I'm – I'm just all over the place, and I'm stressed out.'

'Then you should talk to me! You should tell me these things! I know you said I needed to spend some quality time with Rachel this week, but –'

'Lee . . .'

'If you don't tell me what's wrong, I can't help. I want to help.'

'And I don't want to cause more problems for you and Rachel. You don't need to look after me twenty-four seven. I'm just not having a great week, okay? Everyone gossiping, and talking about college, and . . . It's just getting to me. It's all just getting a little too much to handle.'

'So tell me what I can do.'

'I don't know! I – I just . . .'

'You what? You want to be alone for a while? Do you want me to ask Rachel if she'll tutor you, if you're struggling with your grades?' His voice was gentler now, and his mouth was twisted to one side with sympathy.

I reached up and grabbed at the roots of my hair. I didn't *know* what I wanted or what I needed. That was the problem.

'Things are just weird for me right now. I need you

to understand that. I need you to be normal and I need everyone to stop asking me how I'm feeling, because the truth is, I'm not doing so hot, and . . .' I trailed off, running out of steam. A lump rose in my throat and I hated myself for getting so emotional and so worked up this easily. I just wanted things to be okay, like they had been a few weeks ago. I heard Lee sigh. He tapped on the dashboard agitatedly.

Then Lee said, 'Wanna come round and play video games and order Chinese? We can invite the guys, too. I was meant to catch up with some of the football guys but I can bail. We'll take a night off. We'll both stop thinking about homework and essays and college and grades and studying for a night. Yeah? How about that?'

It sounded perfect. I felt a rush of gratitude toward my best friend. How was he so good at knowing what I needed before I did?

'What about Rachel?'

He shrugged. 'She said she was going to see a movie with some of the girls tonight anyway. It's a win-win.'

I tried not to be hurt that I hadn't received an invite. The girls had been including me more and more in things over the last couple of months, but that had changed now. I'd probably hate me if I were Rachel, so I couldn't really blame her for still being off with me.

'And you *promise* you're going to be normal, and get off my back asking me if I'm okay all the time?'

He held up his hand. 'Scout's honor.'

It made a nice change having a night with the guys. We hadn't done this in a while. Most of the time over the summer, when we'd hung out, there were boyfriends and girlfriends around, too. It had been good, but it was nice to feel like things were back to how they were last year, just for a night.

We separated our food out in the kitchen, and everyone took their plates away into the lounge, until just me and Levi were picking out our orders from the plastic bags.

'Hey,' he said quietly.

I was glad he'd talked first. It was a weight off my chest I hadn't realized was really there; it was a little easier to breathe.

In response, I said, 'I'm sorry about earlier. I didn't mean to yell at you like that.'

'It's okay. You've got a lot going on.'

He smiled at me, his face open and sincere, and I beamed back.

Over dinner, Cam brought up the subject of the Sadie Hawkins dance, which felt like he'd just dumped a bucket of ice water over me. I'd been so focused on asking Noah – and him rejecting me – that the concept of actually *going* to the dance suddenly hit me.

I'd have to ask someone *else* to the dance. Or, actually, I could just go alone. I could do that.

I could also not go at all, but I'd been excited about the dance. I wasn't about to let Noah ruin a night with my friends just because he'd rejected me and we'd broken up. My resolve hardened: I'd *go* to that dance, and I'd make sure there were plenty of pictures on my Instagram from the night showing *just how much* fun I'd had.

Cam was busy complaining about how Lisa wanted him to get a tie to match her dress, but how she'd insisted it had to be *perfect*, an exact match. The theme was red and pink. It was supposed to be cute and flirty and full of romance. Not that the night was going to be very romantic for me any more, but I was happy we'd gone with that as a theme. Simple, and more importantly for the school council budget: cheap.

'Speaking of Sadie Hawkins,' Lee said, 'who's everyone actually going with?'

'Cassidy Thomas,' Warren said. 'She's in my Geography class. She left a note in my locker asking me to go. There were puns involved. I couldn't say no.'

'She's kind of cute,' Dixon said. 'Big nose. Bad taste in guys, too, obviously.'

Warren laughed.

Olly piped up next, saying, 'Kaitlin asked me. I think it's just because she lives a block away from me so it's easy to get home, but she's nice.'

'Oh, yeah, she did tell me she'd asked you,' I said, recalling the school council meeting we'd had where a couple of the girls had been discussing their dates and the guys they wanted to ask.

'What about you?' Cam asked Dixon. 'Someone's asked you, right?'

Dixon, to my surprise, started blushing. 'Um, actually, I – I asked someone.'

'But it's Sadie Hawkins,' I said. 'The girls ask the guys.'

'That's – that's kind of the thing,' he stammered, looking down at his plate of sweet-and-sour chicken and noodles. His cheeks went even redder. 'I asked Danny, a couple of weeks ago.'

'Danny who? Dani Schrader?'

'No, Danny Brown. From the basketball team.'

Several seconds passed in silence as we all let that sink in.

I could see the guys exchanging looks that said, *Dixon's going to the dance with a guy? What? Wait, how did none of us know about this? Did he think he couldn't talk to us?*

I hoped my face didn't look like that too, since Dixon glanced up at me then.

And I smiled, and said, 'The most important question here, Dixon, is what color ties are you two gonna be wearing? Please tell me you're gonna match.'

He smiled back at me, obviously relieved, and said, 'Red, I think.'

Then Cam pitched in, in a voice that sounded totally disbelieving, 'Sorry, but *Danny Brown*?'

Dixon's lips twitched. 'Look, I'm sorry I didn't tell you, or any of you guys, but – I mean, just ... it's ... okay, and –'

'No, no,' Cam said, 'I don't give a shit if you're bi or gay or whatever label you prefer, but my point *is* Dixon, that Danny Brown is *not* a fine piece of ass. You can do a lot better than that. You should've asked Joe Drake. He's into guys *and* he hasn't got a date yet.' Cam shook his head, mock-woeful, and Dixon snorted.

'It's too late now,' Cam said, still shaking his head and pressing his lips into a disapproving line.

'He's a nice guy,' Dixon argued, but he was smiling. 'He's funny.'

'Hey,' Warren said, leaning over to shove Cam's shoulder. 'I don't know why you're laughing. God knows what Lisa sees in you – again, not a fine piece of ass, *and* you're not even funny. What've you got going for you?'

'I can do that trick where you tip a glass of water

upside down without spilling it. The ladies love it, what can I say.'

'It's true,' I joked, looking at Warren with a deadpan expression. I put a hand to my chest. 'I think my heart just skipped a beat thinking about it.'

'How about you, Elle?' Dixon said then, still looking obviously relieved that none of us had made a big deal about him asking a guy to the dance. 'Don't try and change the subject. The dance is, like, a week away.'

'Um . . .'

Levi caught my eye and said pointedly, 'You know, I need a new suit jacket. You guys got any recommendations for where to go?'

Ignoring him, Olly said, 'Yeah, c'mon, Elle. You're single, now. You could, like, have your pick of guys. We can come up with someone for you to ask now you definitely won't be going with No– Ow!' He broke off to scowl at Lee, who'd just elbowed him.

I was grateful for Lee and Levi trying to intervene and spare my feelings, but said, 'I figured I'd just go with you guys. Go *stag*. Or, like, doe, I guess. Is that a thing? Going doe? I'm definitely making that a thing.'

A few of them laughed, then Olly piped up again with, 'Hey, Levi, you don't have a date either, though, do you?'

He shook his head. 'Uh, no, actually.'

I pulled a face at Levi, my eyes bugging. 'Wait, what? I've seen at *least* five girls ask you to the dance.'

He shrugged. 'I figured it was easier to turn them down than try to explain I wasn't really looking for *a date*, you know? I'm cool just going with you guys.'

Lee caught my eye, his mouth pulling and eyebrows raising slightly as he glanced at Levi, as if to say, *Well?*

And honestly, I didn't hate the idea.

I stood up and walked over to where Levi was sitting between Cam and Warren on the couch, picking my way carefully through the plates and glasses and cutlery.

I bent down on one knee in front of Levi, ignoring Lee snickering, and picked up one of his hands in both of mine, putting on my most serious expression. 'Levi Monroe, will you do me the honor of being my date to the dance?'

'Oh, my,' he drawled in a high-pitched, Southern accent. 'Golly gee, ma'am, I'd just love to.'

I raised my eyebrows. 'Don't humiliate me here. I'm trying to be cute.'

'So am I.'

I rolled my eyes, and Levi laughed. 'Sure, Elle, I'll go to the dance with you.'

I fake-swooned backward – and lost my balance, falling into some egg-fried rice.

Chapter 16

I'd spoken to Rachel a little over the last several days, and even though her frosty attitude was thawing, I still felt unusually awkward calling her. But Lee hadn't answered his phone in hours, and that was really unlike him. I'd asked him if he wanted to come to the mall with me tomorrow, and then, more recently, wanted to know if there were plans for getting to Sadie Hawkins. The lack of answer was concerning.

It was only once I was dialing Rachel's number that I realized maybe they were both . . . otherwise occupied. I was about to hang up when she answered.

'Hello?'

'Hey, Rach, is Lee there? Promise it's just a quick question.'

'No, he's . . . He's not with you?'

I frowned. 'Why would he be with me?'

'He told me you guys were hanging out tonight.'

My face scrunched up, an uneasy feeling settling over me. 'Um . . . no. He told me it was date night.'

'He's definitely not with me. Is everything okay? What's up, anyway?'

I rubbed a hand over the back of my neck. 'Oh, it's no big deal. I just thought it was weird he wasn't replying to me. He's *really* not with you?'

'I'm sure it's just a misunderstanding,' Rachel said, her words slow and measured. I could tell she didn't believe it even as she said it. 'Maybe he got a flat tire somewhere?'

'I doubt it, the rat bastard,' I muttered. I put Rachel on speakerphone, and loaded Snapchat, then Instagram. 'Dammit, there's nothing on his story . . . You don't have that Find My Friends thing on his phone, do you?'

'Uh, no. Maybe his mom does?'

'No, the most she can do on her phone is forward me articles via Facebook about which food is gonna give me cancer this week. Last week, it was popcorn.'

'What was it this week?'

'Tofu. The prediction for next week is kale. Anyway, we're getting off topic. You don't have any idea where he'd be? He didn't say anything to you?' Her speculation that he might have a flat tire sent my mind racing. What if he'd got in an accident? What if something awful had happened?

But then – why had he lied to me and Rachel? Where the hell was he?

'No, he just said he was hanging out with you tonight. He said he was having dinner with you and your dad and your brother, and then you were gonna play some video games and chill.'

I stared at my phone for a second. That was a *whole* lie. Not even just a little one. He'd told me it was date night and he was taking Rachel out for dinner.

What was so important that he'd lied to both of us?

'Wait, I've got him,' Rachel said. 'Look at Olivia's Instagram story.'

The first picture was of five kegs of beer, and the caption #*getrekt*. The next one was a selfie of Olivia with two of the guys from the football team. Then there were some videos, of what looked like a party, only, as far as I could tell, it was just the football team and some of the popular girls, mostly cheerleaders.

'He lied to us to go to a party,' Rachel said. Her voice was small.

'He's dead. I'll come pick you up and we're so busting his ass. Give me two minutes to put on some shoes and get in my car.'

Rachel was trying really hard not to cry. She kept sniffling, then wiping the corners of her eyes, then saying,

'I just don't get why he lied? Why didn't he just say he was hanging out with the guys from the team?'

Every trace of animosity she'd held toward me had vanished. This wasn't about Lee trying to juggle his friendship with me and his relationship with her. Tonight, we were a united front.

The house wasn't lit up like a beacon of high school chaos and freedom, like it was for any of the other parties Jon had hosted, but as we walked up the drive we could hear laughter and music through an open window.

Rachel hesitated while I tried the door handle. It was open.

'I don't know, Elle, maybe we should just . . . talk to him tomorrow . . .'

She looked so upset, so betrayed. I knew that feeling all too well, but I was too furious with Lee to even *consider* letting him off the hook easy tonight. Conflict wasn't usually my bag, but this was an exception. Rachel wringing her hands and biting her lip in an attempt not to start sobbing only spurred me on.

'You stay here if you want, but I'm going in.'

I stepped inside and heard Rachel run up after me. She touched my shoulder. I think it was more for her comfort than mine.

We followed the noise to the massive lounge. There

was a video game playing on TV – it looked like *Fortnite*. There was music playing from somewhere too, but nowhere near as loudly as for a usual party. The football team were scattered across the couches, chairs, sitting on the floor or standing around the room. Bottles of beer and cups were scattered on every surface. There were maybe five or six girls around – I recognized them from the cheerleading squad.

Lee was sprawled in the corner of one couch, a cup balanced loosely in his hand on the arm of the couch, with Peggy Bartlett sitting on his knee, pushing his hair back off his face, and giggling.

Rachel made a noise behind me, and I turned just in time to see her run out.

I debated running after her, but I'd deal with Lee first.

I stepped into the room, and people looked up.

'Hey, Flynn, you didn't say you were gonna invite one of your girlfriends!'

'She's not my girlfriend,' he slurred, but grinned at me. 'Sup, Shell?'

'Nah, he's totally boning her on the side,' someone muttered, but by the time I looked up to glare, I couldn't tell who'd said it.

'*This* is date night? This is why you can't answer your phone?'

'Hey, lay off him, alright?' Benny Hope, a guy who'd had to retake sophomore year, called over. 'Go back home to your Build-A-Bear collection.'

'Dude, come on,' Lee said, laughing. 'Mr Wiggles is a cherished member of the family.'

Everyone laughed. My cheeks burned. I balled my hands into fists, trying not to run out of there like Rachel had.

'Lee, we're leaving.'

'But I'm having fun.' His glassy eyes rolled toward me, his mouth an open, slack smile. 'It's fun, Elle. You should stay.'

'Your girlfriend just ran out of here crying. You don't think maybe you should go and talk to her? You don't think maybe you owe both of us an apology?'

'C'mon, I'm not the one who crashed your party and ruined your night.'

Peggy Bartlett laughed, pushing his hair back again. 'Yeah, *Elle*. Maybe you should just leave, before you ruin everybody's night. Nobody invited you, last time I checked. Nobody asked for a stripper.'

More laughter. Lee's was loudest.

There was a hand on my shoulder. I almost expected it to be Rachel, but the hand was too heavy. I looked up to find Jon smiling at me. There was no sympathy in it, but no mockery either. I couldn't help but feel relieved at the intervention, and the fact that at least someone was happy to see me.

'Hey, Evans! What're you doing here? Flynn invite you?'

'She's totally dragging us down, J,' one of the other girls whined. She was a junior and I didn't know her that well. Sara? Sarah? Something like that. She pouted and it looked like one of those overexaggerated Snapchat filters. It wasn't a good look on her. 'Tell her to leave already.'

'You want a beer, Elle?' he asked me instead. 'Stick around, huh? I'll get you a beer.'

'Elle's a bad drunk,' Lee pitched in. 'She should go home.'

'I'm not staying,' I told Jon. 'I'm taking Lee home.'

He eyed Lee. I could smell the beer on Jon's breath, but he didn't look wasted like the rest of the guys. 'He's been drinking for hours. You bring your car? I'll help you get him outside.'

A few people protested, moaning that Jon was ruining the party now too, saying he should leave Flynn where he was, Flynn was fine, they were all having a great time till I showed up and ruined it.

To me, Jon said, 'He's kind of an angry drunk.'

'He didn't used to be. Actually, he didn't used to get any kind of drunk, so much.'

'You drank enough for the two of you, right?' He winked, but moved into the room, and tapped Peggy's waist to make her move. She threw a nasty look at me over her shoulder, nose scrunched up like I'd brought a bad smell in. I was sure she could make my life miserable come school on Monday if she wanted, but right now, I couldn't bring myself to care if I pissed her off. Jon hooked an arm round Lee and dragged him to his feet.

'Get off, Fletcher, I'm fine, I can walk,' Lee protested, but his legs didn't do a lot except stumble along as Jon took him outside. Jon practically carried him down the driveway.

'Where're you parked?'

'There wasn't any space so I'm a block down. It's fine. Thanks. I think he needs to sober up a little. I don't want him puking all over my car, you know?'

'Sure. Hey, you need anything, give me a shout, yeah?'

Much as I appreciated the help, and that Jon hadn't been shitty with me like everyone else had, something still niggled at me. Jon was captain of the football team this year, and . . .

'Did you make him do this?' I called after Jon as he started back toward the house.

He turned, head cocked to the side. 'What, get drunk? I mean, we played a few drinking games, but –'

'Lie to us. I know you guys said he couldn't tell us where he was when you did that initiation thing, so . . .'

I was hoping Lee had a really stupid reason for lying to me and Rachel about tonight – like the fact it was some football team secret party. Any reason.

Jon laughed. 'That's crazy. It was just a low-key thing tonight. Not even a party. I told the guys not to shout about it on Snapchat or anything, because I didn't want things to get too crazy, but I didn't tell him to lie to you about it.'

'Okay. Thanks.'

Lee sat on the edge of the sidewalk where Jon had dropped him, legs stretched out in front of him, hunched forward with his elbows on his thighs. He groaned, mumbling unintelligibly.

I looked at him, hands on my hips, before looking round for Rachel. I spotted her standing by the car, and waved her over. She didn't move, so I kept waving, in case she hadn't seen me.

Then my phone buzzed.

I can't see him right now. You talk to him first.

I sat down on the sidewalk next to Lee. 'You did a really shitty thing tonight, you know that?'

'So did you. I was just *having fun*. Why'd you have to stop me having fun?'

I laughed, the sound dry and bitter. 'Remember how

217

shitty I felt when I saw that picture of Amanda and Noah? That's exactly what you just did to Rachel.'

'Did not.'

'Uh, yes you did. You and Peggy looked pretty cozy. Throw in the fact you lied to Rachel about where you were tonight, and you don't come out of this looking good. And I don't just mean because you look like you might puke.'

'What, and you come out of this looking good for stalking me and tracking me down? Ten points to Sherlock and Holmes.'

'Watson.'

'God,' he snapped.

'Don't be like that,' I snapped back. 'You lied to both of us. You told me you were with Rachel, told Rachel you were with me, just so you could, what, come to a party where you could flirt with Peggy from the cheer-leading squad?'

'Oh, like you're so perfect!'

Lee sat up, putting one hand behind him to lean back on. He looked pasty in the light of the streetlamps, his eyes unfocused and bloodshot, but his mouth was pressed into a tight line.

'What the hell's that supposed to mean?'

'You're making Rachel into such a third wheel. Or you're the third wheel. I don't know, okay, but there's a third wheel somewhere. And now that's my problem to deal with? You're just feeling sorry for yourself for dumping Noah. The guy you lied to me for months about to be with. You lied to me, because you were too busy making out with my brother, and you think that wasn't a crappy thing to do?'

I scoffed, standing up. 'Okay, this is so not the same thing.'

Lee struggled to his feet, too, swaying. 'So you get to be let off the hook, and I don't?'

'I never – Jeez, Lee, this has nothing to do with Noah! This has nothing to do with me feeling lonely! Forget about me! Rachel is so upset she can't even talk to you right now. You don't think you owe her an apology?'

He looked away.

'I get you hate being Noah's little brother, and that he was this big star on the football team, and he left you this big reputation to live up to, but nobody ever said you had to be such a jerk and push away everyone who cares about you. When was the last time you went to see a movie with Warren, and Cam and Dixon, and Olly? When was the last time we went to the mall for a milkshake? I know we all hung out last night, but that was for the first time in months. Literally, in *months*. I'm not trying to ruin your Friday night and tell you to stop hanging out with the jocks, but Jesus, Lee, get some self-respect.'

I turned on my heel, marching off. I thought I heard him say something, but when I looked back, he was just puking his guts up instead.

I hesitated.

I couldn't just *leave* him there like this.

I jogged down the road to Rachel. There were tear-tracks down her face, and she made quiet sobbing sounds. She sniffled, swallowing hard, when I reached her.

'He's in bad shape,' I told her.

'Did he apologize?'

I bit my lip. 'Not . . . exactly . . . Look, Rach, why don't you take my car and go home? I'll sort him out. He's puking. I can't leave him. I'll come get my car from you tomorrow. Hey, I'll come get my car, and we'll go to the mall together, huh? Some girl time. No boy talk, or any of that crap. We'll just hang out.'

'That sounds . . . That sounds good, Elle. Thanks. But are you sure –'

'I'll get a ride home, don't worry. I'll fix this. And I promise that by the time he's sober, he's going to be groveling to you for your forgiveness for weeks.'

Rachel smiled, but it was strained. She took the car keys from me, twiddling them in her fingers and rattling my keychains. 'Elle, do you . . . D'you think I . . . Did I do something wrong?'

'What?'

'Peggy's a cheerleader.'

'He's not interested in Peggy. I don't think he even knew she was sitting on his knee. He's literally so trashed right now, Rach, he can't even stand up. I can promise he's not cheating on you. But he is being a total jerk for some reason, and you have every right to be mad at him.'

'Let me know he's okay? Let me know you're okay, too? Are you sure you can get a ride home? I just . . . I can't see him right now, Elle, I can't.'

'Go home. I'll text you later, okay? Promise. And I'll see you tomorrow.'

Rachel nodded, and once she'd got into my car and had started adjusting the mirrors, I went back to Lee. He was slumped, sat back on the sidewalk with his head in his hands, groaning, and a pool of vomit in front of him.

I took my cell phone back out and called my dad.

I'd told him I was going to see Lee and Rachel, which hadn't been a lie. It took a couple of rings before he answered. 'Elle? Everything okay?'

'No. Dad, I need . . . I need some help.'

'What's wrong? Did you get in a crash? Elle? What –'

'No, I'm fine,' I said quickly, 'but Lee's so drunk he's throwing up, and I can't leave him here.'

'Where are you?'

'Jon Fletcher's house. You know, from the football team. Lee was here for some football party thing. Rachel doesn't want to see him. I gave her my car and she's gone home. I can't leave him here like this, Dad.'

'Text me the address. Give me five minutes. I'll have to get Brad in the car, too.'

'Thanks, Dad.' I hung up, texted him Jon's address and nudged Lee with my toes. 'You owe me big time.'

He just groaned in response.

While we waited, Jon came back out with a bottle of water. 'Thought I saw you still out here. You want a hand getting him in your car?'

'No, thanks, my dad's on his way. Rachel took my car. She couldn't face him.'

'Nothing happened with him and Peggy,' Jon said quickly, earnestly. 'She's a total flirt, but Lee kept saying how he had a girlfriend.'

'Thanks.'

'Let me know if there's anything I can do.'

'Thanks, Jon. I appreciate it. I'm sorry I ruined your night.'

'Nah, you didn't ruin anything.' He grinned at me, then clapped me on the shoulder again. 'I'll see ya.'

I waved as he went back into the house, uncapped the water bottle, and bent down to put it to Lee's mouth. He took it from me with shaky, fumbling hands, and sipped at it until my dad arrived.

'Please don't tell my mom,' was all Lee could say, as my dad hauled him up into the back seat of the car. 'Please don't tell my mom.'

'Buddy, I think you've got bigger things to worry about.' My dad sighed. I climbed into the car after Lee, and my dad said, 'There's a bucket on the floor there. Make sure he pukes into the bucket.'

'I'm not gonna puke,' Lee managed. He groaned once we started driving, though, and took the bucket off me, with one more, 'Please don't tell my mom.'

Chapter 17

Lee stayed the night, sleeping on the couch with the bucket near his head. I stayed awake as long as I could, watching him, but eventually I fell asleep too. We both woke up when my dad came downstairs to make coffee, around eight.

'Shit,' Lee muttered, smacking his lips. 'Shit.'

'I think that's an understatement, but yeah.'

'Shit.'

He dragged himself up, and I gave him the silent treatment while he drank some water, then coffee, then ate six slices of toast. I got dressed while he took a shower, and tossed him one of his sweatshirts from my closet when he came back into my room in his jeans, hair wet. At least he looked more human now. Less ashy and hungover zombie. His voice was rough and his eyes were bloodshot. He dragged his feet as he crossed the room toward me and leaned against me. I pushed him away.

'Elle? Shelly, c'mon. Please. I'm really sorry. I'm sorry I was such a mess and you had to take care of me. I'm sorry I was such a jerk.'

'You know, Lee, that's not even why I'm mad. I'm mad because you really hurt Rachel. She wouldn't have cared that you were at that party. She's hurt because you lied about it. You know how I felt when I heard Noah on the phone to Amanda? That's exactly the kind of hurt Rachel's feeling.'

'I know. I know. God, I know.'

'Don't you have anything else to say? We did this before, remember? You were an asshole at a party, apologized the next day, and we moved on. But I'm not doing this with you again, Lee. I can't do this every time there's a party. You need to get your shit together. I need to get my shit together too, I know, but . . . I'm being an annoying, sad potato. You're –'

'Please don't say wrecking ball. Because you know I'll have to start singing.'

I jutted one hip out, crossing my arms, and Lee's smile disappeared.

'Sorry.'

'Seriously. Next time, I'm not gonna help you out like this. You need to make it up to Rachel.'

'I know. Shelly, honestly, I owe you for, like, the rest of my life. I'll head straight over to Rachel's, and –'

'No, you're not. You're going home to sit there feeling guilty. Me and Rachel are going to the mall. Third wheel, my ass.'

'He's really sorry?'

'Yes, but c'mon. No boy talk. Remember? I'm so sick of feeling sorry for myself and stewing over the whole breakup and, trust me, you don't want me to get started on that.'

I understood now why Levi had deleted all the pictures of him and his ex from his social media. It was tough, seeing them. Remembering how good things had been. How much I'd loved Noah. How much I'd thought he'd loved me.

The less I thought about it, the more I could at least pretend I was moving on.

Rachel squared her shoulders. 'No, you're – you're right. No boys, no pity parties. Can we talk about college? Or is that on your banned list, too?'

'Funny.'

'My mom's been on at me to apply to Yale, but I don't know. I had a cousin who went there and I visited her last year for a weekend, and . . . I just didn't feel it, you know? You know when you know you don't like something?'

'So don't apply.'

'Yeah, but . . . I don't know. There's just something about Yale. The name, I mean. It's so prestigious . . .'

Noah had said something like that to me when he got his acceptance letter to Harvard.

I shook the thought away. I *had* to stop thinking about him.

'A prestigious college won't mean anything if you're miserable for the next four years of your life.'

'Okay, miserable is taking it a little far.' Rachel smiled. 'But yeah, I guess you're right. Have you thought about which colleges you're applying to yet?'

We kept talking about colleges, even talking about Brown, and Rachel assured me she didn't mind me applying. We talked about school, about movies and people and literally anything except our love lives. It was weirdly refreshing.

And it was so good to feel like the air had finally cleared between me and Rachel.

Lee and Rachel, of course, made up. She'd let him sweat over it for a couple of days, but he knew how in the wrong he was, and she forgave him eventually. He hadn't hesitated to tell me how great the make-up sex had been, which I'd teased him about, but it only made me think about Noah.

As the Sadie Hawkins dance crept closer, the

excitement at school built. And the air was filled with the promise of romance. It left a bitter taste in my mouth. I lost count of the number of times I got out my cell phone to text Noah – just wanting to see how he was, tempted to apologize for how things had ended between us, to say maybe we could talk again when he was home for Thanksgiving to make sure things weren't too weird between us.

I checked his Instagram a few times.

He didn't post that much.

Amanda, though, posted a lot, on her feed and her story (which I always watched from Levi's phone, so she wouldn't know I'd been snooping on her account). She seemed to be hanging out with Noah a lot.

I was the one who ended things. I had no right to be jealous. I should be happy for him. I should want him to move on and be happy.

But now, as I was getting ready for the dance, it was impossible not to miss him and regret ending things. I kept thinking about the last school dance, and how we'd gone together, and how I'd daydreamed about him coming home for this dance to do it all again.

I fixed my earrings and pursed my lips. I had to stop thinking about Noah. He hadn't even *wanted* to come to the dance with me anyway. It was better this way.

And I was free to date anyone I wanted.

My thoughts moved to my date for tonight. Everyone assumed something had happened between me and Levi, at some point.

And I couldn't help but let my mind wander. Would I really hate it if something did happen between us? I liked Levi. A lot. He was so easy to be around, and so different from being with Noah. He knew exactly how to make me smile and laugh, and we never argued. It didn't hurt that he was cute, either.

Would it be weird to slow dance with him tonight? If we did, would I want to kiss him?

I'd never kissed anyone except Noah.

And part of me couldn't help but wonder what it might be like to kiss Levi.

My cheeks flushed and I caught sight of my blushing face in the mirror.

Okay, let's maybe not think about that.

Get it together, Elle.

I probably shouldn't be thinking about dating anybody right now. I was definitely in no rush to get my heart broken again.

'Tonight is all about me,' I told my reflection, trying to inject confidence into my voice.

I ran my fingers through my hair, shaking it out to give it some more volume. I smiled, satisfied with my appearance. I hadn't bothered with much jewelry – just the pretty watch my dad gave me for my seventeenth birthday that used to be my mom's, and some small diamond studs.

I rocked back and forth on my feet, wiggling my toes to test my shoes. They were black kitten heels that I hadn't worn in a while, and I couldn't remember if they gave me blisters.

I hoped they wouldn't. I wanted to spend most of my night dancing.

There was a knock on my half-open bedroom door, and my dad stepped in. 'All ready?'

I spun, showing off my deep-red jersey dress with its flared skirt. 'Yep.'

'You look really pretty, Elle.'

'Thanks.'

'Noah doesn't know what he's missing.'

I rolled my eyes, wanting to shrug it off and not let it upset me, but I appreciated the sentiment. 'I broke up with him, remember?'

'I know. But I know you still miss him a lot. Every time your cell phone buzzes, you jump for it, like you're expecting it to be him begging you to take him back.'

I busied myself double-checking the contents of my clutch. Lip gloss, check. Ticket for the dance, check. Cash, check. House key, check . . .

Zero contact from Noah, check.

'Bud, you know you can talk to me, right?'

'There's nothing to talk about, okay? I couldn't deal with the distance and stuff. It got too much. It's better this way.'

'And you're sure there's nothing else going on?'

I looked over at my dad, who was raising his eyebrows at me skeptically behind his glasses. Was this about college? Or had Lee told him about the whole thing with Amanda? Was that what that look was for? So, carefully, I replied, 'Like what?'

'Oh, just . . . You and Levi. You guys seem really close.' He raised his eyebrows even higher, and his lips pressed into a line like he was trying not to smile. 'Hanging out all the time, texting a lot, now you're going to this dance together . . .'

Oh.

OH.

I snorted, as though I hadn't just been thinking about kissing Levi a few minutes before. 'Dad, that's really not what's going on. Levi and I, we're just friends.'

'Sure about that?'

'Yes.'

'Okay. If you say so.'

I rolled my eyes deliberately at him. The sound of a car engine outside drew both our attention, followed by a car door slamming. 'That's him.'

'Are you going to be completely embarrassed if I insist on taking some photos of you two going to the dance together?'

'Yes.'

'Then I'm doing my job as your dad exactly right.'

Once my dad had taken, like, two dozen photos of us, and Brad had told Levi all about soccer practice this week, we finally left.

And I had to admit, Levi did look hot in his suit. It was a plain black suit, with a pink shirt and black tie. Plus, he smelled *really* good. His curly brown hair was tidier than usual, held down with some gel that caught the light.

Something else caught the light, too.

I reached over and ran a finger over his cheekbone when we paused at a stop sign. 'Is that glitter?'

Levi did something between a laugh and a sigh. 'Becca wanted to help me get ready.'

'Right . . .'

'And she persuaded my mom to buy her this glittery moisturizer stuff last week.'

'Ah, I see.'

'You know what she said? It's funny. She said, my face needed to be soft, in case I kissed any pretty girls tonight. Like you.'

I didn't have to pretend to be shocked, but I acted melodramatic about it to play it off. I hoped I wasn't blushing again. 'You were talking about kissing me?'

Did he want to kiss me?

Did I want to kiss him? Or was this some rebound impulse?

'I think Becca thinks I should have a new girlfriend. She really liked having Julie around, because it was kind of like she had a big sister, too. I think she just misses that.'

'I guess I'll have to come babysit again soon, then.'

Levi smiled. 'Thanks, Elle.'

'It's okay. I don't mind.' And I really didn't.

(But did that mean I liked him as more than a friend, or would mind if he kissed me?)

With Noah, I'd always known I had a crush on him. A helpless, and I'd thought hopeless, crush. And I'd never really *liked* another guy. It was hard to work out my feelings toward Levi now.

But I couldn't deny that his comment about kissing me played over and over in my mind on the rest of the ride to the dance.

We didn't have too much trouble parking at the school. We could hear the dull thrum of the music pulsing from the direction of the school gym, and it sent a buzz of adrenaline through my system.

233

As we walked round to the entrance, our arms swinging at our sides and occasionally brushing against each other, I asked, 'Are you planning on going to the after-party?'

The after-party was organized last minute – one of the girls from the school council, Emma, had managed to persuade her parents to let her throw a house party, and I couldn't wait. Lee and Rachel had decided not to go, but that was okay – the rest of the gang would be there. I needed tonight, to try and enjoy myself without thinking about school or college, or too much about Noah. I wanted to let my hair down. Have fun.

'Oh, yeah, Cam text me about it earlier. Uh, I guess, maybe for a little while. I promised my mom and dad I wouldn't stay out too late, though. My mom wants to be up early tomorrow, to take Becca to ballet.'

'Becca does ballet?'

'It's gonna be her first class. Anyway, I promised I wouldn't get in too late, because she'll stay up to make sure I get in okay, and haven't gotten wasted and driven into a ditch somewhere. My dad would sleep through a hurricane, though.'

'You could always crash at mine,' I offered. 'My dad won't mind. You could sleep on the couch.'

'You sure that'd be okay?'

'Yeah. I don't see why not.'

'Thanks, Elle.'

I smiled at him, and he stepped to the side as we reached the doors of the gym, sweeping his arm out in an 'after you' gesture.

The gym had been mostly transformed. Not totally – but mostly. I'd been one of the lucky few to avoid coming early to help set up, but only because I'd had to pick Brad up from soccer practice.

There were balloons and streamers in red and pink and white strung all across the room, and the usual too-bright overhead lights had been turned off, in exchange for some flashy colored lights coming from the corners of the room and the electric lanterns we'd got to put on some tables.

And –

'Oh my God,' Levi exclaimed, grabbing my arm, noticing it at the same time as I did. 'Is that it? Is that the infamous kissing booth?'

I could only gawp, taking in the crowd around the booth Lee and I had created for the Spring Carnival months ago. It looked a little worse for wear now. I'd just assumed they'd scrapped it. People were going inside to pose with their dates for photos.

Ethan Jenkins spotted us and came over to say hi. I didn't let him get out a word before jabbing my finger at the booth and saying, 'What the hell is that doing here?'

'It's great, right? We found it yesterday. Fits *perfectly* with the pink-and-red theme, huh? People are going crazy for it!'

I gave a cracked smile, relieved when Ethan spotted someone else and moved on.

Levi turned to me with a grin. 'You wanna grab a photo?'

'Definitely not,' I said – maybe a little too quickly. I winced.

As if I needed any more reminders of Noah tonight, or any more reason to try and work out how I felt about the idea of kissing Levi. Stepping into the actual kissing booth with him was bound to be a recipe for disaster, I just knew it.

'Come on.' I grabbed Levi's hand, and he tripped after me. 'Let's dance.'

It was warm outside, but I wrapped my arms round myself, hunching over. There were a few clouds in the inky sky, but I could still pick out a few stars. Behind me, the soft noise of the last dance filtered out from the gym.

The night had been fantastic: there were no problems, so even us guys from the school council had been able to enjoy the dance. I mean, someone had tried to spike the punch with vodka, but the teachers and chaperones had been keeping a close eye on that, and sent the guy home before he managed to get away with it.

The kissing booth had been a hit, too. I did cave enough to take a photo in there with Lee. We took one with our arms round each other, one where he kissed my cheek, and one where I leaned toward him for a kiss and he shoved my face away with both hands with an overexaggerated expression of disgust.

'New profile pic,' I'd told him after, zooming in on his face.

Once I was up there to take a picture with Lee, Warren and Cam had shoved Levi up there with me, and I'd stood awkwardly while Rachel snapped a photo of us at the booth. I'd stepped away quickly.

The band we'd picked were awesome. The dancing had been fun, too – but I didn't want to stay for the last one. I didn't feel like being surrounded by cute couples holding each other close.

So here I was – sitting on a bench outside the gym, alone.

A throat cleared behind me, and I looked up as Levi sat down next to me. I hadn't seen him for a little while – I'd been dancing with some of the girls instead.

He was loosening his tie from round his neck, and cocked his head at me.

'You cold?'

I shrugged, and he slipped his arms out of his suit jacket, offering it to me. I put the jacket round my shoulders. It smelled like his aftershave. Which did smell *really* good. I had to work not to bury my face in the shoulder and sniff it.

'Thanks.'

'Guess you didn't feel like taking this last dance?'

'Not so much that. I just didn't want to be around all the couples, you know? Everyone hugging and kissing and being sappy . . . Don't get me wrong, it's adorable, and romantic – but that's exactly what I don't want to see right now.'

'I get it. You know, this is the first school dance I've been to since Julie broke up with me. I know how you feel.'

I leaned sideways, resting my head on Levi's shoulder. 'Breakups suck.'

'Yep.'

'Do you still miss Julie?'

'Sometimes. Less than I used to. It gets easier, don't worry. But maybe it won't be so easy for you because you're going to see Noah again. Like, over the holidays. Thanksgiving and Christmas and stuff. I don't see Julie any more, and I think that helped me get over her.'

I smirked, and laid the sarcasm on thick: 'Wow. Thanks. That's really encouraging, Levi.'

'Sorry.'

I nudged him with my head. 'It's okay.'

'It'll get easier,' he reiterated.

'Yeah.'

'In the meantime, though . . .' Levi eased his shoulder from under my head and stood up. I sat up straighter, and glanced at him, silhouetted against the lights from the parking lot. He looked tall and lean, and his curls a little wild from the night of dancing. He was holding out a hand and smiling at me.

'Wanna dance?'

I smiled back. 'Why not?'

I let Levi pull me up, and set his jacket on the bench, putting my arms round his shoulders. Levi's hands held my waist, and we swayed side to side.

I couldn't help but compare him to Noah. The arms around me weren't as strong, the shoulders not as broad. There was no heat, no spark, no tension between us; no desire to pull myself flush against him, like I was used to feeling with Noah, nothing that made me catch my breath and lean to kiss him. But there was something soft and sweet about it. Something comfortable and easy.

The song was almost over, and so was the dance – but while it lasted, it was *nice*.

*

I groaned, rolling over and burying my face in my pillow. My head hurt. My feet hurt. My throat hurt. I pulled my face out of the pillow, remembering the night before – Sadie Hawkins, dancing with Levi . . .

The after-party, where, after Levi had decided to head home, and I'd had maybe one too many beers, I'd sat outside moaning to Dixon and Cam about how much I missed Noah, and how I shouldn't have broken up with him, and how much I hated that bitch Amanda for coming between us and being everything I wasn't – and, apparently, everything Noah was looking for – and how much of an asshole Noah was for hiding things from me.

I probably deserved the headache.

I hadn't gotten in past curfew, at least. I remembered walking through the door promptly at one a.m. My dad had been awake, asked me how the dance and the party had been, and I'd done a good-enough job of not looking drunk enough to warrant being grounded.

I sat up slowly, rubbing my hands over my face. It was only nine in the morning, according to the clock on my nightstand, so I settled back against my pillows and picked up my cell phone, checking my messages.

There was a notification from Rachel – she'd tagged me in a post. I found she'd uploaded a bunch of photos from the dance last night, including one of me and Lee acting like dorks on the dance floor, and the one of Levi and me in the kissing booth.

I stared at the photo for a while. It was nice. I looked good in it, my dress flattering, my hair cute. And the more I looked at it, the more I thought how good Levi looked beside me. I hit the like button.

When I opened my texts to respond to some in our group chat, my heart stopped for a second and my eyes bugged out of my skull, and then I felt like retching.

There was a text to my dad – to say I was on my way back from the party – and before that . . .

I'd texted Noah.

I miss you sooooo much xxxxx

Shit.

Shit, shit, shit!

I clicked to see what the damage was – and was kind of relieved to find I'd only sent the one text. I'd have been even more mortified if I'd sent him two dozen pining texts. God, that would have been a total disaster.

But even so – one was pretty bad. My cell said that I'd sent the message at 00:24, which I was sure was when I was sitting outside with the guys. I must've been a little more drunk than I'd thought . . .

I was an idiot. My shoulders tensed up as I stared at the message, and the little *Read: 07:58* message underneath it.

What did I do now? Noah had seen it, and there was no way I could take it back. He'd obviously decided to ignore it, since I knew he'd seen it over an hour ago, so what did that mean? Did he hate me? Or did he just figure I wasn't worth replying to?

I swallowed the lump in my throat and ran a hand through my hair, my fingers getting caught in some knots.

Should I text him and apologize, say I was drunk and didn't mean to send it?

Should I ignore it, too?

I tried typing out an apology first: *Hahaha, just seen the text I sent you last night. Sorry about that – had one too many at the party after Sadie Hawkins!*

I looked at the text, hesitating over the send button. It looked forced. It looked fake. I didn't want him to think I was full of regret, pining for him. (Even if I kinda was.) And what if he didn't reply to that, either?

Or what if he did reply and say it was okay, and that he knew I didn't miss him – he didn't miss me either?

Worse: what if he replied and said he missed me too?

I deleted the reply I'd typed out and set down my phone, closing my eyes. If I'd thought being with Noah long-distance was hard, getting over him was so much harder.

Chapter 18

In an attempt to really start getting over Noah, I decided to spend the whole day focusing on myself. After watching some YouTube videos, eating a breakfast big enough to cure my hangover and finishing an essay for my history class, I was feeling pretty collected and motivated. I decided to try tackling my college application essay again. I'd made some progress on it over the last week. Maybe today would be the day I actually finished it.

I typed out a few new paragraphs before I read over the whole thing. It was almost there! All I needed was a good conclusion, but I knew it'd help if I read back over everything I'd written first.

The more words I read, the more I wondered why I'd wasted my time writing this crap in the first place. The elation I'd felt at thinking I'd almost finished vanished. I had to write about something I'd felt had inspired me – and I wasn't feeling very inspired rereading my essay.

I'd been thinking about this damn essay so much, and

rewriting pieces of it for weeks now. All that work and stress, and for what? This piece of crap on the screen now?

The words on the screen started to blur, mushing together until I couldn't see them. I clicked the mouse furiously, highlighting random words, wondering what the hell was going on – until I sniffled, and realized I was on the verge of crying. Again.

God, I was such a loser.

I couldn't even keep it together over a single, stupid essay.

I'd never get into college. I couldn't even write a damn essay! How the hell would I manage to make it through four years of college?

I didn't even know what I wanted to do with my life yet. I had no idea what I wanted to major in.

I'd talked to my dad and the careers counselor they'd brought into school, and they'd reassured me that I'd probably get into a good college without having to declare a major (which, once they pointed it out, was totally obvious, and made me feel like an idiot for stressing over it so much). But they hadn't done a great job of giving me any real, solid advice on writing my application essay to get into college in the first place.

So here I was, sobbing – and wailing a bit, too – over my computer, because *I couldn't even string a decent sentence together.*

My bedroom door opened, and since the figure – blurred beyond recognition by the tears in my eyes that just wouldn't go away – was too short to be my dad, I figured it had to be my brother.

'Get out!' I wailed, my words hitching on a sob. 'Go away! Leave me alone!'

Brad hovered in the doorway, and then I got angry. I didn't know why – I was just suddenly overwhelmingly furious that I couldn't even wallow in self-pity in peace.

'Elle? What's the matter?'

He was being really sweet (for a change). He was genuinely worried about me.

And it only made me feel even angrier.

'Get *out*! Leave me *alone*!'

Eventually, Brad shut the door and I collapsed over my desk, crying into my arms. I probably looked about as pathetic as I felt, but now I'd started crying, I couldn't stop. I hated this kind of crying.

What if I never finished the essay, and never made it to college? I'd disappoint my dad, and myself, and Lee would go to college without me and forget all about me, and –

The thoughts kept swirling, a vicious whirlpool dragging me further and further down. I slammed my laptop shut, unable to take the glare of the screen, the essay on it mocking me.

After a while, the door opened again.

I was ready to tell my little brother, or Dad, to get out and just let me be, but there was someone else standing behind my brother: Levi. The words died on my tongue.

'I thought maybe you could use a friend,' Brad said quietly.

I sniffled again, and managed a teeny tiny smile. Brad smiled back awkwardly – he wasn't used to being this nice to me, either – and then backed out of the room. Levi clapped him on the shoulder and smiled at Brad before coming into my room.

He sat on the end of my bed, facing me, and I moved to sit next to him, leaning my head on his shoulder.

Levi didn't seem to mind.

Then he put his arm round me.

'I was gonna ask if you're okay, but I think that's a pretty redundant question. You look like shit.'

I nudged him half-heartedly. 'It's the college application essay. I can't do it. I don't know what to write about. And what I do write sucks. I want to go to college, but I can't do that if I don't write this essay, and –'

'Hey, c'mon.' He squeezed his arm tighter round my shoulders. 'Your whole life isn't riding on whether you go to college or not, you know. Look at me. I'm not gonna go. I'm taking a year out to work and earn some money and try to figure out what I want to do. I'm not gonna waste four years, and rack up all that debt, for something I'm not sure about. Maybe that's something you wanna think about.'

I picked at a chip in my nail polish. 'Pretty much every time I sit down and hit a block with my essay, I think, *maybe I should just do this next year.*'

'But?'

'But I don't want to get left behind.'

It took him a second. 'Lee.'

Lee had been working so hard to get into Brown, and keeping his grades up, and working hard on the football team, trying to make a name for himself (and, from what I could tell, he was doing a damn good job of it; they'd stopped calling him 'Little' Flynn now).

Lee had football. Rachel had drama club. Some of the other guys did sports, or band. Sure, I had track, now, but I didn't really compete or anything. I'd even given up on hearing back from any of the after-school jobs I'd sent out applications for. I felt like I was a step behind them all, somehow.

'Yeah. And even if Lee didn't factor into it – I want to go to college. I do. It's just . . . Like you said, I'm not sure what I really wanna do with my life after college, and it's terrifying to think that what I do now commits me to that for the next few years, you know?'

'Not really,' he said, sounding disturbingly upbeat

for my current mood. 'You've gotta get through the SATs first and the way you're going, with all the practice tests, you'll ace it. And when you *do* get to college, you'll have ages to pick a major. And you know you can always change it. Hell, you could do anything. Work on the next Mars rover. Run promotion for a baseball team. Open a vineyard. Be a kindergarten teacher.'

I gave a weak smile. 'The sky's the limit?'

'Elle, we've all seen *Mean Girls*. We all know that the limit doesn't exist.'

I did laugh at that.

'Thank you for coming to my TED Talk,' he added, making me laugh again. 'How about this? I'll read your essay. We'll work on it together. It can't be *that* bad that we can't make it work.'

That . . . actually didn't sound so bad. Although it did make me feel like an idiot for not just asking someone for help on it before. I twisted to hug him. 'Thanks, Levi. You're the best.'

He hesitated before hugging me back. 'I'm always here for you, Elle.'

Levi stuck around for dinner, and by the time he left later that evening, my application was pretty much ready to go. I couldn't believe how much better I felt for it, and couldn't thank him enough.

When I thanked him again as he was putting on his shoes to go, he laughed. 'If you really wanna thank me, you can come to the aquarium with me tomorrow. I promised I'd take Becca. It'd be nice to have some company.'

A day at the aquarium sounded great, so the next morning, Levi picked me up, and Becca was totally hyper with excitement the whole ride. She talked a mile a minute about how her first ballet class had gone, and her ballet teacher, and the girls at ballet, and the recital they were putting on at Christmas – which made her start talking about Christmas.

I oohed and aahed in all the right places, asking her questions to prompt her on. Levi caught my eye in the rearview mirror with a shameless smile that said, *Rather you than me.*

Inside the aquarium, it wasn't very busy. There were mostly families around, with young kids. A handful of couples on dates.

Which, I had to admit, did make me feel a little awkward. I knew it wouldn't have been awkward if I were here with Lee, but this wasn't Lee, it was *Levi*. And that made it just a little bit weird.

I must've looked uneasy as we followed Becca, who was dashing between the tanks of manta rays and starfish and eels like they'd disappear soon, because Levi turned and grabbed my elbow gently, looking at me with concern.

'Hey,' he said, voice soft, 'everything okay?'

'Huh? Yeah. It's fine. I'm fine.'

'Are you sure? You look a bit weird.'

'Oh, no, I'm . . .'

'Are you thinking about Noah?'

I wasn't, actually, and was surprised to realize it; I wasn't thinking about what it would be like to come here with Noah, or wishing that Noah and I were one of the couples walking around hand in hand. I was just thinking that, despite Levi's little sister's presence, it felt like this was kind of a date.

But it was easier to say, 'Yeah.'

Levi gave me a sympathetic smile. 'You'll get over him, you know. I'm not saying you'll forget you ever loved him, but it'll get easier to not love him any more.'

'You sound like you write for *Cosmo*, or something.'

Levi just laughed, and Becca drew our attention by squealing loudly, 'Oh my God! Look at this! It's HUGE!'

As we made our way round the aquarium, I relaxed enough to manage to enjoy myself. Becca, it turned out, had a lot of random trivia about jellyfish to tell me. (Like: 'Did you know jellyfish can clone themselves? Like, you can cut one in half and then you just get two jellyfish.

I read it online.' And: 'Jellyfish don't have brains. Just like Levi!')

She kept reading the information cards nailed next to the tanks out loud to us, excited about each new type of fish.

Levi hung back a little as Becca grabbed my hand to haul me after her to the next tank, after giving up on trying to find the hermit crabs in the one we'd just spent ten minutes at. I glanced over my shoulder at him as Becca pressed her nose to the glass, peering in with wide eyes.

'What's that smile for?' I asked him. It was a weird sort of smile, not exactly his usual. Small and thought-ful. A kind of smile that made me feel warm and blush and tuck some hair behind my ear as I smiled back.

It seemed to change quickly, once I'd pointed it out, back to the easy smile I was used to seeing. 'It's just nice for Becca to have a girl to hang out with.'

'What about you? You're not enjoying my company too?' I teased, and he rolled his eyes. I probably shouldn't think about that smile, or what it might mean.

'I always enjoy your company, Elle. Now get over yourself.'

I laughed, and then Becca said, 'Hey, Levi, come look at this!' and broke whatever moment was going on.

*

Later, when we were standing at the shark tank, watching the sharks swim overhead and around us, with Becca occasionally making a soft 'oooh' of appreciation, I felt Levi looking at me. He was close enough that his arm was pressed against mine, a fact I suddenly became hyperaware of.

I had to make an effort not to stare right back at him. Glancing quickly out of the corner of my eye, I noticed he had that same weird smile on his face as he'd had earlier.

And it made my stomach feel strange. I didn't have butterflies, exactly, but . . . it was something similar.

Because it was the kind of look I always saw Lee giving Rachel when he didn't think anyone was looking. And it was the kind of look I used to catch Noah giving me sometimes, when he didn't think I'd seen him.

Becca stood a couple of yards away. I knew that if I turned and looked at Levi now, there would be *something*. Enough of a something that he might kiss me.

I swallowed, my mouth suddenly dry.

I realized that I *wanted* him to kiss me . . .

And then my cell phone rang.

The noise was loud, violent almost, in the quiet of the aquarium tunnel. I flinched, and the people around us looked over at me as I fumbled in my purse for my cell, finally finding it and pulling it out.

It was Lee.

'Hey,' he said, before I could say anything. 'Where are you? I just went round to your house and your dad said you'd gone out for the day with Levi.'

'We're at the aquarium.'

'The aquarium?' The shock in Lee's voice was palpable. 'What, like . . . like . . . just . . . the two of you? Like a date?'

I stole another glance at Levi. Who I'd just been very much thinking about kissing. Who I'd sort of almost kissed. And I told Lee, 'We're with Becca. You know, Levi's little sister. He promised to bring her to the aquarium and wanted some company.'

'Oh,' Lee said, and I was sure I could hear relief in his voice. 'Okay, well . . .' He trailed off, clearing his throat, and I got a nervous feeling in the pit of my stomach. Whatever he'd called me about, it was serious.

'Lee? Is everything okay?'

'I can just tell you later, when you get home. It's okay.'

He tried to sound casual, but totally failed. I knew him too well for him to play something serious off like it was nothing. He'd gone over to my house to look for me, wanting to tell me something. Panic seeped through me.

'Is it Rachel? Did you guys have a fight, or something?'

253

'Oh, no, it's – it isn't about me and Rachel. Seriously, don't worry. It's . . . Look, I'll just tell you when you get back.'

'*Lee,*' I snapped. The way he was avoiding whatever it was – and the fact that it was so important that he wanted to tell me in person – terrified me. 'What's going on? Please.'

He sighed. 'Okay, well, my mom just got off the phone with Noah. About how he's coming home for Thanksgiving . . .' Lee paused – waiting for my reaction.

Even though I was dreading seeing Noah at Thanksgiving dinner, I couldn't avoid it, and I knew that. I just had to suck it up for that one day and be polite to him. Just like I sucked it up now and tried to sound like I didn't care. 'Yeah, well, I figured he would be. What about it?'

Lee drew in a deep breath, and let it out slowly. It whistled, crackling, down the line. My palms began to sweat. 'He's bringing a friend back home for Thanksgiving, too, is all, and I thought you should hear it from me first.'

'A friend?'

But who was Noah that close with that he'd –

No.

No, he wouldn't do that. He *wouldn't*. Not after everything that happened. He wouldn't dare. But maybe

I was jumping to conclusions ... God, I hoped I was jumping to conclusions.

'You mean, like, Steve?' I could hear the desperation in my own voice, and I hated it, hated the way I clutched at my phone with both of my clammy hands. 'His room-mate? Or whatshisname that he hangs out with from football. David? Dave?'

'Yeah. I mean, no. I mean ... that's not who he's bringing home for Thanksgiving.'

'Lee ...'

'Shelly, he's bringing Amanda.'

I'd been expecting it, but even so, the air rushed out of my lungs and I put a hand against the nearest wall – the glass of the tank – for support, feeling dizzy. I was pretty sure that my heart had shattered before, when I broke up with Noah, but that was *nothing* compared to how I felt now. The floor seemed to swim beneath me. There was a ringing in my ears. The tang at the back of my throat made me wonder if I was going to puke.

'Shelly?' Lee was saying. 'You still there? Rochelle? Elle?'

'Yeah,' I said. My voice sounded strangled. I took a few deep breaths, suppressing the feeling of nausea. Something else filled the void pretty quickly, though, as I got hold of myself: anger.

'You okay?'

'Okay?' I hissed, dropping my voice to a whisper. I noticed a couple of people looking at me, and I staggered a few feet further away. 'Of course I'm not fucking okay, Lee! You saw that photo of them on Instagram. I told you about that conversation I overheard between them the day we broke up. And now he's bringing her home for Thanksgiving dinner, when he knows I'll be there? To rub it in my face? I'm pretty fucking far from *okay*.'

'Whoa, whoa, Shelly, okay, I get it. Chill out,' Lee said, sounding frantic. I didn't often use the F-word, same as Lee. But if there was any time for it, it was now. 'I just figured you should know now. Rather than be surprised on Thanksgiving Day.'

'Thanks for telling me,' I said through clenched teeth. But it wasn't Lee I was mad at, and we both knew that. 'I just . . . I can't believe he'd do that to me. I know we're broken up, so now he's totally entitled to sleep with her and date her and whatever, but to bring her home with him like that, this soon after, it's just – God, I can't believe he'd do that! What kind of *asshole* –'

'Elle?'

It was Levi, now, saying my name. He was standing in front of me, touching my shoulder with a frown on his face.

I held up a finger to signal 'one minute' to him, and

focused on what Lee was saying: 'I know you're not over him, Shelly, and that you're heartbroken over the whole breakup but, if it's any consolation, he told my mom she's just a friend.'

'She's not just a friend, Lee! She's not, and we both know that!'

'Well,' he said cautiously, 'we don't know *for sure* they're hooking up.'

'Oh, so now I'm just making stuff up?'

'No, I didn't say that. You know I didn't.'

I let out a deep breath. 'I'm sorry. You know it's not you I'm mad at.'

'I know. Look, text me when you get home and I'll come over and see you, and we can talk about it more then, yeah?'

'Okay.'

'Say hi to Levi for me. See you later.'

'Bye,' I said, hanging up and dropping my cell back into my purse. I looked up at Levi.

'What was that all about? Is everything okay?'

I shook my head, and wasn't surprised when my eyes filled with tears. I blinked them away, but one fell down on to my cheek before I could get rid of it. 'Noah's bringing Amanda home for Thanksgiving.'

Levi just pursed his lips, and said, 'Oh, crap.'

*

I had the same conversation with both Lee and Levi, and now I was having it again with my dad. I just needed to vent about it. A lot. Repeatedly. Like a broken, bitchy record.

Brad was taking a shower before bed, so it was just me and my dad sitting downstairs in the lounge with mugs of hot chocolate as I told him exactly how much I hated Noah. I'd told my dad we'd broken up because of the distance, but now I told him everything. I was too furious to keep it in.

'I mean,' I said, for the billionth time, 'he knows how much trouble she was causing between us. She's practically the reason we broke up. First the photo, and then the phone call. I knew they were close, and I wanted to trust him when he said he didn't cheat on me with her. And I was kind of expecting them to get together once I broke up with him, if they were that close, but the fact that he's bringing her home when he knows I'll be there . . . Like, okay, maybe if she'd come to visit around Christmastime, then fine, because I *might* have moved on by then. But it's only been a couple of weeks.'

My dad wasn't saying much; he just nodded and went *mm-hmm* in the right places and let me get it out of my system.

He nodded again now, while I paused to draw breath.

'And, the fact that he's moved on so quickly that he's already close enough to her to bring her home for the holidays *really* gets me. I mean, he can't have been *that* upset about our breakup if he's already with her seriously enough to do that.'

'Didn't Lee say that they're just friends, though?'

I scoffed. 'That's what Noah told his *mom*. I just *told* you about the phone call I overheard. They've *got* to be together. I mean, she's really pretty. She's *so* pretty. And she's smart, too. They have all these classes together. She can talk about all kinds of stuff with him I just wouldn't get. When are guys like Noah ever not with girls like her?'

'Elle, I know I'm not the best at this, but – well, maybe you're looking at this the wrong way. It didn't work out with you and Noah. And you need to move on, like you've said. This can be your chance to show him you have.'

'But I haven't.'

Well. Not *really*. Just because I'd wanted to kiss Levi earlier didn't mean I'd moved on from Noah completely.

'And, if he's bringing his new girlfriend home for the holidays, do you want him to know you're still hung up on him?'

I hadn't thought about it like that.

'So . . . pretend that I *am* over him?'

My dad shrugged. 'If it makes you feel better.'

I let myself imagine it: me greeting Noah and Amanda really politely, with a big smile that said I didn't care if they were dating now because I was totally over it, and Noah's let-down expression when he realized I wasn't chasing after him any more, that I didn't miss him, actually. He could bring her home to flaunt in front of my face, and I would show him how little I cared about him in return. See how he liked *that*.

'I guess I could do that.'

'It might help you *actually* get over him,' my dad said.

'Maybe.'

Chapter 19

'Maybe I should get a new boyfriend,' I commented to Lee as we walked to class the following week. 'Not anything serious, necessarily, but just, you know, to invite over on Thanksgiving to make a point to Noah.'

'I don't think that's the right reason to get a boyfriend,' Lee said with a warning tone in his voice.

'I'm just saying.'

'Yeah, well, so am I. What next, Elle – revenge sex?'

I laughed. 'With who? His room-mate, Steve, on the other side of the country?' Lee rolled his eyes and I gave him a pointed look. 'I'm not talking about that. Just . . .' I sighed and ran a hand through my hair, tugging on the ends of it in frustration. 'I just can't stop thinking about it. About them.'

I also couldn't stop thinking about how close I'd come to kissing Levi.

'I get that you're feeling betrayed, Shelly, but I really

think you need to try to get over it. You're too hung up on this.'

'I am trying to get over it! I was! Until he decided to bring *her* home for the holidays.' I ground my teeth. I'd been doing that a lot the past few days, whenever I pictured Noah and Amanda sitting together at the table in his parents' dining room, their hands linked together on top of the table, them giving each other soppy, lovestruck looks all the time.

The part I hated most about that picture was how perfectly they seemed to go together.

'What, like it would've been any easier to see Noah on his own if he's in a relationship with Amanda?'

I sighed. 'Well, yeah. It's just . . . bringing her home for the holidays is pretty serious. Right? And it's just making me wonder if maybe they did have something going on while we were still together.'

'One thing I know for sure is that my brother would never cheat on you. He was totally different with you, you know? I mean, he *dated* you – that's more than he did with any other girl. He can be a jackass, but cheating . . . It's just not him. He was *crazy* about you.'

'I'm not saying he *cheated*, necessarily, but maybe they were flirting a little, and – and maybe there was chemistry. And maybe coming home to visit me was just a last-ditch effort to see if we still had chemistry, like they do.'

'Shelly, seriously. You're overthinking this. We don't even know for sure if there is anything going on with them. It's probably nothing.' I waved him off, trying not to let the comment get to me. I knew it was just Lee's way of trying to comfort me, so I didn't push back.

But if it was really nothing to worry about, wouldn't Noah have messaged to tell me himself? The fact he *hadn't* told me felt like a big deal in itself. Either he was too much of a coward to tell me, or he really just . . . didn't care how much this hurt me.

I wished I could stop feeling so strongly about him. I was the one who broke up with *him*. I shouldn't care this much. If he wanted to date Amanda and bring her home for Thanksgiving . . . I wished it didn't bother me this much.

A big part of me was still in love with him, despite everything. And that part was hurting too much to let this go.

Levi tried to reassure me a few days later: 'It won't be so bad on the day. You'll see. He'll walk in with this girl Amanda and you'll realize you're not as hurt as you think you are. Seeing them together might help you get over him.'

263

'But she's perfect,' I whined to Levi. I'd convinced Rachel to take a little snoop on Noah's Facebook and Instagram profiles with me the other night. I'd resisted so far, but now I wanted to look. His relationship status still said 'single', but that didn't mean he didn't have anything going on with Amanda. That just meant he hadn't changed his Facebook status. There were a few updates from him, about a 'great night with the guys' or something similar, and photos that he'd been tagged in.

Amanda was in a lot of those photos with him. They weren't kissing in any of them, but they had their arms round each other and they looked couple-y.

And she looked so much better than I did. She looked so . . . *grown up.*

Like, she could've been a catalog model. Her skin was flawless, her hair looked good in *every single photo* and even in the photos taken at parties where she had a drink in her hand, there wasn't an unattractive shot of her. Not even with her eyes half closed, or her mouth hanging open, or anything.

It was so unfair.

I told Levi so, and he just shrugged. 'Maybe she's got a really bad personality. Maybe she's really, really boring.'

I could only hope.

I doubted it, though.

*

As November slipped away, and Thanksgiving drew closer, I did my best to stop focusing on the whole thing with my ex and his (probably) new girlfriend coming home, and I attacked my college applications with a furious passion.

I even decided to apply for Brown. Mostly because I wanted to be with Lee, I did admit to my dad. I also applied to UC San Diego, and a couple of others close by. I still didn't know what I really wanted to do after college, but my dad reassured me I'd figure it out.

The Sunday before Thanksgiving, I convinced Rachel to come out one afternoon to get mani-pedis with me. We hadn't hung out, just the two of us, outside school and not involving college applications, in a long time – and I needed a girly afternoon before facing Noah and Amanda, I figured.

Plus, I'd been trying to keep Levi at a distance. It didn't feel right to be hanging out with him wondering if there *was* something between us when I was so pre-occupied over Noah.

'How are you feeling about it?' Rachel asked me when we sat down to grab a coffee. 'Okay, or still stressing out?'

'Right now, I'm okay. If he wants to be a total jackass and do this, then fine, but I'm not going to let him know it's getting to me. And, besides, I deserve better than someone who'll get over me that fast.'

'I can't see how he did get over you that fast, though,' Rachel said slowly. 'I mean . . . he loved you. A *lot*. Everyone could see that. I kind of have to agree with Lee – maybe Noah was telling June the truth, and they're just friends.'

'A friend he's bringing home for a major holiday that you usually spend with your family?'

Rachel sighed. 'Yeah, but . . . He loved you so much. You can't just get over a relationship like the one you guys had like *that*.'

'If they're just friends, why wouldn't he *call* and tell me?'

I watched her think on it for a minute. 'After how the breakup went down, maybe he thought if he told you himself, you wouldn't believe him. Maybe he was . . . trying to avoid another fight?'

I scoffed. Sure, maybe, but I couldn't bring myself to believe it.

Rachel went on, 'If they are dating, or just hooking up, or something, at least you can be pretty sure she's just a rebound. It probably won't last that long, if they are together.'

'You think?'

'Yes,' she said with confidence, but when I glanced over at her expression, she didn't look so sure of herself.

266

'Anyway, enough about me for now. I'm done stressing and being mad. I can totally handle it. I'm going to show him he doesn't have a hold on my heart any more, even if that's not exactly true. How are things with you and Lee?'

Rachel's whole face lit up with a smile and, despite myself, I felt a pang of jealousy. 'So great! I really hope we both get into Brown next year, because it kills me to think I might be away from him. And I hope you get in, too, of course. I don't think Lee will be able to function properly if you're not around,' she added quickly with a laugh that was a little awkward. 'But yeah, it's – it's weird. I feel like it's been way longer than the eight months that we've been together. I feel like I've known him my whole life. And it's like, whenever Lee's around, I forget if I'm upset about anything or stressing out. He just makes me feel so much happier.'

'That's great,' I said, though my voice didn't have as much enthusiasm as I'd have liked. I was happy for them, even if I was a little bit jealous. 'Honestly, I'm glad you guys are doing so well. I've never seen Lee happier than when he's with you. Or talking about you. Or texting you. Or thinking about you.' I laughed.

Rachel blushed a little.

'And,' I said, dropping my voice and leaning a little bit closer, 'how's the sex life?'

She blushed even brighter, and I laughed. 'I'm teasing,' I assured her. 'You don't have to answer that if you don't want to. I know it's probably weird talking to me about it, because of how close I am with Lee.'

Rachel smiled at me, biting her lip. 'I honestly don't know what I was so scared about. Seriously. I thought it was going to be this really big deal, and it just ... wasn't.'

'Should I pass that on to Lee?' I joked.

'Oh, God, please don't.' She giggled. 'I just mean, it's like, you hear everyone talking about it like it's such a major thing, and it just wasn't. In a good way, you know? I'd totally built it up in my head that it was something to be nervous about, and there was *nothing* to be nervous about.'

'I know *exactly* what you mean.'

'Yeah. Okay, so enough talk about my bedroom business,' she said. 'Since the topic of the afternoon seems to be guys – I've been dying to ask, but I didn't really want to do it at school with everyone around. What's going on with you and Levi?'

I couldn't help the way my eyes narrowed at her. 'What about me and Levi?'

'Well, you're always together. And you act all flirty.'

'I don't flirt with him!'

Did everyone else notice that? Did he notice? (*I* had barely even noticed I was doing it.)

'Mm.' Rachel pulled a face, unconvinced. 'You kind of do. And he flirts back. I'm telling you, Elle, everyone is convinced you're together.'

'I – I don't . . .'

The last thing I needed was Rachel telling Lee that I had a crush on Levi, and it getting out – especially when I hadn't even really worked out what my feelings toward him were yet.

'I don't have a crush on him, if that's what you're getting at,' I told her, adding, 'Besides, what's wrong with a little harmless flirting?'

She didn't look overly convinced, but she let it go, and I breathed a sigh of relief.

I made Rachel come over to help me pick an outfit for Thanksgiving dinner after our mani-pedis.

'I know I said I'm not stressing out,' I told her, opening my closet, 'but this is different. This is my outfit. And I want something that screams "I'm totally happy with myself and totally over you."'

'And "Look at what you're missing out on now, Noah Flynn"?' Rachel added with a sly smile.

'Well, that too.'

She laughed, and settled down comfortably at the foot of my bed. 'Okay, so what are the options?'

I pulled out one dress, which I'd bought about a year ago, that was mustard yellow and had long sleeves and a figure-hugging skirt.

Rachel pulled a face. 'So not a fan. It looks like dog puke.'

'What? But it's such a fall color!'

'And I'm sure you can do better. Next!'

I pulled out a floaty black blouse made out of thin linen. The buttons only did up partway, because my boobs had grown since I'd last worn it. I tried it on to show Rachel what I meant.

She scrunched her nose up. 'Hot, but might look like you're trying too hard? And black seems kind of dull for Thanksgiving, unless you're going for a classy LBD. Like you're in mourning, or something.'

'Okay . . .' I put the blouse back in the closet, and pulled out a few more shirts to show her. Too casual, too summery, too brightly and garishly patterned, too conservative, too try-hard . . .

I found another dress buried in the back of my closet, one I'd almost forgotten I owned. I hadn't worn it in a while.

'Ooh, cute,' Rachel said, as I pulled it out. The dress was light cotton and deep burgundy, with a scoop neckline and sleeves to my elbows. I pulled it on for Rachel's verdict.

'I think we've just found the perfect outfit,' Rachel declared.

'You think?' I twisted in front of my mirror, examining my legs, butt, waist and arms in the dress.

'Wear it with some cute flats and nice earrings and Noah will be practically drooling,' she assured me.

I grinned. 'That's exactly the look I'm going for.'

Chapter 20

I smoothed down my skirt, but really, it was an excuse to wipe the sweat off my clammy palms. My breath came in short puffs, like I'd been running. I'd been feeling really great this morning, while I was getting ready. I'd been feeling so good, in fact, that I'd almost managed to convince myself that I actually *was* over Noah, and it didn't even bother me to think I'd be seeing him today.

I was in the bathroom at the Flynns' for the hundredth time in the last hour, since Matthew had gone to get his son and his son's probably-girlfriend from the airport. I lifted my arms to check I didn't have pit stains. That was the last thing I needed today.

I checked my messages again, even though my phone hadn't buzzed since Levi had texted me a few hours ago to wish me good luck seeing Noah and Amanda today.

I kept hoping that a text would appear on my phone from Noah. Nothing serious, no big apology to tell me that he wanted me back, no explanation that he and Amanda were just friends.

All I wanted was a message from him that said: *Just to let you know, I'm bringing Amanda home for Thanksgiving. Thought you should know.*

Because, really, that was only polite. Wasn't it? He had to have known that I'd heard about it from Lee; I couldn't help but be a *little* pissed that he didn't even have the courtesy to text me and warn me about it himself. (Okay, a lot pissed. Because seriously? After everything, and after the way we broke up, he wimped out and let Lee tell me? I'd really thought more of him.)

There was a knock on the bathroom door, making me almost drop my cell. 'Just a sec!'

I opened the door and forced a smile for Lee. His face was full of pity. 'Shelly, seriously, you need to stop worrying. It's going to be fine. You'll see him with Amanda and realize he was a dick to you and you deserve better, and you'll be fine.'

'Mm-hmm.'

'Plus, you look *hot*,' Lee told me. 'He'll be wondering how he ever let you go for some boring, preppy goody-two-shoes.'

I managed an actual smile at that, and hugged Lee. 'How do you always know what to say to make me feel better?'

'I guess our minds are just so in sync, I can't help it. If I were a girl too, I bet we'd even have our periods at the *exact* same time.' I pulled away from the hug to see Lee grinning at me, his blue eyes gleaming. His freckles weren't so prominent any more, I noticed. They'd faded away a bit. He'd built up even more muscle lately, being part of the football team. (He'd also stopped going to their parties so much, which seemed to help him not act like such a jackass.)

I ruffled his hair, which he'd painstakingly artfully messed up with product this morning, and he yelped in protest, batting me away.

'Mercy, mercy!' he exclaimed, and I laughed, backing away.

'Are you seeing Rachel today?'

'I'm going over this evening, after dinner. But only if you're okay. I told her I might not, if you want me to stick around here, if things are weird with you and Noah. And Amanda. She totally understood, though.'

I shrugged. 'With any luck, it won't be. And then you can go see Rachel.'

Lee smiled at me, but it wasn't impish any more, it was sad. 'You know I'm always here when you need me, Elle.'

'I know.'

I hugged him again, and then we heard, 'Oh, not interrupting anything, am I?'

It was one of Lee's aunties, Maureen, who was raising her eyebrows at us like she'd just caught us making
out or something instead of hugging. Lee crossed his
eyes at me, and I bit back a giggle.

'Can I just get through to the bathroom, hon?'

'Sorry,' I said, stepping away from Lee and out of
the way of the bathroom door. 'All yours.'

Maureen smiled at us conspiratorially and shut the
bathroom door behind her. She had been convinced
for years that Lee and I would end up married with
a dozen kids. She told us so, every Christmas.

'I guess we should go downstairs, see if your mom
needs any help,' I told Lee.

Lee's mom always hosted Thanksgiving for their
family, and for us.

The usual crowd was here: a handful of aunties and
uncles and grandparents, most of the cousins. Right
now, we passed one of Lee's cousins, Liam, who was
about Brad's age, and was trying to explain why the fan-
tasy series he was reading was even cooler than the
video game Brad had been talking about all day. Somehow, I didn't think he'd have much luck persuading
Brad to give the books a try.

June always said she found making Thanksgiving
dinner fun, but from the stressed-beyond-belief look
on her face when we walked into the steamy kitchen

you'd never have guessed it. She snapped at us to make sure the table was laid properly, that there were enough knives and forks and plates and chairs, enough place mats and empty glasses and napkins. And was the wine in the fridge? Could *someone* please check?

Thanksgiving was always totally chaotic.

There was no other way to describe it.

But boy, did we love every second of it.

It was a bigger affair than Christmas at the Flynn household, because of all the extra family members. Christmas was usually just us, without the grand-parents and aunties and uncles and cousins.

Uncle Pete and Aunty Rose were helping June in the kitchen, and Pete's new wife, Linda, was standing off to the side, trying not to get in the way. This was only her second Thanksgiving with us, so I didn't blame her for still feeling a little out of place. But she caught my eye as I scooted out to the dining room, and I smiled.

She drifted after me while I laid out the cutlery, swirling the wine round in her glass. Lee said some-thing about getting more spoons and left. Linda was about fifteen years younger than Pete – closer to mine and Lee's age than to Pete's. 'I heard you and Noah split up.'

'Yeah,' I said. I hadn't really talked to Linda much. Not one-to-one, anyway. I mean, she was nice, sure, but

I didn't feel comfortable telling her all the ins and outs of the breakup.

'It's probably for the best,' she told me, sipping her wine. She leaned down to straighten a knife. 'When I went to college, I was about four hours away from the college my boyfriend at the time was going to. We'd been together since the tenth grade, but we just couldn't hack it, not that far apart. I think you did the right thing to call it off. I tried to keep my relationship going. We tried to see each other every weekend, and my grades suffered for it, but after a while there wasn't any relationship to keep going.'

'I'm sorry,' I said, because I didn't know what else to say.

Linda shrugged, and sipped more wine. 'I got over it. I'm just saying, you will too, even if it seems hard right now.'

'Thanks,' I said, sincerely. 'I appreciate it.'

'Kind of an asshole move for him to bring his side-piece home, though,' Linda said, then grinned and winked at me. 'But don't tell June I said that.'

I laughed. 'My lips are sealed.'

'What are you two gossiping about?' Pete asked, walking in and going straight to kiss his wife on the cheek.

'Oh, just girl stuff,' Linda said passively.

Pete nodded, like this was a very comprehensive answer. Then he looked at me. 'You feeling okay about seeing Noah, kiddo?'

He was always calling us 'kiddo'. He even called Noah 'kiddo'.

'Uh, yeah, I guess so. I knew I'd have to see him if things didn't work out right from the start.'

'Elle's a tough girl,' Lee pitched in, coming back into the room. 'She can handle anything.'

Pete laughed, and June yelled from the kitchen to ask where the hell he'd disappeared to – the carrots were burning.

'Better go,' he said, disappearing out of the room before any of us could say another word. Linda wandered out after him, our conversation apparently over.

Lee looked across at me as we set out the last of the cutlery and the basket of warm bread rolls he'd brought back from the kitchen. 'Hey,' he said softly, 'are you sure you're okay?'

'Just dandy,' I told him, and, at least for a moment, I was.

We all heard the car pull up in the drive, and June shot out of the kitchen, wiping her hands on the gravy-spattered apron round her waist before opening the door. Lee and I moved to the doorway of the lounge to look out into the hallway.

Matthew came in first, with a bulky purple duffel bag, and Noah came in with his plain gray one after. Followed by *her*.

The first thing that hit me was how good Noah looked. Like, he looked even more incredible than I was used to. I was used to seeing him with a bit of stubble, but now he had a full beard going on – and it really suited him, made him look older, more mature. He was wearing a white T-shirt under a red-and-gray flannel shirt, the sleeves on it rolled up to his elbows. And the big biker boots he normally wore had been changed for a simple pair of black Converse. His jeans must've been new, too – they didn't even have any holes.

I'd never seen Noah dressed so well, or so casually – with the exception of when he'd taken me to the Summer Dance. He usually dressed to intimidate with the boots, and his T-shirts were mostly worn and old, his shirts usually faded and jeans ripped from wear.

'Hi, sweetie,' June said, kissing Noah on the cheek. She looked totally ecstatic to have him home, and I saw the expectant smile she gave Noah, glancing at Amanda.

'Hi, Mom. This is Amanda,' Noah introduced the girl by his side.

Amanda was a tall, leggy blonde, with an upturned nose and sweeping bangs across her forehead. Her lipstick was bubblegum pink and her eyeliner immaculately flicked at the corners of her eyes.

And, just like in her photos, she looked like the catalog model for preppy college girls everywhere (at least, I thought so): a white blouse underneath a periwinkle-blue sweater that was probably cashmere, with black skinny jeans and delicate gray pumps. She had this huge square beige purse with black handles and piping – the kind I half expected a small dog to pop its head out of.

She was so beautiful.

I hated her so much.

'Hello, hon,' June said affably, holding out a hand to Amanda and kissing her on the cheek. 'It's so lovely to finally meet you. Noah's told us so much about you.'

He has?

I glanced at Lee, who pointedly didn't meet my eyes. Lee had told me that he didn't really know anything about Amanda, that Noah hadn't said much. Now I got the feeling he had just been saying that to make me feel better.

Amanda smiled, a big toothy smile that only made

her look prettier. 'Thank you so much for having me, Mrs Flynn. Your home is absolutely lovely.'

Oh, God.

She was *British*.

Just when I thought she couldn't get any more perfect, she had a cute dang accent, too.

I was about to scrunch up my face in disgust, when I caught Noah's eye. His piercing blue eyes locked with mine, his expression incomprehensible.

Was he mad at me? Was he missing me? Was he totally over his little brother's best friend and just didn't care?

The longer we stared at each other, the less I wanted to find out.

I turned away, and made a hasty escape through the lounge to the kitchen, before I had to be introduced to Amanda properly, too. She could meet the rest of Noah's family first. There were certainly enough of them to keep her busy for a while.

Lee followed me, catching my arm by the island in the kitchen and linking his fingers through mine. He squeezed my hand tight. 'Hey, hey, it's okay. Look. I'm right here.'

I blinked a few times, just to make sure I wasn't going to cry. Because I wasn't; I'd promised myself last night that, no matter what, I wouldn't shed a tear over Noah Flynn today.

I'd thought I could handle it. Convinced myself I totally could. But getting used to the idea of Noah being with another girl was a lot different from actually seeing him with her. This hurt so much more than I'd been expecting.

'All you need to do is get through dinner,' Lee told me. 'Show them you don't care. Hell, she'll probably be intimidated that my family love you so much that you're here for Thanksgiving.' I managed a snort of laughter at that. 'And then we'll get out of here for a while, later. Go for a drive somewhere, maybe.'

'But you were going to see Rachel later.'

'And I told you already, I'm here for you today, because I think you need me more.'

June popped into the kitchen before we could talk any more, so I just squeezed Lee's hand by way of thanks that he was picking me over Rachel today. She said, 'Lee, you should go and say hi to Amanda.'

He got the message, and saluted his mom. 'Yes, ma'am.'

Once he was gone, June came up to me and squeezed my shoulders gently. 'You okay, honey?'

'I'll live.'

'She's very nice.'

'That's the worst part,' I said, managing a nervous laugh. June had been very sympathetic to me about the breakup; she'd heard everything from Lee, and told me she understood completely, and that she hoped I knew I was still very welcome any time – that just because things were over with Noah didn't mean I wasn't still part of the family. But I'd totally avoided having to talk to her about Amanda, and Noah bringing her home for the holidays.

'He's told me they're just friends.'

'Lee said. I'm just having a hard time believing it, that's all. But it's okay. I'm okay.'

'Are you sure?'

I nodded. The last thing I needed was for her to tell Noah how badly I was taking this, and to be considerate of me and my stupid, broken heart. 'I'll even go say hi. In a minute. Unless you need any help with the, um, cooking, or – like, literally anything? I'll take the trash out.'

June laughed. 'I think you need to go and say hi. You don't have to chat, just say hi. But I'll hold you to that offer – you can take the trash out later.'

'Gee, thanks,' I mumbled, and she gave my shoulder a squeeze before letting me go.

I sucked in a deep breath, and prepared myself to plaster on a big, warm and totally fake smile to go and say hi to Amanda.

She was shaking hands with Lee's Uncle Colin when

I neared her. Noah was across the room, squatting to talk to Brad and Liam.

Amanda looked at me, smiling.

'Hi,' I choked out. I cleared my throat. 'I'm –'

'Elle!' she exclaimed, with her fancy damn accent, her smile stretching wider. I was so shocked my own forced smile faltered. The smile even reached her eyes. It didn't look fake at all. 'It's so wonderful to finally meet you! I've heard *so* much about you!'

And then she hugged me.

She *hugged* me.

She hugged *me*.

I stood there for a second before deciding it was probably best to hug her back. Noah caught my eye again, and then he looked away, obviously uncomfortable.

Well, that made two of us.

Amanda pulled away, still beaming. 'It really is just *so* lovely to meet you, Elle. How *are* you?'

'Um, I'm – I'm great, thanks.'

My whole 'I'm super confident in myself and totally over everything that happened because of you, you total bitch' persona had vanished into thin air and I couldn't find it again. I was floundering without it. She beamed at me, and suddenly all I could do was smile back and say, 'How are you? How was the flight?'

'I slept the *whole* way.' She laughed. She even had the

same laugh as I'd expected – all high and tinkly and musical. 'I don't really like flying much, to be honest.'

'Oh, really?'

'Noah will tell you. I was awful during takeoff! How about you? How are you? You're in senior year now, aren't you? How are college applications going? I swear, I've never been *so* stressed out in my entire life as I was when I was trying to pick a university. Ugh.'

'Um, yeah, well, I've just sent off some applications. I think I want to be a kindergarten teacher, or something.' I listed off the colleges I'd applied for, too – because I was too dumbstruck by her reaction to do anything else.

What was I *doing*?

Talking to her like we could be friends? Like she wasn't part of the reason I'd broken up with Noah? Okay, the *main* reason.

Why was she so nice? Why did she sound like she actually cared? And why was I still giving her this bland smile, nodding along like *I* cared?

I wanted to think there was some ulterior motive on her part – to get all friendly with the ex-girlfriend so I wouldn't try to get back together with Noah now that she was with him.

But she just seemed so genuine and so damn *nice* that it was getting harder to hate her. She asked me more about how I was finding senior year, and what my plans for college were, and she shared stories of how her room-mate was a total *nightmare* but had left college because she couldn't hack it so now Amanda had a room to herself.

I was pretty sure that I hated Amanda for the fact that I couldn't possibly hate someone so nice.

I stood there talking to her, stunned and unable to do anything but laugh and smile and chatter like we were really getting on (and maybe we were?) until June called that dinner was ready.

Noah came over and touched Amanda's elbow. My eyes flicked to the gesture and he dropped his hand away. I didn't know what that meant. I glanced back up to his face, but he'd turned to Amanda. 'Come on, it's just this way.'

I clenched my jaw as he led her away, and balled my hands into fists so tight that my nails dug into my palms.

He couldn't even look at me? Couldn't even say *hello*? Did he hate me that much?

Or was he so ashamed of himself for realizing that he'd brought his new girlfriend home to meet his whole family, all in front of his recently ex-girlfriend?

I kind of hoped he was. I wanted him to realize just how much this was hurting me.

A hand waved in front of my face, and Lee came into focus. 'Earth to Shelly. What was that all about?'

'What?'

'You and Amanda. I thought you wanted to rip her throat out and then I look over and see you laughing like you're suddenly best friends?'

'She's . . . nice,' I defended myself, and bit my lip, looking guiltily at Lee. 'She just hugged me and started asking about college, and chatting, and – and I didn't know what else to do. She's hard not to get on with. And did you hear her accent? It's, like, impossible to hate anything she says in that accent. I'm kind of starting to hate myself for ever hating her.'

Lee shook his head in dismay, looking disappointed in me.

'Hey, better we get on than have a catfight over the dinner table, right?' I said.

Lee cracked a grin, then nudged me. 'You know I can't resist seeing a good catfight, Shelly.'

I settled for swatting him over the head, then I looped my arm through his. My friendship with Lee might have been a little rocky the last few months, but right now it was as concrete as ever.

Even if I'd lost Noah, at least I'd always have Lee.

Chapter 21

The dining table at the Flynns' was huge – so huge that there were three centerpieces. Like always. There was the big one with fake flowers and waxed fruit, all with gold edging, which June's mom had passed on to her when she stopped hosting Thanksgiving; and the ones that Brad and Liam had made in school.

The rest of the table sagged under the weight of all the food. Dishes of buttery roasted vegetables, still-steaming bread rolls and the huge turkey covered every inch of the table.

My dad said grace this year. Neither Lee's nor my family were very religious, but we always said grace on Thanksgiving. The whole time, when I had my head bowed, I tried not to steal a glance at Amanda and Noah, who were sitting on the other side of the table from Lee and me. Were they holding hands? Were their legs pressed together under the table?

As I thought this, I felt Lee bump my knee underneath the table.

I could do this.

I could totally do this.

As the turkey was carved, and dishes of vegetables were swapped across the table, I had to make a conscious effort not to keep looking at Noah. But it was so hard not to when he sat directly opposite me.

Conversation wasn't half so uneasy and stiff as I'd expected it to be. The grown-ups asked us all about school and college. Lee and I didn't have much to say that people didn't already know; Brad and Liam were so excitable that they kept talking over each other with their mouths full; and all anybody got from Liam's older sister, Hilary, was a surly half-response. (Her parents affectionately rolled their eyes and told us she was going through a 'goth phase'. She'd told us she'd had better places to be today; we didn't take it personally.)

Mostly, everyone talked to Amanda and Noah, wanting to know all about how they were getting on at college, and how football was going for Noah, and did Amanda have any hobbies?

She smiled when Colin asked her that, and said, 'Actually, I'm really into horse riding. There's this riding school back home where I go. I *really* miss it, and the horses. I don't have my own horse, but I'd like to, some day.'

'Not much of a city girl then, eh?' Pete said.

'Oh, I don't mind the city, but I think long-term I'd prefer somewhere in the country. I could see myself in the city for my five-year plan, but not to, like, settle down.'

She had a five-year plan.

I was starting to think that she was actually flawless.

That led everyone to ask about her plans after college, whether she planned to stay or move back to the UK, and while everyone was preoccupied, Lee whispered in my ear, 'Jeez, I see what you mean. She *is* nice. It's infuriating, but I can't actually get mad at her.'

'I know,' I whispered back. I turned my head away so Noah couldn't lip-read.

'Noah keeps looking at you,' Lee added. 'He's looking now.'

'I know,' I repeated, giving him a rigid smile and a wide-eyed, unimpressed look. 'I'm trying not to notice.'

'Why?'

'He didn't even say hi to me,' I mumbled. 'I'm getting the feeling he's pissed at me.'

'He's *definitely* not mad at you, Shelly. He just looks kind of sad.'

Sad? What right did *he* have to be sad about all this?

I turned away from Lee; I wasn't going to get into that. I didn't want to feel sorry for Noah. Especially not today, when he least deserved it.

I tried not to let it get to me whenever Amanda laid a hand on Noah's arm or on his hand, or when she brought up a story about a mutual friend, or a story that started, 'Do you remember that time when . . .'

Whenever she touched him, it looked so natural, so familiar. Like *we* used to be.

And that hurt, too.

I poked some yams around on my plate, losing my appetite.

Then Noah distracted me, by actually speaking to me. The grown-ups had all moved on to talking about work and about their bosses or colleagues, Hilary was talking to her grandma, and Liam and Brad had finally found common ground with a shared love of Marvel and were arguing about whether Iron Man or Thor would win in a fight, so nobody really noticed Noah had spoken to me.

Like, directly to me.

For the first time since we'd broken up.

And he said, 'So, uh, Elle . . . How's Levi?'

Really? Was he serious? Of all the things to talk to me about – why Levi? He couldn't say hi, but he could ask me about Levi?

Lee coughed and said, 'Hey, Brad, Liam, you guys know that the Hulk would beat them both, right? Elle, back me up here.'

I turned back at Noah. God, he looked so good. Why did he have to look so good?

Why did he care so much about Levi when he was here with his new girlfriend?

'Yeah. He's good.'

Noah nodded. And kept nodding.

And I bit my lip, staring back at him and waiting for him to say something else, but also wanting that to be the end of it.

Amanda intervened, luckily – because things were starting to get really awkward. 'Is Levi the boy who moved from Detroit? You had all those nicknames for him, Noah. The jeans guy. True Religion, Diesel, stuff like that. He lives by your friend, um . . . Is it Carl? I want to say Carl.'

'Cam,' I corrected her, slightly stunned.

Noah had talked to her about Levi? What the hell was that about? It was weird that it was easier to talk to Amanda than Noah, but I went ahead and said, 'Yeah, that's him. We just got to be really good friends. We keep each other company when we have to babysit. He's got a little sister a few years younger than Brad.'

'That's nice, though.' Amanda smiled brightly. 'And

I suppose it makes babysitting easier, too.'

'Uh-huh.' And then, because I couldn't resist, I said, 'I asked him to the Sadie Hawkins dance a couple of weeks ago. That was really nice. It was only in the school gym, but it was cute.'

I wasn't exactly sure why I said it. I just couldn't help myself. I guess I wanted to make Noah feel as bad as I did.

Or I wanted to make him jealous.

I wasn't sure which, and I really didn't want to spend too long thinking about it.

'Yeah,' Noah said, obviously making an effort to keep his voice casual – it came out sounding sort of strained, though. His eyebrows pulled together almost into one straight line because of the frown on his face. 'I saw. There was that photo of you guys in the kissing booth.'

Oh my God. He'd seen the photo. And judging by the look on his face, it *bothered* him.

Well, so what? What damn right did he have to be mad about a photo? Did he hear what a hypocrite that made him? And at least I was *single* when that photo was taken.

I stared back at him, chin jutting out. 'Yeah. Cute, right?'

Noah scowled down at his plate; I saw his Adam's apple bob as he gulped. Amanda glanced between us, then smiled again, reaching an arm across the table to me and waving it excitedly. 'Oh my goodness,' she said, all bubbly, 'my school never did dances like you guys have over here. Tell me *all* about it. Was there a theme? Noah said you're on the planning committee for stuff like that, what did you have to do?'

She kept on babbling – and I was pretty sure she knew she was babbling. I figured she was doing it on purpose, trying to alleviate the tension between me and Noah, which was tangible now. I bristled.

I locked eyes with him, and felt the urge to start crying again. I felt Lee bump my leg with his again, and I inhaled deeply through my nose, trying to keep my eyes from drifting back to Noah.

We were over.

I had to move on.

I couldn't let him keep getting to me.

I swallowed hard, smiled politely at Amanda, and told her, in the most upbeat voice I could manage, all about the Sadie Hawkins dance.

I helped clear away the dishes when we were all done. Lee asked me quietly if I was okay, and I assured him I was (although I wasn't so convinced myself). He went outside to play football with Brad and Liam in the backyard.

'I'll help,' Amanda volunteered, standing and starting to pick up plates, too.

'Oh, no, hon, honestly,' June protested. 'You're our guest! There's no need.'

'It's the least I can do,' Amanda said cheerfully.

Hell, I thought. *Everything she says is cheerful.* I guessed she was just one of those people. Or maybe it was the accent. 'It's so generous of you to have me stay for Thanksgiving.'

'It's nothing, Amanda,' Matthew said. 'What's one more mouth to feed when there's already seventeen of us?'

'Says you,' June said, tutting at her husband but smiling. 'All you did was the cranberry sauce!'

'The cranberry sauce is a vital component of any turkey dinner,' Matthew assured us.

'Well, it was absolutely delicious, Mr Flynn.' Amanda laughed, picking up more plates. Linda and Colin started gathering some, too.

June's sister Rose said, 'Hilary, why don't you help?' and Hilary glared at her mom, saying, *'Fine.'* She grabbed some glasses and stormed out to the kitchen.

Rose sighed, and drank a little more wine. 'I don't know what to do with that girl, honestly. Just because she wanted to go to the movies with her friends later, and – what did she call it, Colin? FOMO? – You'd think I'd signed a death warrant for her social life.'

Amanda and I walked to the kitchen together, even though I'd stalled to try and avoid doing so. Just because she was so frustratingly easy to get along with didn't mean I wanted to spend more time with her than I had to.

We put the dishes by the dishwasher, stacking them carefully. 'June will kill us if we scratch her best china,' I commented.

'My mum's just the same.'

'Why didn't you go home for Thanksgiving?' I asked her. It came out sounding rude, but I didn't mean it to. I just wanted to know. I looked away, sheepish.

Instead of the kind of answer I was looking for – 'Noah and I are super serious now and we thought I should come here to meet his family' or 'Noah and I are just great friends' – Amanda said, 'Well, we don't celebrate Thanksgiving.'

'Oh, right, yeah. Of course . . .'

'Noah didn't want me stuck at college all by myself for the holidays. And I thought it'd be fun to see a real American Thanksgiving.'

I wanted to ask, 'Yeah, but are you here as Noah's friend, or his girlfriend?'

Instead, what came out of my mouth was, 'That was nice of him.'

Then Amanda said, 'I hope you don't mind me saying, but it was a bit awkward between you and Noah. At least, it felt like it was.'

Wow. Straight to it, huh?

I clenched my jaw. 'Sort of.'

'Do you still have feelings for him?'

Seriously, how did anybody sound that nice when they were asking such a blunt, personal question of someone they'd literally just met a couple of hours ago? And to their boyfriend's ex, of all people? It wasn't fair.

I looked at Amanda, at the genuine concern and open curiosity on her face, and I narrowed my eyes at her. 'I don't really feel like talking about this.'

I turned and walked out of the kitchen just as some of the grown-ups came in, juggling glasses and empty wine bottles and plates, like they were part of a circus act.

'Elle,' I heard her say, my name an apology, as I was by the doorway.

I didn't look back.

When I returned to the dining room to collect what was left of the dishes, Noah was just leaving. I bumped right into him, bouncing back and stumbling. He caught my arm to steady me, and I jerked it away like he'd given me an electric shock.

And, if I was going to be totally honest, it felt like he had.

It made me think of Levi, and the fact that we didn't have this kind of thing between us. That spark. Although, right now, it was definitely not a good kind of spark. Maybe I was better off without it.

I looked up at him, unimpressed when he didn't move out of my way. 'What?'

'Elle, I just . . .'

'Just what?'

He clamped his mouth shut, looking away.

Fine. If he wasn't going to talk to me, then I'd . . . I could . . .

I didn't know what.

'Why don't you go play football with the boys, son?' Matthew said, appearing behind Noah and clapping his hand on Noah's shoulder.

Noah looked at me again, with those electric blue eyes searing right through me, and then he strode away. The door to the backyard banged behind him.

I gave his dad an awkward smile. 'Uh, thanks.'

'You two will sort things out,' he said, looking as uncomfortable as I felt.

'Oh, I – I really don't think we'll ever get back together,' I mumbled, looking in the direction Noah had just gone in. 'I don't think either of us could go back after all this.'

'I just meant you guys will both get over it and move past it. Eventually.'

'Oh.' I rubbed a hand across the back of my neck, which felt like it was burning just like the rest of my face. 'Well, yeah. Some day.'

Matthew clapped me on the shoulder, then left the room with the remainder of the turkey on the dish in his other hand.

I looked at the few things left on the table, and back in the direction of the kitchen, where I could hear Amanda's laugh.

I really, *really* couldn't do this.

I walked toward the front door, pulling on my ankle boots and already calling Levi.

'Hey,' Levi said, answering on the second ring. 'What's up?'

What *was* up? I couldn't pinpoint it exactly. I just needed to see him and get out of here for a while. I needed to not be around Noah, or Amanda, and pretending I was fine.

I told him so. 'Can you meet me at the park? I just need to get out of here for a while. I can't handle this.'

'Sure. I'll leave in a couple of minutes.'

'Great. I'll meet you in the parking lot.'

I hung up, and turned to grab my coat off the hook on the wall. I jumped when I saw Lee standing in the hallway. 'Jesus, Lee,' I gasped, putting a hand over my racing heart. 'You scared me.'

'Going somewhere?'

I hadn't even considered asking Lee to get out of here with me. I'd just gone straight to Levi. I was feeling shitty enough without having to think into that one, too.

'Um, yeah. I'm just going to go to the park. Get a little air. You know.'

'On your own?'

'. . . Yeah.'

Lee raised his eyebrows, crossing his arms. The sleeves of his green woolen sweater rode up his arms with the motion. 'Shelly, please don't lie to me.'

I slipped my arms into my coat, and walked up to Lee. 'Fine. I'm going to see Levi, but I – I really don't need to hear anything about that from you right now, that's all. I'm sorry, but I really need to go. I can't handle this like I thought I could and . . .' I sighed, and kissed his cheek. 'Go see Rachel, huh? I'll be okay.'

'Elle . . .'

I was already grabbing my purse and opening the door.

'Shelly!' he yelled after me, but the door closed before he could say another word.

Chapter 22

The park wasn't particularly far away, but far enough that I drove. I took a detour to make it last longer. I turned up the volume on my stereo and sang along to the new Taylor Swift song the radio station was playing. I sang half the words wrong, shouting non-sense instead. It kept my mind off the Flynn brothers, at least.

But when I parked up and killed the engine, I had to think about them.

I wasn't sure if I was mad at Noah, or just upset. I couldn't tell if I was pissed at Amanda for asking if I still had feelings for Noah, or if that just made me edgy because I *did* still have feelings for Noah.

I didn't *want* to still have feelings for him. I wanted to be over him.

But it was so, so hard.

And Lee . . . I really didn't want to put him in the middle of all this. Mostly because I had the feeling he'd pick me. But he wasn't who I wanted to see right now. He wasn't who I needed to be around.

I leaned forward on to the steering wheel, kneading my forehead with my knuckles.

I felt like such a mess.

But I still wasn't about to cry over him. Not if I could help it.

I jerked upright when someone rapped on my window. Levi stood outside, the collar on his jacket turned up, hair tousled, smiling at me.

I climbed out of the car. 'Hey.'

'Hi. Happy Thanksgiving.'

'You too. I'm sorry I called you and dragged you away from your family, it's just – I needed a friend.'

Levi didn't look remotely annoyed, though. 'That's okay. Besides, my mom was busy watching *La La Land* again and my sister was too busy trying to do a puzzle for them to miss me for a while.'

'What about your dad?'

'He's taking a nap. I think it was an excuse to get out of watching *La La Land*, but it might just be his meds making him tired again.'

I smiled at him, but didn't speak.

'Wanna go for a walk?'

I nodded, and we ambled through the park gates. It was quiet: there were some kids playing tag, their family sitting on a nearby bench, and an old couple was taking a walk hand in hand. The breeze rustled through the trees, making it rain leaves on us.

'Do you want to talk about it?' Levi asked.

'Not right now.'

He held out a hand toward me, and I took it. We'd never held hands like this before, but . . . it was nice. It felt like the right thing to be doing. There was no spark when we touched, no electricity. But I thought again about how, maybe, that wasn't such a bad thing.

We walked round the park for a little while before going to the swings and sitting down. I rocked back and forth, my toes anchoring me to the ground. Levi stayed still, running his fingers over the rusted spots on the chain.

After another heartbeat of silence, I spilled my guts out. Told him how sucky my Thanksgiving Day had been, and how I hated that Amanda was so nice, and that she'd even asked if I still have feelings for Noah, and –

'Do you?' he interrupted me.

'Huh?'

'Do you still have feelings for Noah?'

'You know what the worst part is?' I said instead. 'He didn't even say hi to me. And half the time he couldn't even look me in the eye.'

'Are you sure he's *actually* in a relationship with Amanda?'

The question startled me.

'Well – he's . . . he's got to be. I mean . . .'

All the evidence suggested he was. Or that they had something going on. That picture, the phone call, all the parties they went to together, the casual touches, the fact he brought her home for the holidays . . . That she'd wanted to know if I still had feelings for him . . .

And yet.

No relationship status on Facebook. No introduction of her as his girlfriend. No mention of her being his girlfriend or anything else. No kissing. Not even really any hugging. No soppy looks between them.

I'd convinced myself so easily that I'd forgotten nobody had actually called her his girlfriend.

I glared at the ground, kicking off sideways so that the chains of my swing twisted around. I bit my lip.

So what if they weren't officially anything? There had to be something there. Otherwise – otherwise . . .

I picked both my feet up off the ground, letting myself spin round so fast that I got a little dizzy. Levi's voice floated around me.

'If you don't wanna talk about it, I can change the topic. Let's see . . . There's football, the parade, um . . . *Frozen*. I can quote *Frozen* off by heart now. We can sing one of the duets, if you want, but I get to sing Anna's parts. Or there's the French Revolution. Spanish Civil War. The episode of *Jeopardy!* I watched last night . . .'

I'd stopped spinning now, and he was still rambling.

'Levi –'

'Embarrassing stories from my childhood –'

What I meant to do was tell him to shut up, tell him I'd rather not talk at all right now.

That's not what happened though.

On some reckless, crazy impulse, I reached across to his swing, grabbed his coat collar, and pulled him toward me.

And just like that, we were kissing.

I'd only ever kissed Noah. His kisses were familiar; they made my skin tingle with that firework feeling I'd always read about in books. His kisses were the only ones I'd known.

And kissing Levi was so different and so weirdly similar all at once.

I pushed all thoughts of Noah from my mind and concentrated on kissing Levi. It was all soft and hesitant – he'd stayed still for a second at first, but now his hand was on my face and he was kissing me back.

I knew I was doing this for all the wrong reasons. I knew it wasn't fair on Levi. But I couldn't seem to stop. I was a horrible, horrible person.

And all I could think about was how it was nice, and exactly like I'd expected it to be when I'd thought about kissing him, but it wasn't like kissing Noah.

My thoughts still plagued by Noah, I kissed Levi harder. I needed to forget about Noah. I needed to move on. And I liked Levi, so why not move on with Levi?

I was the worst person in the world.

I was the one who stopped kissing him, though. Eventually.

When I did, I felt beyond ashamed of myself. Levi looked a little happy and a lot confused. His eyelids were heavy, his breathing shallow.

I'd started to open my mouth to apologize when the park gate clanged loudly, like someone had slammed it shut. I looked round and saw a tall, broad figure striding away. It was getting dark, so I couldn't see him properly – but I didn't need to.

Noah had followed me here – or Lee had told him and he'd come after me. And he'd seen.

My stomach lurched. My lips formed his name and it felt like someone had punched the air straight out of my lungs.

It wasn't like we were still dating, like I couldn't or shouldn't kiss Levi if that was what I wanted to do, but still – knowing he'd seen us somehow made me feel every bit as terrible as if I *had* cheated.

I turned back to Levi. The poor guy looked so confused by the interruption and my sudden shift in demeanor, and I felt . . . *awful.* He didn't deserve this. I never should have asked him to meet me. I heard my breath shudder.

'I'm sorry. I shouldn't have done that. I mean – I don't mean it's anything against you, but I just . . . I'm really sorry. God, I've screwed up everything. I'm sorry. I'm such a bad person.'

Levi looked even more sheepish than I did. 'No, it's – it's my fault, too. I shouldn't have kissed you back.'

I shook my head. 'This wasn't . . . This was a mistake. Not because of you, or anything, but – I mean . . . I can't do this right now. Do you think we could just . . . forget that happened? For now, anyway? I don't want to screw things up with us, and I know making out kind of already screwed things up but –'

'Elle,' he said, cutting across me. I looked up from my knees to see Levi smiling at me, the usual easy smile I was used to. But there was no missing the hurt in his eyes, the way he couldn't quite look at me, or the way his smile faded after a moment. 'I get it.'

'I'm sorry. Fuck, Levi, I'm . . . I don't even know what I was . . .' I bit my lip, then fixed him with a determined stare. 'No, you know what? I do know what I was thinking. And it was a shitty thing to do.'

'It's okay.'

'It's not.'

'Well.' His lips twitched. 'Yeah, it's not. But I won't hold it against you. We all do stupid things when we're in love.'

I opened my mouth to object and faltered.

'You really need to stop being right so much,' I mumbled, trying to clear the air a little. 'One day it's gonna bite you in the ass.'

'It's because I'm a Ravenclaw. It's what we do. Being right, I mean.'

I let myself smile again, raising my eyebrows. 'Oh, please. You're such a Hufflepuff.'

We stayed on the swings a while longer, watching dusk bleed pink and red through the sky and the wind blow more leaves from the trees.

'I should probably be getting back,' Levi said after a while. 'I promised my mom I wouldn't be gone too long. Are you gonna be okay?'

I nodded. 'Sure. Thanks for coming to meet me. And – I'm sorry. Again. I really am.'

He shrugged. 'I'll get over it. In fairness, you did call me so you could vent about your ex. I should've seen it coming. Come on, I'll walk you back to your car.'

I let him, but this time we didn't hold hands.

He gave me a hug before leaving, though. 'You know you can call me if you need anything, right?'

I nodded. 'I think I'm just gonna head home. I don't much feel like facing up to Noah and Amanda right now, you know?'

'Okay.'

'Say hi to your mom and dad and Becca for me.'

'Will do. See you, Elle.'

'Yeah. See you.'

I didn't drive off straight away. I sat there staring blankly at the park, wondering why Noah had come after me.

Was it because he wanted to talk? Did he just feel bad that he'd chased me out of the house and wanted to apologize? Or was it something more?

He'd asked me about Levi. He'd seen the photo and it had obviously bugged him enough to comment on it like he had. And then he'd come after me.

I stopped before my mind ran away with itself. Noah and I were over. And I had to remember: I'd been the one to end things. He had no right to be mad if I snuck away from Thanksgiving to make out with Levi, and I had no right to want him to miss me.

Turning the key in the ignition so violently that I stalled the car, I ground my teeth. I really had to stop wondering if there was still anything between us, or if there ever would be again, no matter how I felt.

It just hurt so much because he'd been the first guy I'd fallen in love with. That was all. Right? In a few more months, I'd look back and laugh at how stupid I'd been about this whole thing. And it was so hard because he was going to be a part of my life whether we were together or not.

I turned the car on again and an Imagine Dragons song was on the radio. Then, I made my way home.

When I got home, I called my dad.

'Is everything okay, bud? Where are you? Lee said you went to hang out with Levi.'

'Yeah, I did. I'm home now.'

'Aren't you coming back here?'

'I've got really bad cramps, Dad. I'm just gonna head to bed.'

'Oh. Um, okay. If you're sure. Do you want us to come home?'

'No, no, you guys stay there. I'm fine.'

In a lower tone, my dad asked, 'This doesn't have anything to do with You-Know-Who, right?'

'No, Dad, Voldemort has nothing to do with this.'

'Oh, ha-ha, very funny.' I could practically hear him rolling his eyes at me down the line. 'You know what I mean. I know it must've been hard for you today, seeing them together, but –'

'It's just cramps, Dad.'

'If you say so. Well, we won't get home too late if you're not feeling well.'

'Okay,' I said, because there was no point arguing. 'I'll see you later. Can you say bye to everyone for me, and sorry I had to leave?'

'Of course. They'll understand.'

I hung up, and within ten minutes I had a text from Lee.

Liar. I know you had your period last week.

Then another: *Noah looks pissed. Did he talk to you?*

He said he wanted to say sorry to you because he knew you left cos of him. What did you say to him?

And: *SHELLY STOP IGNORING ME.*

Okay. I hope you 'feel better' soon. When you do, text me back and tell me what happened.

Love ya, even if you are ignoring me.

When the texts stopped coming through, I put my cell phone to one side and ran my hands through my hair. I could really have done with a reset button for today.

I took my time removing my makeup and getting changed. I had a raging headache from overthinking everything, so took some Advil and climbed into bed.

I'd just pulled the comforter over my head when I heard my dad's car pull up outside.

A couple of minutes later, there was a knock on my door.

'Elle? Can I come in?'

'Yeah.'

I sat up as my dad came in, calling over his shoulder to Brad to take a shower before bed. Then, to me, he said, 'How're you feeling?'

'Okay.'

It wasn't entirely a lie. Physically, I felt okay, anyway.

'Look, bud, I know how hard it must've been for you today, because I know how much you liked Noah, but –'

'Oh my God, Dad, I'm not having this conversation right now.'

Not when my headache was just starting to ease off.

'Alright, alright . . .' He held his hands up in surrender. 'But you know I'm here if you want to talk about it.'

'I don't. Jeez. I don't care about Noah or his precious new girlfriend.'

He sighed. 'Okay, fine. Well, just in case you *do* care, they're leaving on Sunday afternoon, and Noah said he'd like to talk to you before he goes, if you're okay with that. You know, he seemed really upset about something.'

'I can't imagine what.'

I was a horrible, horrible person to hope he'd been jealous.

'Elle . . .'

'Dad,' I snapped back, then felt bad for snapping. I pursed my lips. 'I don't want to talk to or about Noah. Can we drop it now?'

'Fine. Do you want some hot chocolate? I'm making me and Brad some.'

'No, I'm good. I think I'm just gonna get some sleep.'

Another sigh, and Dad pushed his glasses up his nose. 'Alright. Night, bud. Happy Thanksgiving.'

'You too.'

He snapped off the light on his way out, leaving me alone in the growing darkness.

My phone buzzed again, rattling across my nightstand. I glanced at it, expecting another text from Lee, or maybe Levi. It was neither.

Can you meet me tomorrow? Want to talk x

I stared at the screen in shock, thinking, *He must be desperate to talk if he spoke to my dad AND text me.*

But I ignored it, and ignored the kiss at the end, and he didn't send any more. I lay on the edge of sleep until past midnight, trying not to think about the fiasco that was the entire day, and unable to think of anything but.

Chapter 23

By some miracle, I managed to avoid Noah the whole next day – and Lee, too. I messaged Levi a little, neither of us mentioning the kiss; I was relieved things were (relatively) normal between us. After a while, I turned off my cell phone, and spent a few hours surfing online through the Black Friday sales, and then watched a movie with my dad and brother before helping Brad with some homework, because I was so desperate for any kind of distraction.

When I turned my phone on before dinner, I had a couple of texts. One was from Levi; another three were from Lee asking me to reply already, or was I actually mad at him for something; one from Rachel, asking me to please get back to Lee because he was worrying about me but didn't want to come over in case I was pissed at him for some reason; and another from Noah, asking if I could please reply to him, he just wanted to talk to me before he went back to college.

I replied to Lee first.

I kept it vague, just apologizing for not getting back sooner, saying that I hadn't spoken to Noah yesterday after dinner, and that I'd just needed space today.

Then I text Rachel to let her know I'd replied to Lee and to ask how her Thanksgiving had been. I replied to Levi, too – his had only been something about a quiz he found called 'Which classic Thanksgiving dish are you?'

I hesitated, looking at Noah's previous texts.

And I ignored them.

So what if all he wanted was to apologize for his behavior yesterday and for bringing Amanda home with him when that was totally insensitive? So what if he wanted to apologize for how things ended between us and for keeping things from me? I didn't want to hear from him. Not even that. I needed him out of my life for a while to get over him, and if that meant pushing him away when he was just trying to be nice, then so be it.

After dinner (leftover yams, carrots and broccoli that June had sent my dad home with, and meatloaf), we were back in the lounge channel-surfing, none of us able to agree on what to watch, when the doorbell rang.

My dad glanced at me before saying, 'I'll get it.'

Like he thought it'd be Noah.

And, to be totally honest, I thought it was, too. If he was so desperate to talk to me, there was nothing stopping him from coming over here to talk face-to-face when I ignored his texts. But then I told myself maybe it was Lee – because why wouldn't it be Lee?

I could tell it wasn't either of them, though, from the look my dad gave me as he put his head round the door. 'Elle, you've, er, got a visitor,' he said, looking as confused as I felt.

I stood up and walked into the hallway. Was it Levi, maybe? Or –

Or not.

'Oh. Um – uh, hi,' I stammered, facing a smiling, rosy-cheeked Amanda. Her hair was braided, but the wind had blown a few strands free round her face.

I wanted to be mad at her just for looking so damn pretty, even windswept.

'Hey. I was, um, hoping we could talk, if that's okay? I don't mean to intrude or anything, but I thought it'd be a bit weird to just call . . .'

'No, that's, um, that's fine.' I gave my dad a look, and he ducked back into the lounge, closing the door.

What was she doing here?

And what could she possibly want to talk about?

I composed myself. 'Can I get you a drink?'

'Some water would be great, please.'

She said 'water' so weird.

'Sure,' I mumbled, still kind of shell-shocked.

She followed me into the kitchen, and I handed her a glass of water. We stood facing each other, and I flexed my fingers nervously. My heart thundered, and I swallowed the lump in my throat, uneasy.

'I know this is probably very strange for you, but I wanted to talk about Noah.'

Well, there wasn't much else that she could want to talk to me about, but still – what the hell?

I just looked at her, waiting, not knowing what to say.

Amanda sipped her water and then dropped her shoulders back, as if squaring herself for something. Was she here to tell me to back off? Insist that I keep away from Noah or something? Tell me to get over him already and stop mooning around like some silly little girl?

'Why won't you talk to him?'

'What?'

Okay, whatever I'd expected, that was *not* it.

Far from it.

'He didn't send me over here or anything like that, but I just thought – well, I thought maybe you could talk to *me* if you couldn't talk to him. He *really* misses you, you know. And I *know* he feels bad about what happened between you, and about yesterday. For goodness' sake, *all* he's been able to talk about since we booked flights to come was what he was going to say to you. You're all he talks about. I understand that you probably don't want to see him, but he really does just want to talk. He says you deserve an explanation.'

I stared at her, gaping, for probably a full minute. Maybe more.

Amanda, looking awkward for a change, sipped some more water, and looked around the kitchen.

'I don't get it,' I said finally. 'Why are *you* talking to me about this?'

'I know, I *know* it's not really my place, but I care about Noah, and he's really cut up about what happened, so I thought –'

'Yeah, yeah, you thought you'd try to get me to talk to him. I just don't get why *you* care. I mean, I thought . . . You guys . . . It just doesn't make any sense.'

She stared at me for a moment, a quizzical expression on her pretty face.

Shit, was she really going to make me say it?

'I don't get why this is such a big deal to you now you guys are, you know . . . *a thing.*'

Amanda made a weird choking noise, her eyes blown wide, and her hand flew to her mouth. A giggle escaped her lips. 'Oh my God. He didn't tell you. Did he? He didn't tell you?'

'Tell me *what*?'

'Oh, shit. Sorry. I mean . . . No, it's . . .' She looked flustered, her hands waving around her erratically, and she bit her lip between words. Finally, she composed herself, looking calm and collected and – and like she was almost about to laugh. 'We're definitely *not* a thing. We never were.'

Now it was my turn to look like an idiot and gawp at her. Her face was open, sincere, her blue eyes wide and apologetic.

'Honestly. I thought he told you. I mean . . . He never *said* he told you but I thought he must've done. He said you thought we were together and that was part of the reason you guys broke up but I assumed he told you we *weren't*.'

'I mean, he said you were . . . friends. He said you were lab partners. That you were close and I wouldn't get it. And he brought you home for Thanksgiving.'

'Yes, because he didn't want me to stay on my own back in the dorms. We *are* close. You try spending hours in labs and classes with someone and not bonding. Of course he invited me for Thanksgiving when he heard I planned to spend it alone. He's a nice guy.'

'No kidding,' I said, my voice sounding weird, like it didn't belong to me. It sounded detached, and flat, and not half as confused as I felt right now.

'Oh, God, I can't *believe* this. No *wonder* you looked so awkward yesterday. I thought it was just because of Noah. I didn't think it was because you thought we were together. I'm *so* sorry.'

'It's not your fault,' I said, in the voice that didn't sound like mine.

'I didn't even think. I'm so sorry, Elle. But I promise you, there's nothing going on with us. There never has been. He's like . . . He's like a little brother, or something. Kind of helpless. You know he can barely work out how to do his own laundry? He tries to wingman for me at parties, set me up with guys.'

I didn't know what to do with this information.

I tried to digest it, but the words just swirled around in my head. I felt numb. My mouth had gone dry.

'He feels *awful* about what happened with you two. And about yesterday. He was really upset about you leaving. He went to go and look for you, but he said he couldn't find you. I don't know if he means to just clear the air so you can both move on, or what. He wasn't really in the mood for talking to me or Lee about it yesterday.'

I stared at her a while longer.

'You're not together.'

'No.'

'You're not his girlfriend.'

'No. Trust me, he's not my type.'

I stared again.

Oh my God.

What the hell had I done?

'I'm really sorry if I've made things weird now,' Amanda said nervously. 'I thought you knew. I thought maybe you just didn't want to talk to him because you were angry with him, or just really upset, or . . .'

I shook my head.

She reached over to squeeze my hand. 'I feel awful. I'm so sorry, Elle.'

'No, don't, it's – it's not your fault. He should've told me. Okay, I mean – he – he did. He told me there was nothing going on with you two but I didn't really believe him. But that was when we broke up. He hasn't spoken to me since.'

'He's sort of clueless when it comes to girls,' Amanda said, smiling and rolling her eyes. 'He acts like a womanizer and he's just *not*. He's like a lost puppy. He acts like a badass out on the football field but then he watered my fern for me when I went on a trip to DC for the weekend.'

I laughed, and it seemed to take some of the weight off my chest.

Amanda smiled, too. 'So, will you talk to him?'

'I –'

I faltered. Okay, so they weren't together, but that didn't change the fact that he hadn't tried to talk to me since the breakup, and he hadn't really talked to me yesterday. He hadn't bothered to warn me he'd be bringing Amanda home for the holidays, whether they were together or not. If anything, he'd done it knowing I believed they were a thing.

Plus . . . if it wasn't Amanda he'd been hiding from me, what had it been?

Amanda was looking at me expectantly, waiting for an answer.

Was I going to talk to Noah?

'I don't know. It's complicated.'

She nodded with a sympathetic smile. 'That's okay. I understand. He probably won't, but can I let him know you'll talk to him when you're ready to?'

'Sure. Thanks. I guess.'

'I'm really, really sorry,' she said again.

'What for?'

'Well, I know that I was one of the problems between you guys. He told me about the photo. And I'm sorry I didn't say yesterday that we weren't together. I honestly thought you knew. It might've made you feel less – well, it might've made you feel *better* yesterday. I bet it was pretty rubbish thinking he'd brought his new girlfriend home so soon after you guys split.'

'*Rubbish* doesn't even begin to cover it.'

Amanda laughed. 'Yes. Well, I'll get out of your hair. Thanks for the water.'

'No problem.'

I walked her to the door, and as she was stepping outside I said, 'Amanda?'

'Yeah?'

'Thanks. For telling me. And explaining.'

'Of course. I'll see you around!' she added, in the bubbly, cheerful tone she'd used all yesterday, and she gave me an equally bright grin before walking down the street.

I still felt stunned when I went back into the lounge. My dad pounced immediately, muting the movie. Brad shouted 'Hey!' but my dad didn't react.

'What did she want?'

'Was it Noah's new girlfriend?' Brad asked, forgetting about the TV.

'She's – she's not – they're not together.'

My dad raised his eyebrows, but he didn't actually look too surprised. 'Huh.'

Brad said, 'Does that mean you're going to be his girlfriend again now?'

'I don't think so. I don't know. We didn't – she just wanted . . .'

Dad said, 'I thought you said they were dating.'

'I thought they were. I mean, I just assumed . . .
I mean, he did try to tell me when we broke up, but . . .'

'I see. So what are you going to do? Are you going
to talk to him?'

I huffed, pursing my lips for a moment. 'I don't
know, Dad, jeez.'

'I just don't want you to do anything stupid.'

'What, like get back together with him?'

'No, like get your heart broken again.'

Chapter 24

The crowds at the mall were worse than ever as people poured into stores for the sales and to start their Christmas shopping, now that Thanksgiving was officially over. It was almost three o'clock before Lee and I had managed to grab a seat for lunch.

I still hadn't talked to Lee about what had happened with Levi, but I'd told him all about my chat with Amanda.

'Well,' he'd said, 'to be fair to Noah, we all just assumed . . .'

'Yeah. Well, he could've mentioned it. Like, to me.'

'He *did* tell you there was nothing going on between them.'

I shot a glare at him for that. 'Which is exactly what he would've said if something had been going on. And then he brought her home for Thanksgiving. What was I *supposed* to think?'

'I know, I know. I'm not blaming you. I thought they

were together, too. I'm sure my mom and dad were convinced as well, even though Noah said they were just friends.'

After we'd given the waitress our orders, Lee looked serious. 'What actually happened after you ran out on Thanksgiving?'

'Did you tell Noah where I'd gone?'

'He asked. He heard your car leave. I said you were going to the park because you were sick of his attitude –'

'Oh my God, tell me you didn't actually say that.'

'– and he went after you. He didn't say anything. When he got back, he looked really pissed. I figured you guys had had another fight or something, especially after you didn't come back. I tried asking him, and he just told me to leave it. So? Did you have a fight?'

'I never spoke to him.'

'Then what happened? Did he pick a fight with Levi?'

'No.' Oh, man. I didn't want to lie to Lee or hide things from him, but . . . I squirmed in my seat. 'Okay, you have to promise not to laugh.'

'Why?'

'*Promise me.*'

'I promise.'

'So I met Levi at the park. I wanted to let off some

steam about Noah and Amanda, and we ended up . . . making out.'

Lee stared at me a moment before his mouth pinched and contorted side to side, and the muscles in his jaw and cheeks twitched as he tried really hard not to laugh. I glared at him.

'You promised not to laugh.'

I watched him draw a deep breath through his nose and let it out before he said, 'Sorry, but you kissed *Levi*? Like, Levi Monroe? The same Levi you've been hanging out with all semester and swearing you don't *like* like?'

I groaned, burying my head in my hands. 'I know. It was a shitty thing to do. Especially if I *did* want to date him. I'd have totally ruined anything now.'

'I cannot believe you made out with Levi Monroe.'

'Will you stop saying his full name? It's weird.'

'Was it good?'

'What kind of question is that?'

'Okay – was it weird?'

'Not as much as it could've been. But it just . . . wasn't . . .' I sighed. 'He wasn't Noah.'

Lee's mouth twisted in sympathy. 'So what happened then?'

'Noah saw. I didn't know he was there until I heard him leaving. I don't think he overheard anything but he definitely saw us kissing.'

'Damn,' Lee said, and let out a long, low whistle. 'You guys really need to talk and sort your shit out.'

I grunted, unimpressed with the suggestion – especially since he was probably right – and we moved on to talk about something else instead. Although every five minutes was punctuated with Lee saying, 'I can't believe you made out with Levi' or 'Wait till the guys hear. *Levi*.'

'If you tell anybody, I swear to God I'm going to tell Rachel something you don't want her to know.'

'I tell Rachel everything.'

'Oh yeah? Does she know that you cried harder than me when we watched *Marley & Me*? Or what about the time I got my first bra and you wore it for a day to see what it was like?'

The laughter disappeared from Lee's face and he raised a fry threateningly at me. 'You dare . . .'

I raised my eyebrows, grinning at him triumphantly.

Lee came back to my house after the mall. He didn't even suggest we go back to his, where I might bump into Noah. He'd tried to get me to talk about Noah again – what I was going to do and if I was going to talk to him – but I stayed mute on the subject.

The truth was, I still didn't know myself.

I knew I was still in love with Noah; somehow that

made it all so much worse. I was torn between wanting to get back together with him and wanting to never have to talk to him again until I was officially one hundred per cent over him.

But what if I couldn't get over him until we'd talked things through and he'd explained the whole thing with Amanda was just a horrible misunderstanding? What if seeing him alone was the best way to get over him?

And what if it just made things worse?

My head was spinning with what-ifs and I knew I could think about it for weeks and still not figure out the right thing to do.

Lee was only trying to be helpful – I knew that.

But he didn't *just* have my best interests at heart; he was looking out for his brother, too. And he knew his brother wanted to talk to me.

I ignored the two missed calls I had from Noah and the text that said: *If you don't want to talk, I get it, but let me know?*

'I think you should at least call him and say you don't want to talk,' Lee said. 'Or, for God's sake, at least *text* the poor sap.'

I still didn't know what I wanted to do when I was lying in bed, tossing and turning, later that night. I couldn't sleep for thinking about it.

I'll go see him early tomorrow, before he leaves.

I'll text him in the morning to say I think it's better if we don't talk, and I hope he and Amanda had a nice time here.

I'll ignore everything to do with him.

I'll see him in the morning.

I'll call him when he's back at college.

I won't speak to him.

I'll –

There was a rattle at my window.

I sat up, twisting toward the sound, and stared at the closed drapes.

Another one. Kind of like a tap, but whatever it was hit the gutter on the way down.

I frowned at the window for three more taps before I got up to see what it was.

I scrambled out from under the covers and threw open the curtains, peering down through the darkness. The streetlamp cast an amber glow over the guy in my front yard, and I clenched my jaw tight while my heart did a somersault and his name jumped to my lips.

Seeing me, he waved.

I fumbled for the latch and opened the window.

'What are you doing? It's two in the morning!'

'Yeah, I know.'

I gawped at him for a second. 'What do you want?'

'I have to talk to you. My flight leaves at twelve and

I couldn't not talk to you before I left. I figured this was the only way to get you to talk to me.'

I stared at him for a split second longer before closing the window. I found some sneakers and a hoodie, pulled them on, and crept downstairs to the front door. I closed it quietly behind me, leaving it on the latch so I could get back in.

'You've got two minutes, Noah Flynn.'

'I almost didn't think you were coming.'

He was holding a bag of Skittles – they must've been what he was throwing at my window.

Noah strode toward me, coming up on to the porch. I took a half step back. I forgot how tall he was, up close like this. I noticed, in the porch light, that he was wearing flannel pajama pants and a hoodie, and sneakers with no socks, almost exactly like me: he'd come straight here from lying in bed.

I stared up at him, resolute. 'Time's ticking.'

It sounded lamer than I expected it to. Noah just looked determined. Serious.

I counted my heartbeats. I got to sixteen before he spoke.

'Cramps, huh?'

'Excuse me?'

'On Thanksgiving. We both know that was a load of bull.'

'You followed me,' I accused instead.

'I felt like you'd left because of me. I thought I should . . . apologize, or something. It wasn't fair on you to have to leave because of me. And from talking to Lee, he made it sound like you weren't over me, so I thought maybe I should clear the air. But obviously he was wrong.'

I stuck my chin out. 'What difference does it make? We broke up. Who I kiss isn't any of your business any more. I thought that was pretty clear when you didn't even call me to tell me you were coming home for Thanksgiving, let alone with Amanda.'

Noah sighed, the sound broken, and he ran a hand back and forth through his already tousled hair, making it stick out even more. 'I didn't think you *wanted* me to call.'

Of course I wanted you to call! I wanted you to call and I wanted you to tell me you missed me and tell me how much you loved me and tell me I'd made a mistake in breaking up with you!

Instead, what I said was, 'If you followed me to the park to talk to me, why didn't you talk to me? Why did you leave?'

He scoffed, almost scornful, but he couldn't hide the hurt expression on his face. 'You're really asking me that? I thought you two were *just friends*. You told me you weren't interested in him like that. Told Lee, too. I wasn't convinced when you kept sharing photos and stuff with him, and when I saw that photo of you guys at the dance . . . But Lee told me. "Nothing going on," he said. Looks like you're making a habit of lying to him about guys you like.'

My jaw clenched, teeth grinding. I could feel the muscles in my face twitching, not sure which expression to settle on. I was breathing hard, trembling all over, but that had nothing to do with the chill in the air.

'You have no right to . . . to say that to me. It shouldn't matter to you any more if I *am* dating Levi, but just FYI I'm not. I asked him to meet me because I needed a friend who wasn't Lee, for once. Yeah, I kissed him. So what? It was a stupid decision but it was *my* decision to make. And anyway, what about you and Amanda? You didn't think to tell me you were bringing her home for Thanksgiving.'

'You're . . . not dating him.'

'No,' I said, more softly, some of the tension in my shoulders easing. 'I'm not.'

'Well, what was I supposed to think when I saw you two all over each other, Elle?'

'Well, what was I supposed to think when I saw all those pictures of you and Amanda, and then you bring her home for Thanksgiving? You could've told me. You could've at least told me you two weren't dating.'

'I did! And you didn't want to hear it!'

'Did you really expect me to believe you when you brought her home for Thanksgiving?'

'She was going to be all alone for the holidays! It had nothing to do with you, nothing to do with – with making you jealous, or anything else!' he exclaimed, and I was shocked into silence. 'You broke up with me, remember? I didn't think you'd *care*. I didn't realize that me having a good friend who also happens to be a girl was such a big deal, so when you broke up with me out of the blue like that, I thought there had to be someone else. It was the only thing that made sense.'

I was suddenly breathless.

And had never felt like more of an idiot.

'What did you expect me to think, after you broke up with me?' he carried on, exasperated. 'I thought you were just looking for an excuse. I thought there was someone else. I knew you and Levi were getting close, and when I saw the photos from Sadie Hawkins, and when I saw you two the other night –' Noah broke off with a sigh. His forehead was lined, his eyes shining and sad and desperate, and it made my heart ache. 'I mean, you and Lee are so close. So honestly? I

334

thought you'd be the last person to get jealous of me being friends with another girl, when I told you about Amanda. And I know, I – I know I should've told you about her before, but . . . I was an idiot. Okay? I don't . . .'

We'd *both* been such idiots.

'I can't believe you thought I'd broken up with you to be with Levi.'

'You kissed him.'

'Because I was trying to get over you! And it didn't work! It was stupid and I regretted it as soon as it happened. I thought, maybe, there was something, but . . .' I shook my head. 'There was never anybody else, Noah. There still isn't. We broke up because we couldn't trust each other.'

'I trust you!' He reached out as if to grab my shoulders, then dropped his hands to his sides, before shoving them in the pockets of his hoodie instead, where the Skittles packet crinkled. 'Of course I trusted you. But I was never good enough for you. I was never the right guy, and I was terrified the whole time that we were together that the right guy would come along, and I felt like I was just waiting for you to realize that, and to see that the right guy for you isn't me. And . . .'

'And what?'

'And I loved you too much to let you go,' he said

quietly, looking up at me from under his eyelashes. His eyes looked unnaturally bright blue. 'I still do.'

I sucked in my lower lip, biting it hard. Why, why did I feel like crying? Why were my eyes prickling and my throat itching like I was about to sob? Just because he'd said he loved me . . .

He still loves me.

But I had more questions. The fact that he hadn't stopped loving me – and that I still loved him – didn't change anything right now.

'You let me think something was going on with you and Amanda.'

He shrugged one shoulder. 'I was jealous. I was mad. It hurt me, Elle, when you broke up with me. You flipped out so much over her, I thought . . . I didn't think you'd get it. That we were just friends.'

'I flipped out because you were keeping secrets from me. That phone call I overheard – if it wasn't about you being with Amanda, what the hell *was* it about?'

Noah blushed, looking distressed. He shifted from foot to foot and ran a hand through his hair again. Now he looked like the one on the verge of crying.

As angry as I was, and had been, it fell away in an instant.

'Noah?' I said softly, reaching out to touch his arm

impulsively. He jumped when I did, and we sprang apart like we'd been electrocuted.

'I was failing some of my classes,' he said finally. 'I was going to get kicked off the football team. I was stressed. I wasn't getting good grades as easily as I did in high school, which stressed me out so much it affected my work. Amanda was helping me a lot. She knew, because she'd see the grades I got in class, or in our lab. I was too embarrassed to tell you. I didn't want you to think I was . . . stupid. I didn't want you to be disappointed. And I didn't want to tell you when I was with her because then I'd have to explain why we were always studying so much, and I couldn't bring myself to do that.'

And suddenly everything made sense.

It made so much sense, especially given that he'd told me all about how he'd put so much pressure on himself at school before he'd built up his bad-boy persona. I couldn't understand how I hadn't even considered it before.

'You shouldn't have been embarrassed to tell me,' I said quietly. 'I wouldn't have thought you were stupid. I don't. I just wish you'd *told* me.'

'Would it have made a difference?'

'Yes!' I exclaimed, and then I checked myself. I didn't want to wake anybody up. I blinked a few more times

337

but a tear spilled over. I took a second to try and steady my voice.

'Noah, I . . . Before we broke up, it felt like you were hardly talking to me. You kept avoiding talking to me about classes, and it felt like you were cutting me out of your life. Like I didn't belong in it any more. I get it, now, but I didn't know, and that scared me. I thought we were drifting apart and that you didn't love me so much any more, and . . . When you wouldn't talk to me about that call, of course I thought you had something going on with Amanda. It was the only thing that made sense.'

'I'm sorry,' he whispered, and I was shocked to see him crying. Actual *tears* hanging on his lower lashes. One of them splashed on to his cheek. His Adam's apple bobbed as he gulped. 'I'm sorry. I should've told you. About college, about Amanda . . . I know there was nothing going on with you and Levi but I started convincing myself that there might've been after we broke up, and on Thanksgiving I . . .'

Noah trailed off when I stepped closer.

'You're *such* an idiot, Noah Flynn.'

He chuckled, and I brought my hand to his face, running my thumb across the tear-track on his cheek.

'But you're my idiot.'

I didn't kiss him. I waited, every one of my nerves coiled and ready to spring.

338

And, when he kissed me, I ignited.

His lips were tender and insistent against mine, his arms wrapping round me tight, his hair soft through my fingers.

I thought I'd remembered what it was like to kiss him, but those memories were pale imitations of the real thing. And I'd been right to think that kissing Noah was just so much *more* than kissing Levi. I felt like I was burning up from the inside out, in the best way possible. My fingertips trailed over his face and back through his hair and down his arms, and I was sure I'd never felt more alive than I did while kissing him.

When we stopped, I clung to him, and he didn't loosen his hold on me.

'I love you,' he whispered, the words rushing out as though he couldn't say them fast enough, the look in his eyes so intense it was like the words didn't mean enough. 'I fucked up. I should've just talked to you. I know that. I messed everything up. I just got so scared of losing you that I made things worse.'

I managed a laugh. 'That was why I broke up with you. Because I was scared that you'd find someone better and forget about me, and I couldn't lose you like that. *I* got scared and made things worse.'

Noah chuckled, the sound soft, his breath tickling my nose. I closed my eyes, pressing my head into his shoulder and inhaling deeply. He still smelled the same. Still felt the same. He was still my Noah.

Dragging my head back up, I stepped back so that I could see him properly. 'I'm still in love with you, too, Noah Flynn. Just, you know. In case you were wondering.'

'So . . .'

'So.'

He kissed me; this time, just a lingering peck on the lips. Even that made my heart do somersaults. 'If you still don't want to be together, I get it. I understand. It's horrible being away from you and I miss you all the damn time, but I don't want to be with anyone but you. If you find it too hard, then I get it. Just tell me.'

'I think . . .'

Oh, God. What *did* I think? I missed Noah so much while he was at college, but . . .

But however hard I'd tried, I hadn't been able to get over him, not even a little tiny bit.

I didn't want to lose him, but maybe I'd done the right thing by breaking up with him, in case this didn't work, in case we were just wasting our time . . .

Only, looking at Noah, I didn't feel like I was wasting my time. Standing in his arms, I felt like I was right where I wanted to be. I beamed at him.

'I think we can make it work.'

Chapter 25

Noah kissed my nose for the billionth time. Mm, he smelled so good. 'I'll be back after my exams for Christmas. Not even a month away. It'll fly by.'

'It better.' I kissed him again. We were making up for weeks and weeks of missing out. Last night, he'd come inside and we'd talked for a while longer about everything. We talked until we fell asleep on the couch, with me drifting off first, Noah's fingers running through my hair and his arms tucked tight round me.

I could *feel* how much he loved me. How could I have ever doubted him or thought there was anybody else?

My dad had woken us up around eight, not looking overly surprised to find Noah in the house when he'd come downstairs, and just said, 'What do you kids want for breakfast? You'd better head back home soon, Noah. You'll have to leave for the airport in a while.'

Once Noah had left, I'd explained everything to my dad, who'd sighed and said, 'Don't get me wrong, I like

Noah – he's a good, smart kid, and I know you're in love with him – but I did like Levi.'

Now, we stood on the Flynns' driveway. Noah's fingers ran absent-mindedly up and down my arm, and I tried to memorize every freckle on his face. He'd shaved this morning, his cheek smooth under my hand.

God, I'd missed him so much.

Amanda came out of the house then, and grinned at us. 'You see, Noah? I *told* you that you'd work things out.' To me, she said, 'And I'm so glad that you did. He was *miserable* without you. He was *always* moping around. It was making the rest of us feel shitty, too. I'm not even joking.'

I laughed, breaking away from Noah for a moment to face Amanda. 'I'm really sorry if I was horrible to you when you got here.'

She waved a hand, a silver ring on her middle finger catching the light, and beamed at me. 'Don't mention it. I'd have done the same in your place. But you weren't, for the record.'

Then, before I could reply, she threw her arms round me and said, 'Ooh, it was *so* great to meet you!'

'You too,' I said, surprised to find I really meant it as I hugged her back.

Then she went back to the house, where we could hear her thanking June again for having her to stay and making her feel so welcome, and Noah kissed the side of my head, pulling me back into his side.

'I'll call you later, when I'm back at the dorms.'

'Okay.'

'And I'll be back in a couple of weeks.'

'Maybe I can come out to Boston, to see you, after Christmas?'

'Maybe you could look at some colleges out there,' he said, and even though his tone was playful his eyes were serious, hopeful. I kissed him by way of reply, rising up on my tiptoes and clutching at the front of his jacket.

'Alright, lovebirds, break it up. That plane *will* leave without you,' Matthew announced, clapping his hands and shutting the trunk of the car. Amanda came out of the house with her oversized purse and said a last thank you to June, and Noah gave me one more kiss.

Lee stood next to me as we waved them off, and it felt weirdly like it had in the summer, when we'd watched Noah's plane take off. But it felt better than that; more peaceful, more comfortable. This time we knew exactly what we were in for with the long-distance thing. And we were determined to make it work.

Lee sighed, slinging an arm round my shoulders. 'I still can't believe you made out with Levi.'

'I'll tell everyone I know what a snotty mess you

were over *Marley & Me* if you breathe a word to anyone. And don't forget about the bra story, either. I'll tell your buddies on the football team, too.'

Lee nudged me in the shoulder. 'Yeah, yeah. Don't worry, I'm not telling. That doesn't mean I don't still find it hilarious.'

'It's not funny. God.'

'It really kind of is.'

When I caught up with Levi in the parking lot on Monday morning, he didn't bring up our kiss at all – he just grinned at me knowingly and said, 'I see you've changed your relationship status again.'

'I have.'

'Tell all.'

And he sounded so genuinely interested – so genuinely happy for me – I relaxed. I'd been worried about seeing him again, even if things were normal between us over text, but everything really was exactly like it had been before. (Only now I wasn't wondering about kissing him, or wondering if we had any chemistry, or if I wanted to date him. I knew for sure where my heart lay now.)

So I told him all about how Noah had come by in the middle of the night, how cut up he was about the breakup, how we'd cleared the air.

'I'm really happy for you,' Levi said, and he was; I could tell by his smile. 'But don't look now – I think there are some girls heading over here who want you to spill the beans, too.'

I looked round to see a couple of the girls making their way toward me. Levi had ducked away from my side by the time the girls reached me. Lisa was grinning almost manically, and Rachel grabbed my hand.

'We want to hear *everything*!'

I was going to be in for a very long morning.

But I wasn't the only one with good news: Dixon couldn't stop smiling. He'd had this stupid grin on his face all day long, but I didn't get the chance to ask him about it until we all sat down for lunch.

'Oh, come on,' I said, throwing a fry at him. 'You can't be *that* happy for me that things worked out with Noah. Spill.'

Dixon blushed. Bright pink. And then he bit his lip. 'Um, well – it's, I mean, it's no big deal, but – it kind of is, though, like . . .'

'Jesus Christ. At this rate, we still won't know by Christmas. Come on, man, spit it out.' Warren laughed, and Dixon seemed to be steeling himself for something. He looked all serious for a second, before his face split into another huge smile.

345

'Danny asked me to be his boyfriend. You know, officially. So . . . yeah.'

'Ohmigod,' I said.

'No way,' said Rachel.

'I didn't realize you two were so much of a thing,' said Warren, while Olly started belting out 'Love Is in the Air', and Lee and Lisa pitched in with *doo-doo-doo*.

Dixon shrugged, looking down, still with that big, goofy smile on his face. I shared a look with Rachel, and we both had to bite back giggles. I didn't think any of us had ever seen Dixon looking so *giddy*.

'Well, yeah, I mean, I didn't want to make a big thing of it, but we've been on a few dates, and . . . I really like him.'

'That's so great, man,' Lee pitched in, their singsong done now.

'Yeah, we're really happy for you,' said Levi.

'As long as we're sharing good news,' said Cam, 'I finally sent off my college applications. I know it's not exactly on the same scale, but I finally hauled ass and did it.'

'Jeez, what's with all the good karma?' Warren laughed. 'And when is it coming my way?'

A week before school let out for Christmas vacation, I was hanging out with Levi. We were baking cookies with Becca. They were supposed to be for the bake sale at her school tomorrow, but she kept eating them almost as fast as we could make them. Then, his mom had called to ask if we could bake extra, so she could take them into work.

As I helped Becca press the gingerbread-man cookie cutter into the mixture, and Levi whipped up another batch, the front door opened and closed.

'Hey, kids,' Levi's dad called.

Levi's dad had been in and out of hospital appointments for the last month. But he was getting better, Levi kept telling me – some days were good, some days not so good. He was doing better, and that was the important thing.

'Something smells good,' his voice boomed again, and Becca jumped down from her seat to go and hug her dad.

Mr Monroe was tall, and he had the look of someone who used to be pretty well built but had lost a lot of weight in a short space of time. His face was thin, and so was his hair. He was just wearing jeans and a plain blue T-shirt, and when he smiled he looked like Levi.

'Hey, sweetiepie,' he said, hugging Becca. He stood back up, smiling at us. 'Alright, Levi? Elle? How was school?'

'Oh, sure,' Levi deadpanned. 'Best days of our lives, you know?'

Becca came back over to sit next to me, taking the cookie cutter out of my hands. 'Elle's helping us bake.'

'Well, I'm not doing much actual baking,' I said. 'I'm a disaster in the kitchen.'

'She really is,' Levi said. I knew he was thinking about the time I'd tried to cook lasagna just after Thanksgiving, and the result had been inedible mush that probably would've given us food poisoning if we'd eaten it. My dad had ordered takeout instead. Noah had laughed for five minutes solid when I'd FaceTimed him to show off the disaster of my cooking.

Mr Monroe picked up one of the gingerbread men from an open Tupperware container. The cookie snapped as he bit the head off.

'Mm,' he said, mouth full. Swallowing, he went on, 'Don't suppose you kids could make me some of these for my support group?' To me, he said, 'My doctor and wife insist I go to these support groups for people in remission. Waste of a Monday evening if you ask me. I keep telling them I don't need to go.'

'Oh. Right. But . . . some Christmas cookies should make it a bit better though, right?'

He smiled again. 'Christmas cookies make *everything* better.'

'Sure, what's a few dozen more?' Levi sighed melodramatically, and then the oven timer went off for the sixth or seventh time that afternoon.

I just laughed.

And Becca ate another cookie when she thought none of us were looking.

'I'm sorry about my dad,' Levi said later, when we were playing video games in his room. We both had studying to do, which we'd said we would do after we'd baked the cookies, but neither of us felt like memorizing facts. 'If he made things awkward or anything. I think his support group have this thing about not making cancer taboo, so they can all talk about it more.'

'It's okay. Really. It wasn't awkward.' Levi's relief was palpable. 'You still haven't told the other guys, have you?' I asked, even though I already knew the answer.

'I just don't see the point.'

'Maybe you need to go to these support groups,' I said, but not in a mean way. 'None of the guys are going to look at you differently or anything. I swear. They'd understand. Like when Dixon came out, you know? Everyone just kind of . . . acknowledged it and carried on. It doesn't change anything.'

He mumbled in response so I didn't push the issue, but a couple of minutes later, Levi sighed, paused the game, and said to me in a taut voice, 'I just find it kind of hard to deal with. So, like, the fewer people asking me how he is all the time, the better I cope. It used to be like that in my old school, where everyone would just bring it up all the time. I knew they were trying to be nice, but it just pissed me off.'

I shrugged. 'It's your choice. But, even if you don't want to tell the other guys, you know you can talk to me about it, right? If it's ever, like, getting you down, or whatever.'

'Yeah,' he said softly. 'Yeah, I know.'

We carried on playing the video game and didn't bring it up again.

But he did say, 'Elle? I'm glad we're still friends. Even after . . .'

'After I used you to try to get over my boyfriend?' We caught each other's eye and Levi grinned. I was so damn *glad* he wasn't holding it against me. 'At least I've stopped getting nasty looks in the hallways from the girls who have a crush on you, now that I'm back with Noah.'

He looked way too pleased with himself, hearing about girls having crushes on him, but I just rolled my eyes.

The next day at school, Levi told the guys about his dad.

And, just like I'd predicted, they didn't look at him any differently. Just told him that if he ever needed to take his mind off things, they were always up for a few beers and pizza, or a game of football in the park.

'See,' I said to Levi, smiling smugly. 'I told you.'

'Now who's the Ravenclaw?' he shot back, with such a haughty, teasing tone, I had to laugh. 'If only you could predict what questions will come up in the biology final, that'd be great.'

'I bet they'll ask us what mitochondria are.' Our bio teacher had been embedding that fact into our head for the last few months relentlessly. I swore I'd still know the definition when I was fifty.

'Remind me?'

I rolled my eyes, laughing, and Levi cracked up, too.

Maybe he would've been the kind of guy I would've dated, if things had ended up different between me and Noah, if Noah hadn't been so determined to see me and fix things. Maybe if Thanksgiving had gone differently, I would have been with Levi.

I don't imagine we would have ever lasted long as a couple.

I needed that spark, that passion, that I had with Noah. It just wasn't there with Levi.

We were way better off as friends; I was just grateful that he seemed to be on the same page.

And then I thought: even with finals looming over my head, and the ongoing wait for a response to my college applications, the rest of the school year would be okay. I'd hit my rock bottom. The only way I was going was up.

Epilogue

The sun blazed overhead. There were even birds singing somewhere. The sky was as blue as his eyes and there wasn't a cloud in sight. I felt lighter than I had for months, like I hadn't known just how much was weighing down on my shoulders until now.

Lee and I had our arms wrapped round each other, both of us jumping up and down, out of sync for once, my head knocking against his chin and shoulders.

It kind of hurt, but I didn't care.

I was delirious.

People were calling out, laughing, crying, trying to talk to everyone and anyone.

'WE DID IT!' a voice screamed, and then Cam threw himself on top of us. 'We're done! We're going to college!'

'College!' Lee yelled back.

'College!' I yelled.

'COLLEGE,' Cam yelled again. There was a lot of yelling. And we weren't the only ones.

Lee and I let go of each other – Cam had already run off, probably to yell 'COLLEGE!' at more people – and, just when I thought the hugging was done, Lee slung an arm round my shoulder and kissed the top of my head with a loud smacking noise.

'This is it. The beginning of a glorious, golden summer, the kind they make indie teen movies about, and then we're thrown into the soul-sucking pit of college.'

'College *so* won't be soul-sucking.'

'How do you know?'

'Well, how do you know it *will* be?'

Lee just laughed. 'You're right. It's going to be so great. It really is.'

'Don't jinx it. I don't want to end up with some awful room-mate. What if my room-mate is someone like you? Oh, God, just kill me now.'

Lee laughed again; he sounded as delirious as I felt. It was beautiful. Everything was so beautiful.

Right now, I felt high on life, and I didn't ever want this feeling to end.

I got into Berkeley. So did Lee.

He didn't get into Brown.

Rachel had been devastated, but I knew Lee was

secretly relieved. Brown would've been too much pressure for him, he'd told me after the rejection – although he was disappointed to end up so far away from Rachel. They'd make it work, though. If a couple as turbulent as Noah and me could, Lee and Rachel definitely would.

I looked around for Noah. I'd heard him cheering so loudly for me when my name got called – and when Lee's name was called. (He'd also sent a balloon bouquet to me at school when I got my SAT results, the big softy.) I hadn't seen him since before the graduation ceremony started, though, as I got lost in the crowd of graduation gowns.

Just as I was thinking about him, Noah slid up behind me, his arms enveloping me and turning me around, his touch sending a thrill through me. He kissed me firmly on the lips before saying, 'Congrats, Shelly. Officially a high school graduate!' Then he glanced up and smoothed down my hair. I'd taken the time to straighten it to sleek perfection this morning, but I bet I had some hat hair going on after wearing the graduation cap.

'Thanks!'

The last six months hadn't exactly been easy. Not that we'd had any more arguments, but I just missed him so damn much – and I knew how much he missed me, too. He'd surprised me with a visit home for Valentine's

Day so we could celebrate together, even bringing me a giant teddy bear in a Harvard sweatshirt and cap.

But we'd done it. We'd managed the long-distance thing since Thanksgiving, and it was all completely worth it now we were standing here with the whole summer stretching out ahead of us, the sun warm on my cheeks and my fingertips playing with the ends of Noah's hair, and his lips on mine.

'Alright, you two, break it up,' said my dad. I heard June laughing, and buried my face in Noah's shoulder for a second before turning to our parents. 'Come on, we want more photos. I'd rather not have to get my daughter's graduation photo from a selfie on her Twitter feed.'

Noah stepped aside, and I fixed my hair before holding up my crisp high school diploma and smiling for the camera. My dad had barely snapped the photo when a blur in graduation robes barreled toward us, stopping short when he noticed the camera, arms spinning for balance and almost falling flat on his face.

'Sorry! Sorry! Did I ruin the photo?'

'No, we're good,' my dad said, checking the camera. 'Hey, well done, Levi.'

'Thanks.' He grinned, then turned to me, and when I thought he was about to say congrats to me, he opened his mouth and screamed.

Not even words. Just one long 'AAAAAAHHH!'

So I screamed back.

And then we were both laughing and hugging and he was saying, 'I'm so visiting you at college next year. I don't mind sleeping on the floor. I'll bring a sleeping bag.'

'You'd better.'

We grinned at each other. Levi had been working at a 7-Eleven for the last month or so, just a couple of hours a week, and he'd be working there more now that we were done with school. He also had a job at a bakery he was crazy excited about, which he was due to start next week.

He still hadn't decided what he wanted to do. So, he said, he was just going to work until he made up his mind. His mom had told me when I was over at their place for dinner a few days ago that she'd hoped he'd change his mind and apply to college like most of us, but she sighed resignedly. 'I suppose I can't force him to go, though.'

Someone yelled 'Hey, Monroe! Get your skinny ass over here!' and we both looked to see a group of guys waiting to take a photo – the baseball team. Levi had joined up at the start of the season.

He ducked away, skirting through the crowds to be part of the photo, and then Noah was back beside me, holding my hand. I caught him looking after Levi – they'd met a couple of times and had been polite enough, but there was always something stiff and forced about it. Right now, Noah's eyes narrowed slightly. I squeezed his hand and he turned back to me, his expression relaxing. The sun behind his head gave the edges of his dark hair an almost golden glow, and his eyes crinkled at the corners with the beaming smile that took over his face as he looked at me.

I wrapped my free hand round his bicep (because, boy, that *bicep*) and grinned back. Before I could pull him down for another kiss, Lee jumped at my back, hands on my shoulders pushing me forward as I cushioned his leap, staggering under his weight so neither of us went down, Noah half holding me up and chuckling. I knew it was Lee without having to look round; the elated laugh in my ear gave him away.

The Flynn brothers started chatting over my head about a party we were all going to later tonight to celebrate graduation, and Lee mentioned that he'd heard a rumor about a kissing booth being set up there. I was only half listening.

I felt kind of detached. Dreamy. My eyes drifted between families embracing, friends taking selfies and trying to fit everyone in the photo, people running to try to talk to each other in case they never saw these people again after today, and my two favorite guys in the world right beside me.

Levi caught my eye from where he was talking with his parents. His dad looked so much better lately – his face not so skinny and his skin not so gray. I saw Dixon chatting to a group of people – not with Danny, though; they broke up back in January. Rachel was crying, hugging her mom. She'd got into Brown, of course, on early admission. And I knew she and Lee had talked a lot; after they'd seen how turbulent things had been for me and Noah, they both knew how much work it would be to commit to staying together through college.

And as for Noah and me?

We'd already gone through the worst of it. I was sure we had what it took to go the distance, whatever came next.

Noah kissed the side of my head and Lee held my arm, talking excitedly about something.

I kept hearing about how high school was supposed to be the best years of your life – and then how it really wasn't. And I decided that, if this wasn't the best time of my life, the rest of it couldn't get much better than it was right now.

Acknowledgements

There are so many people I need to thank for this book. It's been about seven years in the making. That it's finally made it to this point – being published – feels so strange. It's been a long time since I first sat in my room and decided to start *The Kissing Booth* and honestly, I'm just so excited for how much more there is to come.

First, thanks to my utterly incredible agent, Clare, for being so patient and helpful throughout this whole process. Thanks to my editors, Naomi and Kelsey, for all your hard work in making this book the best it could be.

When I was editing an earlier draft of this in 2017 and stuck on my characters, the crowd in Cape Town were a huge inspiration. Joey, Joel, Jacob, and everyone else – you brought my characters to life, and helped spur me on when I was feeling drained. Vince, Andrew and Ed, you gave me a renewed passion for my story. 'Thanks' doesn't even begin to cover it, but . . . thanks.

Thanks to my friends and all our group chats, for putting up with me when I'm having a crisis or when I'm spamming you with my latest news because I can't post it on Twitter yet. You guys always know how to lift me right back up when I need it. So, thanks to: Lauren and Jen; Katie and Amy; Emily and Jack and my lab buddy Harrison (special thanks to you for all the memes); and Ellie and Hannah, without whom Levi would still be Kevin.

The journey to this point has been wild. From the idea of the scene at Thanksgiving, to several rounds of edits, to an unexpectedly popular Netflix movie and more, so much has gone into this book, and my family have been a rock throughout it all. (Especially while I've been juggling two jobs, a few moves around the country, and then some.)

A special thanks to my sister, Kat, because one of us has to be the cool one in the family when I'm out here glued to my laptop and phone. Thanks for loving my book and keeping me grounded.

Thank you to my parents, my auntie and uncle, and my granddad. (I'm sorry sometimes you get my latest news from Twitter first. But in my defence, it's usually something you knew about, like, a year before I announced it.)

Finally, thank you to you, my readers. Whether you

only discovered Elle's story after the first Netflix film in May 2018, or whether you've been with her since the very first chapters on Wattpad in 2011, your support and love has meant so much to me – and I honestly don't think this second book would have been possible without you all. Honestly: you have changed my life.